Homeward Trails  Book Three

THE
SISTER'S
Search

Susan Page Davis

Scrivenings
PRESS
Quench your thirst for story.
www.ScriveningsPress.com

©2022 Susan Page Davis

Published by Scrivenings Press LLC
15 Lucky Lane
Morrilton, Arkansas 72110
https://ScriveningsPress.com

Printed in the United States of America

Paperback ISBN 978-1-64917-222-8

eBook ISBN 978-1-64917-223-5

Library of Congress Control Number: 2022941834

Editors: Elena Hill and Linda Fulkerson

Cover by www.bookmarketinggraphics.com.

All scriptures are taken from the KING JAMES VERSION (KJV): KING JAMES VERSION, public domain.

All characters are fictional, and any resemblance to real people, either factual or historical, is purely coincidental.

1

July 1865
Near Columbus, Ohio

Black never suited Molly Weaver. She hated the mourning dresses she and her mother had worn for the past four weeks, ever since her father's death.

Black shoes and stockings she could stand, but not the black skirts and bodice, black gloves, black hat, even black-edged handkerchiefs. Besides all that, her mother had bought a few blacked-bordered envelopes for the letters announcing Pa's death. For a young woman who could shoot a Colt revolver and harness a team by herself, black was terribly staid. Boring, even. But for Pa, she would wear it. For now.

Mrs. Wilcox, a friend of her mother, stepped out into the aisle in front of them as they left the little clapboard church.

"Emma, I heard you've sold the house as well as the store."

"That's right," her mother said.

"My dear, what will you do now?" Mrs. Wilcox squeezed Ma's wrist, her face contorted with concern.

"Molly and I plan to join Andrew in Texas," Ma said with a fixed smile. She knew her friend well.

Surely enough, Mrs. Wilcox drew back in alarm. "Texas? I hear that's a wild place. Full of robbers and army deserters and—and—Confederate sympathizers." She spat out the last two words as if they were the worst thing you could call someone. Three months after the War Between the States ended, maybe it was.

Molly managed a tight smile when Mrs. Wilcox looked her way.

"We're eager to see Andrew again," Ma said. "He's bought some land down there."

"I hope you've given it considerable thought, and you won't leave real soon." Mrs. Wilcox peered closely at Ma.

"Actually, we don't plan to wait long. We'll be setting out within the week."

Mrs. Wilcox gasped and stood staring after them as Ma herded Molly among the lingerers toward the church door.

The pastor, in his own version of mourning clothes, stood on the top step outside, shaking hands with the members of his congregation as they filed out.

"Mrs. Weaver." He took Ma's hand, bestowing a gentle smile on her. "How are you?"

"Fine, Pastor."

"And Molly." He took Molly's hand briefly. "Have you heard from Andrew yet?"

Molly shook her head and looked away. Her brother Andrew should have received the black-bordered envelope by now. A week or more ago. But then, Mrs. Wilcox was right about some things. The mails to the western states were notoriously slow, unless your correspondent lived along the railway lines. And in Texas, what few railroads existed were in chaos, or so the newspaper had told them.

Still, was it unreasonable to think that Andrew would have received the dreary letter bearing the news of his father's death and hurried to the nearest post office to send a reply?

Ma let out a sigh. "Not yet," she told the minister. "We hope to hear something tomorrow."

"Of course. My prayers are with you."

Molly trudged down the steps in her mother's wake and headed beside her toward the road. Ma veered off into the graveyard beside the church, and Molly followed, tears forming in her eyes before they came anywhere near Pa's grave.

The modest headstone had been set only a few days ago. Simeon Weaver, 1815-1865.

Molly groped up her sleeve for her handkerchief with the somber tatted edging. Ma was crying, too, but her tears slipped out from beneath her closed eyelids and streamed down her cheeks. Ma's moving lips told Molly that she was praying.

Goodbye, Pa. She would probably never visit his grave again, at least not after this week. Ma would come every day until they left for Texas, and Molly would come with her if she could. She would never stop being thankful for her wonderful parents, and she could only imagine how empty Ma must feel. Their lives were shattered the day Pa died. Molly pulled in a deep breath.

Ma had her own kind of strength. She'd always held their family together and made a pleasant home for her, Andrew, and Pa. But in some ways, Ma was fragile too. Molly had heard her crying in the night several times since the funeral. She was determined to do whatever Ma needed done right now, and the first thing was a big challenge—a long, arduous journey.

Ma wiped her face, and they left the cemetery, headed for their little home. They must be completely removed from it by Friday. There was packing to do. Things to give away. Decisions to make. Molly was excited about their coming adventure, but the preparations involved a great deal of hard work.

"Andrew should have had time to answer." Molly wished her only sibling had been at home when the tragedy happened, or at least for Pa's funeral, but that was impossible. Andrew was at least a thousand miles away.

"We must be patient, dear."

Somehow, Ma didn't look horrible in the bleak mourning dress like Molly did. She looked delicate and brave at the same time. And she probably wouldn't discard her black clothing for at least a year. Not Molly. She planned to wear anything but black on their train trip.

Her eyes stung with tears as she remembered how happy Ma had been a month ago—so excited at Pa's news that he'd sold the mercantile and they could soon leave to join Andrew in Texas. They'd help him enlarge his little ranch house and stock his land with fine cattle. But Pa had dropped dead on his way to the bank the next morning.

They walked down the street and turned the corner.

"As soon as we hear from Andrew, we'll set out," Ma said confidently.

Molly threw her a sidelong glance. "What if we don't hear from him?"

Ma pulled in a deep breath and looked straight ahead. "I'm sure we will."

On Thursday morning, Molly ran eagerly to the door to meet the postman.

"There you go, Miss Molly," the postman said with a smile, placing two envelopes in her hand.

She forced herself not to look at them while he was still standing there. "You know we won't be here after tomorrow?"

"Yes. You've left a forwarding address at the post office?"

"My mother has."

"Are you moving out of town?" he asked.

"We're going to join my brother in Texas."

"Oh! I wish you a good journey then."

"Thank you. We're going by train as far as Kansas City."

"That's quite a trip. How will you go on from there?"

"We're told there are stagecoaches."

The postman raised his eyebrows. "Have a safe journey."

"Thank you." She closed the door, trying not to think he'd sounded doubtful. She looked at the envelopes and walked into the kitchen.

Her mother stood at the table, adding a few final items to a box they would give a neighbor. "Was that the postman?"

"Yes." Molly held out the envelopes.

Her mother took them the letters and gazed sadly down at them. "The one from the bank is no doubt a final statement. The other appears to be from Cousin Pearl in Brooklyn. Condolences, I'm sure."

Molly swallowed hard. "But nothing from Andrew."

"No."

"Ma, we have to be out tomorrow. What will we do?"

"We'll finish our packing tonight and go to the station in the morning, as planned. The sooner we begin our journey, the sooner we get to Texas."

"But ..." Molly reached for the back of a chair to steady herself. They'd discussed their options, and they'd prayed hard all week that they'd hear from Andrew. The letter hadn't come. She looked around. The man who'd bought the house had given them extra money for the furnishings. She and her mother were planning to stay in Texas, and they'd reduced their belongings to two trunks and two leather satchels.

"Come, let's check each room to be sure we haven't forgotten anything," Ma said. "I'll leave the key where I told Mr. Endicott he'd find it."

"But, Ma ..."

"We must trust the Lord, Molly. We must leave first thing in the morning to make our train. I'll dash off one last note to Andrew today, just in case we don't hear from him, and you can take it to the post office while I finish up here. And then I'll arrange for someone to come in the morning and take the trunks to the station for us." Ma frowned. "I doubt any message we send Andrew now will reach him before we do, but at least we will have tried."

Molly dutifully walked through the house, peering into each cupboard and under the beds. They'd sold or given away what personal belongings they weren't taking with them. Everything left now would go to Mr. Endicott and his family. She hoped they enjoyed the house the way the Weavers had while their family was intact.

When she returned to the kitchen, Ma stood and handed her a sheet of paper. "You'll have to get an envelope and a stamp at the post office. Mine are all packed in my trunk, and I hate to open it again."

Molly took the paper and put on her shawl.

"Hurry back," Ma said. "Mrs. Wilcox invited us to take dinner with them."

"How will we get to the station tomorrow?" Molly asked.

"I'm sure we can ride in the freight wagon when they take the trunks."

On her way to the post office, Molly passed the mercantile. She'd been so excited when Pa announced he'd sold it for a good price, and now they could take the money to Texas and help Andrew build up the ranch.

Her brother had told them in his letters that his ranch was a small one, but there was adjoining land he might be able to acquire later. Ma and Pa had talked about purchasing the land next to Andrew's and combining it in one large ranch. He had only a small, two-room cabin, but they could build a new house nearby. It would be an adventure for the family. Molly could hardly wait to ride the range with him, tending to the cattle.

But now ...

Her heart was heavy as she entered the post office. If she knew all was well with Andrew, she would still be glad. But his last letter had arrived four weeks ago, and it was written before Andrew received the news of his father's death.

What if he'd received the sorrowful news and left

immediately to support his mother? What if he was on his way back to Ohio? They could easily miss him.

Surely, as soon as he reached a town with telegraph wires, Andrew would send a telegram telling them to wait for him. But a month had passed, and they'd received no wire from him, though they'd sent several more letters in the interim. Nothing. When he wrote his last letter, Andrew hadn't known the mercantile was sold. He might think they wouldn't come for some time yet.

So now she and Ma were heading out into uncertainty.

Molly squared her shoulders and walked to the counter.

"OHIO, YOU SAY?" Ryland Atkins's pulse leaped. After two years of trying, was he finally finding a clue to Jane Cooper's whereabouts?

"Yes, just outside Columbus. I received a letter from Emma not two weeks ago saying her husband had passed away." The woman's eyes glistened. "I feel so bad for her. She has two grown children out there to support her, of course. Still, it must be hard. Emma said something about selling their store."

"They have a store out there?"

"Land, yes. Fifteen years or more now. Let me get you their address."

Mrs. Hillier came back a minute later with a scrap of paper in her hand. "I'm sorry you've been to all this trouble."

"It's all right," Ryland said. "I did ask all around their old neighborhood, but folks who remembered them didn't seem to know where they'd gone."

"And none of them knew Emma had a cousin living five miles away." Mrs. Hillier gave him a sad smile. "I hope she and the children are all right. That Molly was a right pert little thing. And Andrew—oh, he could get into mischief."

Ryland smiled. He had the Weavers' new address, and he had

names and information about the family. He could find them. He was sure he could.

"Thank you so much, Mrs. Hillier."

He hurried to the nearest commercial street, swinging his trusty sword cane. A cab driver pulled his horse smartly to the curb when Ryland whistled.

"Take me to the nearest telegraph office, please." He climbed into the cab, and the driver set the horse to moving.

Too bad he had no time to write to Abigail. Ryland smiled, thinking of the lovely young woman he'd left behind in Maine when he started out on this latest quest. Abigail Benson was no doubt sitting primly in her grandmother's parlor doing needlework this afternoon. His chest tightened. He would write her a quick letter while he waited for his train west.

The driver stopped before a hotel.

"Telegraph office in the lobby, sir."

"Thank you." Ryland handed him some coins. "I'll want to go to the railway depot next, if you'd like to wait while I send a wire."

"I'll be here, sir."

Ryland nodded and strode into the hotel. He spotted the telegrapher's grille right away. He'd become an expert at locating them in his travels over the last two years. Quickly he filled in the form with his employer's address in Portland, Maine.

FOUND WEAVERS NEW ADDRESS. HEADING FOR
OHIO.

He was thankful for the freedom with which Mr. Turner entrusted him. Ryland had plenty of funds at his disposal to buy the train ticket to Columbus. With any luck, he'd be speaking to Abby's cousin Jane within a couple of days. He whistled as he rode in the cab toward the train station.

2

Molly listened carefully as her mother inquired of the conductor how they could continue their journey.

"Well, ma'am, we're coming up on the last stop on this line. They're planning to add on, but that probably won't be in operation until next year. Now, there is a local railroad that can take you twenty miles or so farther south, and I'm told you can get a stagecoach from there." The gray-haired man shook his head. "I'm afraid there's just no direct way to get to Texas these days."

"Perhaps we should have traveled south sooner." A frown etched lines on Ma's brow.

"Maybe, but I don't think so. A lot of rail lines were torn up during the war, and east of the Mississippi River it's hard to go very far without delays. No, I think you did the right thing. But short of joining a wagon train, this is probably best."

"A wagon train?" Ma said. "Wouldn't that take months?"

"Yes, ma'am. A lot of hassle too. Stagecoaches are definitely faster. You just never know how reliable it will be once you get off the main lines. They'll be taking you out around the Indian Territory."

"I see."

Molly had never considered that they might encounter Indians on the journey. She hoped not. Maybe they'd see a buffalo. That would be interesting. And Andrew had written about the strange birds and creatures in Texas. She wanted to see an armadillo, but not too close.

She leaned against the window and closed her eyes while Ma continued to chat with the conductor. They'd been nearly a week on the road already, changing trains often and waiting overnight to be ferried across the huge river that separated the civilized world from the vast, unpredictable West.

Changes had slowly emerged in her mother. Pa had always cushioned his womenfolk from the worst in life, she realized. Yes, Ma had uprooted with him to move to Ohio, and she'd helped at the mercantile. But she'd never had to make all the arrangements or endure an undertaking like this. While Ma seemed ready now to break out of her placid routine and set out for a new life on the frontier, Molly had concerns.

Ma's not as young as me. Lord, help me carry the worst of the burden on this trip. Please get us there safely, and let Ma still have some vim left at the other end.

Molly was tired, but she'd expected that. More than once, Ma had cautioned her about how rough and difficult the journey might be. Molly was afraid she would give up on the plan to join Andrew on the ranch after Pa died, but Ma had clung to the dream too. She was probably worried that Molly would go off alone unless she accompanied her. Finding Andrew was of utmost importance, but Molly would never go off and leave her mother alone.

And she'd heard tales of how dangerous traveling was for a woman alone. Although she considered herself adventurous, she didn't want to experience a long trip without her mother's companionship. The trip was safer and more pleasant together.

She opened her eyes and scrutinized her ma. True, she looked tired, but not any more than she used to after a long day at the store. Her somber clothing made her face look pale. She must think about Pa constantly and how they'd planned this journey together.

Molly sat up straight, more determined than ever to look after her mother. Andrew had given her shooting lessons before he left last year, and she was thankful. On his advice, she'd reserved a revolver, a shotgun, and ammunition for both from the inventory when they sold the mercantile. Those were all safely packed in the bottom of her trunk. Perhaps she should get out the revolver before they boarded a stagecoach.

The conductor ambled off down the aisle, swaying with the train's rhythm. Ma turned toward her, brushing her skirt into place as she shifted. The black fabric nestled against the lavender of Molly's skirt, and she suppressed a smile. Ma had let her give up her mourning dress the second day of the trip, once they were away from the chance of meeting anyone they knew.

"Wearing mourning on the trip will make us appear more empathetic," she'd said, trying one last time to reason with her daughter.

"It would make us appear more vulnerable," was Molly's reply, and Ma had said no more except that Molly should eschew bright hues for at least three months. She could do that.

Now Ma gazed at her with a wary smile. "We're in for another big change, it seems."

"It won't be as comfortable as the train." If one could call the train comfortable.

"No, but it may be as fast, from what that gentleman said. If all goes well, we'll keep moving day and night, except for when they change out the teams. No more sitting in railroad stations, waiting for the next train."

"How far will we go in a day?" Molly asked.

"Perhaps as much as a hundred and fifty miles."

Molly thought about that. They were already more than halfway to the Texas border. Of course, Texas was very large, and Andrew's ranch was a long way into its vast territory. And they wouldn't be going in a straight line.

"We must pray for wisdom and safety," Ma said.

Molly nodded. Ma would never think they deserved to pray for comfort. If one had to choose, she supposed safety was more important. Wisdom would be welcome too. She closed her eyes, determined to sleep through the last hour on the train. Sleep might be a scarce commodity once they got to the stagecoach line.

RYLAND STEPPED DOWN from the local stagecoach in a small town just outside Columbus.

The driver waved down the street. "The mercantile's yonder."

"Thank you." Ryland could see the sign from where he stood. One of the stage tenders tossed down his bag. He retrieved it and trudged down the block.

He walked into the store and looked around. It seemed well stocked, and several customers were browsing. A man whose clothing declared him a farmer stood talking to the one presiding behind the counter. When he turned away, Ryland stepped up and smiled.

"Hello, I'm looking for the Weaver family."

The man's smile slipped. "Uh, did you know Simeon?"

"Not personally, no." Ryland tried to add a mournful air to his smile. "I understand Mr. Weaver passed away recently. I'd like to find the family."

"Well, as I understand it, Mrs. Weaver and her daughter have left the area. Maybe her neighbors would have more information."

Too late. He would have to start all over. Ryland tried to keep his voice steady.

"If you could tell me where they lived?"

The man told him where the house was, and he started out on foot, lugging his leather satchel and cane, glad he'd packed light. He kept watch along the way for a hotel but didn't spot one before he found the snug little house. It looked well kept, and a sprightly woman opened the door to his knock.

"Hello, my name is Atkins, and I'm looking for the Weaver family. I understand they used to live here?"

"That's right. I'm Mrs. Endicott. My husband bought the place last week."

Ryland's hope rose a notch. "Last week? Then the family hasn't been gone long?" She hesitated, and he added quickly, "I heard Mr. Weaver passed away. It's important that I find his family."

Her eyes narrowed. "May I ask why?"

"Of course. I'm employed by an attorney in New England. It's a family matter. Nothing sinister, I assure you."

"Hmm." She looked him up and down. "I have to ask, since you're not the first to inquire."

"I'm not?" Ryland swallowed hard. "Someone else has been asking for the Weavers?"

"Yesterday. A man not as stylish as you. A bit down at heel, I'd say."

"Did he give his name?"

"Cooper."

A shock of anxiety zinged through Ryland. "May I ask what you told him?"

"Is he a bad one?"

"I fear he might be, Mrs. Endicott. It's vital that I find the Weavers quickly."

She pursed her lips for a moment. "As I told him, they've moved away. Perhaps you can learn more from the minister at their church on the main street, or from the folks who bought the mercantile from Mr. Weaver."

Ryland nodded. "I've been there. The new owner directed me here."

"I see."

"Let me show you my credentials." He could tell she would

not be an easy nut to crack, so he set down his bag and cane and took his wallet from his inside jacket pocket. "This is a letter from my employer, Mr. Jeremiah Turner, Esquire."

She took the paper and peered at it. "In Maine. You're a long way from home."

"Indeed. But I assure you, my mission is honorable, and I mean only the best for the Weavers."

Again, she scrutinized him. "Bit of an inheritance, eh?"

Ryland opened his mouth and closed it.

She chuckled. "Why else would a lawyer be so keen on finding a body? Well, I like you, Mr. Atkins, and I hope my instincts are right about you. Emma Weaver and her daughter took the train a few days ago. They planned to go to Texas, to the Weavers' son Andrew's place."

Ryland caught his breath. Texas. A new destination, and no doubt new adventures were in store.

The next stagecoach into Columbus wouldn't come through until the next day, so he rented a horse, arranging to leave it at a stable in the city, and set out for the ride. Less than an hour later, he left his mount at a livery near the depot and went to the ticket window.

"Can you advise me on the quickest way to get to Texas?"

"Well, as I told the gentleman yesterday, unless you want to ride horseback all the way, I'd take the train either south to Arkansas—I believe you can get through that far now—or west to Kansas City. After that, you'll have to arrange your transportation to Texas." He shook his head. "It's not the easiest journey, I fear."

Ryland's jaw clenched when he heard that another man had inquired about trains to Texas the day before. Cooper, no doubt.

"And which way did the other gentleman choose?"

"I believe he headed for Kansas City, Missouri."

Ryland nodded and decided to stretch the truth. "Well, I'm a friend of the Weaver family. The widow and her daughter Molly bought tickets a few days ago, but they neglected to leave me word on which route they were taking. Since I hope to reunite with them, I'd like the same itinerary they chose.

The man hesitated. "I'm not sure—"

"It's very important that I overtake them as soon as possible." Ryland took out his credential letter. "I've been sent by the family's attorney to find them. I have important news for them, but it must be delivered in person. I assure you I have the Weavers' best interests at heart."

The clerk scanned the letter and eyed him pensively then turned away with it in his hand.

"Oh—" Ryland reached toward the opening at the bottom of the grille, but the clerk was lost in the busy office behind the window. He sighed. He would have to wait for his letter, if nothing else. A train whistle blew, and a locomotive's departure, loud enough to awaken everyone from Columbus to Cincinnati, shook the station. Ryland winced and put his fingers in his ears.

After about five minutes, during which a line of sour-faced people formed behind him, the clerk returned with another man.

"Mr. Atkins, this is my supervisor. He will speak to you by the door to your left."

Since the supervisor began moving that way with Ryland's letter in hand, he had no choice. He looked along the station wall. Spotting the door in question a few yards away, he picked up his luggage and hurried to it.

The door opened, and a man in a business suit stepped out carrying the letter.

"Mr. Atkins?"

"Yes, sir."

The gentleman frowned at him. "You understand, sir, that the railroad tries to protect its passengers, particularly its female passengers."

"I would expect no less."

"And this is a legal matter?"

"Yes, sir. A family matter of some importance. I would

appreciate your assistance, and I can assure you of my discretion and my desire for the family's wellbeing."

"I'm told there was another man yesterday ..."

"So I've heard, sir, and I'm doubtful his intentions are as honorable as mine." Ryland straightened his shoulders. "This knowledge makes me even more anxious to find Mrs. Weaver and her daughter."

"You would accompany them to Texas?"

He hesitated. "Well, if that was their wish after they hear what I have to say, but I suspect they would want to consult my employer first, if only through telegrams."

"I see. Well, I've been assured—" The supervisor paused as another train roared in on the closest track and screeched to a stop. He gave a tight smile. "I'm assured our ticket agent did not release the ladies' exact destination. But for you, sir ..." He handed Ryland the letter and reached into his pocket. "You must hurry. That is your train to Kansas City, and it leaves in ten minutes. The cost of the ticket ..."

He named the price, which seemed enormous to Ryland, but he whipped out his wallet and counted out the sum then put Mr. Turner's letter away.

"Very good," the supervisor said, pocketing the money and holding out a ticket. "I assumed you'd want this."

Ryland looked down at it.

"Mrs. Weaver mentioned Austin, Texas," the supervisor said. "She was told there were no railroads going there at this time, but she and her daughter were determined to go as far as they could by rail and then make their way to that area. It would perhaps have been better for her to head for New Orleans and go from there, but ..." He shrugged. "I'm told Austin has telegraph service through New Orleans."

"Well, that's something. Thank you very much, sir." Ryland grabbed the ticket, his cane, and his bag and hurried to the platform. No time to send a telegram now, but perhaps if he was quick, he could write a brief message and entrust it to a porter.

With a handsome tip, of course. He would have time to write letters on the train.

MOLLY JERKED upright on the wagon seat. She was supposed to be driving, but she was so fatigued she nodded off several times when she should have paid attention. The journey had worn out both her and Ma, but she was determined to see her mother safely to Andrew's. Today.

The horse they'd hired in Austin knew nothing of their grueling trip and plodded along the dusty road without much guidance. If she'd had the energy, Molly would have urged him into a trot, but she sat, drained and listless, watching his hind feet trudge along.

"We're a sight," Ma said with a little chuckle.

Molly adjusted the slack reins that had slid through her fingers. Both their skirts and their hats were layered with dust. "I don't know about you, but the first thing I want when we find the ranch is a bath."

"If your brother has a bathtub."

Her wry comment surprised Molly. Andrew had always been fastidious, but that was under his mother's eyes. Perhaps Ma was right. They'd seen some very unkempt characters along the way. She didn't want to remember the reeking cattleman she'd been forced to sit next to in a stagecoach, or the leers from foul-smelling men they'd endured.

She'd lost count of the stage stops. Some were fairly comfortable houses with decent facilities and meals to rival Ma's cooking. Others were shacks in the wilderness with nothing but a rickety outhouse a few yards behind the station and a poor excuse for a dinner.

"I'm trying not to get my expectations up," she admitted.

"We should have splurged and stayed overnight in Austin."

Ma gazed ahead, her eyes crinkling at the corners against the merciless sun.

"No, we were right to save the money." Molly put the reins together in one hand and reached over to pat her mother's arm.

"I do worry about road agents," Ma confessed.

"The banker said we ought to be safe, as long as we get there before dark."

"Ought to be." Ma sounded uncertain. At least they'd left half their money at the bank in Austin. The town was within a day's drive of Andrew's ranch, and they'd agreed it might be best to split up their assets. An encounter with a pickpocket along the way had made them extremely wary, and Ma's relief when they banked half their funds safely had shown Molly how very worried she'd been.

Off to their right, water trickled. "That must be the stream the man mentioned." Molly stood for a moment, fighting for balance. "He said that one usually runs all summer."

"Yes, and there's only one ranch between here and Andrew's place." Ma smiled at her. "We're almost there."

"Hallelujah." Molly sat and smacked the horse's rump with the reins. He extended his stride a bit, but never broke out of a walk.

"Come on," she wheedled. "We've been on the road nearly a month, and we want to finish this journey today. I'll give you a nice feed when we get there, I promise."

Ma chuckled. "I guess you don't speak horse."

"You're right. This is the first time I've driven one for half a day."

"At least you know how to hitch him up again if we need to in the morning."

Molly shook her head emphatically. "Andrew will hitch up for us when we need to go somewhere, but I intend to stay put for a while."

A trail led off the dirt track, and she could make out a roofline at the bottom of a slope.

"That's got to be the other ranch."

Ma nodded. "Andrew's nearest neighbor, I'd say. Didn't he mention someone in one of his letters?"

"He did, but I'm not sure it was the fellow who owns that place."

A handful of thin cattle were grazing fifty yards off the road. One raised its head and looked balefully at the creaking wagon.

"You stay put," Molly said firmly, though probably not loud enough for the bovine to hear.

"It seems odd how they let their livestock run loose out here," Ma said. "Wouldn't you think they'd lose a lot?"

"I don't know. Andrew said it takes a lot of land to raise cattle out here, because the grass is so poor."

"I hope he hasn't chosen a spot where he can't make a living."

Molly pulled in a deep breath. "I'm sure he talked to people and looked around before he bought the ranch." Still, the grass all around them looked brownish, and there weren't many true trees nearby, just scrubby bushes.

"There were trees near that stream." Ma peered off to the side. "I wonder if it runs through his land. That would be an asset."

"There!" Molly pointed to a cabin set back from the road. A rail fence enclosed a small corral nearby. "That's got to be it."

She guided the horse into the lane and stared at the house as the wagon rolled toward it.

"It's awfully small."

"We'll have to make do," Ma said.

"If it *is* his place." Molly swallowed hard, hoping this wasn't Andrew's cabin. He'd told them the house was small, but he hoped when Pa came they could add on.

Movement caught her eye. "Ma, look. There's horses in the corral."

Her mother seized her forearm, grinning. "He must be here."

Molly's heart jumped as she stared at the two dusty horses. "Then why didn't he pick up his mail?"

They'd inquired in Austin but were disappointed to learn Andrew hadn't claimed his mail for more than a month. Their last three letters, including the black-edged one, rested in a pigeonhole at the post office. After she'd shown him her new bank book, the postmaster had allowed Emma to take her son's mail.

Neither of them had wanted to talk about the possible reasons why Andrew hadn't picked it up. Anxiety had festered between them unspoken all day as they rode toward his home.

Molly urged the horse to within ten yards of the front door then pulled back on the reins. "Whoa."

The little cabin was a motley composition of stone, brick, and logs. The roof, on this side at least, was shingled. Andrew had told about replacing the roof in one of his early letters. They'd all laughed when they read how his bedding had been leaked on during the first rainstorm.

The door swung open, and a large, bearded man filled the opening.

"State yer business."

Molly gulped.

"I'm Mrs. Weaver," her mother said firmly. "I'm looking for my son Andrew. Is he here?"

"Don't know anyone named Weaver."

"I understand he owns this property."

"First I heard of it," the man said. Behind him, another figure loomed, as tall as the first and even broader. "We're the owners," the first one said. He shut the door with a thud.

3

M olly stared at her mother. Her throat ached.
       "Well," Ma said.

"What do we do?" Molly whispered.

"We can't storm the cabin, that's for sure. Let's head back to that first house and see what we can learn."

Molly painstakingly turned the horse and wagon in the cramped yard and flicked the reins. Headed toward home, the horse set out at a jog. Uneasily, she eyed the lowering sun.

"We can't get back to Austin before dark."

"That much is true. Let's just find out if we've mistaken the location." Ma gave a little chuckle. "It might actually be a blessing to find out we were wrong."

Molly nodded. Anything would be better than learning that really was Andrew's land and he wasn't there.

"Maybe we didn't go far enough, and someone else built that cabin recently," she ventured.

Ma shook her head. "It's not a new dwelling."

Molly drove on toward Austin, her lips pressed tightly together. She slapped the reins and yelled at the horse, and he actually trotted faster. They approached the ranch they'd seen earlier. Ma nudged her with an elbow, and Molly followed her gaze. A man dressed in a cotton shirt, a wide-brimmed hat, and boots, with leather chaps over his pants, rode across the open land where the cattle grazed.

"Whoa." She hauled back on the reins.

Their horse stopped, and Molly gazed with unrestrained envy at the compact, muscular bay horse the man rode. That animal could outrun their hired horse easily, and its glossy coat and rounded hindquarters bespoke good care.

Ma stood up, removed her shawl, and waved it over her head. "Yoo-hoo!"

After a moment, the horseman changed direction and jogged toward them. When he reached the edge of the roadway, he halted, surveying them with pensive brown eyes.

"Howdy, ma'am."

"Hello," Ma said in her most gracious tone. "I wonder if you could tell us who owns the next ranch to the east—the one with the little cabin."

He grinned. "Sure. That's Andrew Weaver's place."

Molly drew a quick breath and looked at Ma, who seemed speechless.

"That's what we thought," Molly said quickly. "But he's not there. Two men came to the door and said they don't know Andrew and that they own the place."

The man's whole face crumpled into a troubled frown. "That's downright odd. Andrew's away, and I've been riding over there every now and then just to keep an eye on things."

"When was the last time you went?" Ma asked.

He sighed. "About three days ago. I was planning on taking a look-see tomorrow morning."

Molly exchanged another look with her mother, and Emma faced the man.

"I'm Andrew's mother, Emma Weaver, and this is my daughter, Molly—Andrew's sister."

"How do you do, ma'am?" He rode a bit closer and leaned

down to offer his hand. "Joe Noyes. I've known Andrew since he came to these parts last year."

Ma shook his hand, but Molly just gave him a nod.

"I believe Andrew mentioned you in some of his letters home," Ma said.

"To Ohio?" Joe asked.

"That's right."

"Well, I'm pleased to meet you." Joe hesitated and glanced toward the rapidly dropping sun.

"Do you know where Andrew is?"

"He's gone to buy some cattle. I admit, I expected him back before this." Noyes pushed back his hat, frowning. "Listen, why don't I ride over there with you and see if we can sort this out. I've heard there's been some trouble with squatters lately."

"Squatters?" Molly asked, a bolt of alarm shooting through her.

Joe nodded with a reluctant air. "Since the war ended, there's a lot of drifters and such."

He wore a revolver in a holster on his hip. Molly wondered if she ought to dig her guns out of the luggage.

Joe smiled. "I expect we can clear things up."

"What if we can't?" Molly asked.

He shrugged. "You can sleep at my place if necessary. I'll sleep in my barn, and we'll go for the sheriff in the morning."

"We couldn't ask you to do that," Ma said.

"And you didn't ask me, ma'am. I offered. Andrew's a friend of mine."

Molly liked him, but she wouldn't admit it if asked. She wanted to trust him. Still, in this wild country where strangers took over your house when you weren't looking, could they really trust anyone?

"Well, thank you," Ma said. "I trust it won't come to that. Molly, can you turn the wagon around in Mr. Noyes's farm lane?"

She made no move to set the horse in motion. Not yet. "Do you know where my brother went to buy these cattle?"

"I know where he intended to buy them." Noyes's brow wrinkled. "He must have hit a snag and had to go farther than he planned. I offered to go with him, but he said one of us should stay here. I guess I should have kept a closer eye on his place."

"We appreciate your help in the matter," Ma said and gave Molly a meaningful nod.

She slapped the reins on the horse's rump. "Up."

The horse dragged his feet as they headed back toward Andrew's ranch. Molly studied her mother's profile. Emma rode with her eyes shut tight. Molly felt a surge of protectiveness for her. She'd lost her husband. She couldn't lose her only son. If they couldn't find Andrew, Molly would be all the family she had. A lump formed in her throat, and tears scalded her eyes.

Joe Noyes rode ahead of them, keeping to a steady jog. The livery's horse seemed willing to follow, but Joe had to pause several times, allowing the wagon to catch up. They should have hired a team, but that would have cost more.

He turned when he was nearly to Andrew's lane and waited for them.

"Are you all right, Ma?" Molly asked.

Her mother nodded. "I'm praying, that's all." She opened her eyes. "The Lord will sort it out."

Molly hoped she was right. Were they wrong to put their trust in Joe, a complete stranger?

He rode his bay back to them, and Molly stopped their horse when she came even with the rancher.

"Stay back here," Joe said. "I'll see what's what."

Molly had a million questions. What if they thought Joe was Andrew? Would they give way to him, or would they attack him?

Another, bleaker thought immediately crossed her mind. What if Andrew had returned from his trip and found them there? Those men could have killed her brother already, in which case they wouldn't welcome further inquiries.

She leaned toward him. "I have two guns in my trunk. Should I get them out?"

"You know how to use them?"

Molly nodded.

He hesitated and looked toward Andrew's place. "Get them. I'll keep watch while you do."

Her mother caught her breath but said nothing. Molly climbed over the back of the seat, into the wagon bed, where she opened her trunk. After rummaging under her clothing and other personal items, she pulled out the shotgun, the revolver, and two boxes of cartridges. She loaded the shotgun first.

"Ma," she said.

Emma looked at her, and Molly handed the shotgun to her over the seat. Then she loaded the revolver. Carrying the handgun and extra ammunition, she climbed back into the driver's seat, careful to lift her legs in Ma's direction, not Joe's. She managed it quite modestly, but even so, Ma reached out and tucked a fold of her skirt around her leg.

Molly placed the revolver on the seat, between her and Ma. The cartridge boxes went on the floor at her feet. Picking up the reins, she looked over at Joe. "Ready."

"We're going to do this peacefully if we can," Joe said.

"Right," Molly replied. "I hate to have you go down there alone, though."

"I guess you can come, but not too close."

Her mother carefully stowed the shotgun out of sight at her feet.

Joe nodded and pivoted his horse. As he rode toward the cabin alone, Molly looked around. If Andrew had come back, the cattle he'd bought would be somewhere close by. She didn't see any livestock except the two horses in the pen. She swallowed hard and flicked the reins.

They were still a good way from the house when Ma touched her arm. "Let Mr. Noyes do the talking."

"Yes, Ma."

Molly stopped the wagon where the lane to the house started and let Joe ride closer to the door without them. She could see the wisdom of not taking the wagon down there where it would be hard to turn around quickly. He glanced over his shoulder and nodded to her.

"Hello the house," he yelled. He sat on his horse not two yards from the stoop—one rough wooden step.

Would he get down out of the saddle? Molly held her breath.

After several tense seconds, the cabin's door opened. The big man who'd talked to them before held a shotgun in his hands.

"Whatchoo want?"

"This is my house."

The bearded man's eyes narrowed.

Molly swallowed hard. She hadn't expected an outright lie. Would the squatter know Joe wasn't Andrew? If Joe could toss out a falsehood that quickly, was he a man they could trust? A wave of fear swept over her. That man wouldn't shoot Joe, would he? What would she and Ma do if that happened? She reached down and fingered her revolver's grip.

The man cast a glance toward the wagon and lowered his shotgun a little. He said something to Joe that Molly couldn't hear, but she noticed Joe's hand hovered near the butt of his revolver.

A moment later, the bearded man cursed, and Joe drew his gun.

"You get out of my house now."

"Make me!" The big man leveled the shotgun.

Joe hauled back on his reins, and the bay backed up so fast Molly thought it would sit down on its haunches.

The shotgun blasted, the horse jumped and squealed, and Joe let off a round. He pivoted his horse and galloped toward the wagon.

"Go," he yelled. "Get out of range."

In the cabin's doorway, the bearded man fumbled with his shotgun, probably reloading. Then the second squatter yanked him out of the way and stuck a handgun out the door and fired.

"Go," Joe shouted again as his horse pounded toward them.

Ma had already dived over the side of the wagon and was crouched below the sideboards. Molly couldn't drive off and leave her. But if she stayed put, the horse would present a large target. She wavered, then dropped the reins and jumped off the far side of the wagon, sinking to her knees beside her mother.

4

E nd of the line. Ryland couldn't travel any farther by train. After finding a small hotel and a meal, he sat down and wrote a two-page letter to Mr. Turner, explaining the circumstances in detail and assuring him that he had enough funds for the journey to Austin, Texas.

He took a fresh sheet of paper for a note to Abby, daring to open it with *My dearest Abigail*. In the past, he'd always opened with *Dear Miss Benson* or addressed the letters to her grandmother, Edith Rose. But during his last stay in Maine, they'd progressed to where he felt the more flowery greeting was justified.

After a few lines assuring her that he was all right and still on the trail of her last missing cousin, he came to the letter's conclusion. But how to close? Did a man who'd stolen one brief kiss on their last parting have the right to sign *with love*? Because he did love her. He had no doubt of that. But was it too forward? And would her grandmother see the letter? With a sigh, he signed off with *Affectionately yours, Ryland Atkins*.

He addressed and stamped the envelope, his mind filled with images of Abby. He enjoyed his travels, but he must be maturing. He was looking forward to times at home more than adventures in the far-flung places Mr. Turner sent him. He hoped the lawyer's next assignment for him would keep him closer to Portland.

He ambled to the local post office, where he entrusted the two letters to the postmaster to be sent out on the next day's eastbound train.

As for Ryland, he would be on a stagecoach south at six in the morning. He wasn't looking forward to that. His stagecoach experiences in the past had somewhat soured him on frontier travel. But he no longer had his friend Mory with him to look after the mounts if they bought horses. Mory had found a job at a livery stable in New Hampshire. Ryland wished him well, but he'd miss his amiable companion, and he certainly didn't want to travel alone on horseback out here.

A short stroll took him to the stage depot, and as expected, he found a large barn behind it, where they housed extra teams and equipment. He walked in and found one of the station's tenders rationing feed for the horses.

"Afternoon," Ryland said.

The man nodded. "You takin' the stage?"

"In the morning, yes."

The tender's eyes narrowed, and he drawled, "You from back East?"

Ryland smiled. "How can you tell?"

They both laughed.

"I'm from the state of Maine."

"I'm from Tennessee, but they say it's not a state now." The man shook his head.

Ryland almost asked him if he'd served in the war but held back. If this man had served, it was no doubt with the Rebs. And he'd probably ask if Ryland had served, and he'd have to admit he hadn't. That knowledge antagonized some people worse than having worn the wrong color uniform.

"I've been to Tennessee." He leaned against a post that supported two stall dividers.

"What part?"

"Well, I was in Chattanooga last winter."

The man grunted. "I'm from Memphis."

"Hmm, that's over on the river, isn't it? The Mississippi, I mean."

"I know what you mean." The tender poured grain into a big chestnut's feedbox. "Yeah, it is. I may go back there."

"I intend to go back to Maine myself, but I have to go to Texas first."

"You goin' all the way on the stage?"

"Hope to. The line's open all the way to Austin, isn't it?"

"Well, you'll have to change a few times. It's all local lines down there, patched together, or so I hear."

"Are they planning to run a railroad through?"

He shook his head. "I misdoubt that'll happen for a while yet. The gov'ment's got a few kinks to work out. And money's kinda tight right now for ever'body, I reckon."

Ryland nodded. He wasn't looking forward to going into such wild country, especially where a lot of the inhabitants bore a grudge against anyone from the North. But he'd ventured into Tennessee and Georgia when hostilities were still underway to find Abby's cousin Jack, and he'd made it back alive. The war was over. He could live through a jaunt to Texas.

"You got a gun?"

Ryland jerked his chin up. "No. Why?"

"You should."

He frowned, recalling some no-goods he'd encountered on his previous trip to Colorado Territory. Stagecoaches weren't exactly the most secure forms of travel. Occasionally they were attacked from outside, and sometimes passengers got trapped in a box with some pretty rough types.

He nodded. "I'll surely consider it."

"Well, at least have a knife on you."

"Oh?" That might make sense, but Ryland wasn't sure he liked the idea. Still, his sword cane wasn't good in close quarters.

"You ever throw one?"

"Er, no."

The man dumped the last horse's ration and eyed him critically. "Let's see if you got a knack for it. Name's Quincy, by the way."

"Ryland Atkins."

They shook hands, and Quincy led him out the back door of the stable. Next to a large manure pile stood a stack of straw. Quincy stuck a rag on the front, tucking an edge into the straw and anchoring it with a stick.

He led Ryland to a spot about four yards away from his target and pulled a wicked-looking knife from a sheath on his belt. "You hold it like this."

Stepping back, Ryland watched him balance the weapon and focus on the target. Quincy's eyes narrowed, and he let the knife fly. The blade sank into the target, pinning the rag to the straw and disappearing except for the end of the hilt.

Ryland whistled softly. "Very nice."

"Let's see you try."

Quincy retrieved the knife and passed it to Ryland. He gave him advice on his grip and the position of his throwing arm. On his first throw, Ryland was surprised that the knife actually stuck into the straw, though it was six inches to the right of the rag.

"Not bad," Quincy said. "Try again."

Ryland had been pretty good with a slingshot as a boy, and at marbles too. Both had probably helped him develop a true aim. He spent the next half hour practicing under his new friend's tutelage. After the first dozen throws, Quincy moved his rag target to the boarded back wall of a shed.

"Had to make sure you'd come within a mile at least," he said with a nod at the straw pile. "Now stick it into something solid." The battered siding on the shed bore testament to the efforts of several other sessions in the past.

They stopped the lesson only when Quincy had to help switch out the horses on a coach heading eastward. Ryland's arm was tired, but toward the end of the session, he was able to place the blade in the rag, or within a couple of inches, nearly every time. Once it fell short of the wall, and another time it flew off to the right.

Despite the occasional miss, Ryland had gained confidence with the weapon. He walked out through the barn and watched Quincy and a coworker lead in the tired team from the waiting coach and take the fresh horses out and hitch them up.

As the stage rolled away, he nodded to Quincy. "You fellows are quick."

"Have to be. Look, you ought to get over to Jackson's store before they close for the night. You can get a good knife there."

"Good idea." Ryland reached for his pocket watch. Quincy probably knew the time to the minute without checking, when the stagecoaches were on time. "What's a good price for a blade like yours?"

Quincy directed him to the general store, and twenty minutes later, Ryland was the proud owner of a new weapon. Amazing how much more comfortable he felt with it now. He went to his hotel. If he found the climate in Texas too dangerous, he might invest in a revolver, but this should see him through the next part of the journey.

MOLLY STARED into her ma's huge eyes.

"Joe said to drive off out of range."

"I didn't think of that." Ma cringed behind the wagon's side and lowered her gaze. "What do we do now?"

Joe rode a few yards away from them and dropped his horse's reins. Molly could see blood on the bay's front left shoulder.

He stroked the horse's face and neck, then hurried, crouched down, to the wagon.

"They shot your horse," Molly said.

33

"A pellet grazed him. It's not serious, but he'll be shy for certain. Why'd you stop here?"

Molly flicked a glance toward her mother.

Joe nodded. "Let's pray they don't shoot your horse too. Maybe we can ease him along slowly. Are you ladies all right?"

"I'm fine," Molly said. "Ma?"

She nodded. "Do you think they've hurt Andrew, Mr. Noyes?"

"Call me Joe. And no, I don't. Andrew's horse would be here, but there are only two horses in the corral, and neither of them is Andrew's gray."

Molly thought about that. "They would keep the extra horse if they'd done away with its owner, wouldn't they?"

"Don't say that, child!" Ma clutched at Molly's sleeve.

"Sorry, Ma."

"I think she's right. They wouldn't give up a free horse. They're too valuable out here." Joe eased past the wagon, keeping himself stooped and sheltered behind the harnessed horse's body. Patting the animal's side and neck, he worked his way to where he could stretch out and grasp the trailing reins. He looked back at Molly. "You two move with the wagon."

She nodded and turned to her mother. "You heard him. When the wagon rolls, we go with it."

They both took hold of the sideboard and duck-walked as the wagon slowly moved forward. They'd only gone a couple of yards when another blast came and lead pellets splintered the board near Emma's hand and threw up pebbles in the roadway.

"Ma!"

"I'm fine," her mother said, but her voice quivered.

Molly edged past her and peeked around the back of the wagon, leading with her revolver. She studied the scene for a moment, choosing a target. The bearded man was reloading. Twilight was upon them, but she thought she could make the shot. She pulled in a deep breath and yelled, "Mister, you see that rock by the corral yonder?"

The man's head jerked as she shouted, and he stared toward the wagon, then toward the corral.

Molly aimed carefully and pulled the trigger. Pieces of the rock she'd chosen flew into the air, and the horses in the corral gave shrill whinnies and jumped away, to the far side of the enclosure.

"The next one will be in your filthy face," she yelled and ducked down behind the wagon wheel, hastily replacing the spent cartridge.

"Molly!" Her mother's tone was a rebuke, but she didn't scold her for being rude to the squatter. Instead, she said a bit incredulously, "What will Mr. Noyes think?"

Joe. She'd forgotten all about him for a few seconds.

Now his deep voice rang out as he yelled to the men in the cabin, "That's right. Now, get yer stuff and go. And don't take none of my stuff."

The door closed.

"Come on." Joe rose and grabbed the horse's bridle.

Molly scrambled up to the wagon seat and took the reins. "I can drive. Bring Ma."

She quickly moved the horse and wagon along the road until they were out of sight of the cabin. Joe and her ma were right there beside her. Joe picked up her mother like a sack of flour and plopped her on the seat beside Molly.

"Keep going until you find a place to turn around. Do it, and then wait for me. I'm going to get Ranger."

Molly surmised that Ranger was his horse. She stayed where she was long enough to watch Joe dart back along the road, across the stretch where the squatters could see him if they were looking. When he reached Ranger's side, she turned forward and slapped the reins. "Up!"

The horse was willing to get away from the noisy area and trotted along until Molly found a spot where she could easily drive out into a level patch of prairie and circle around. By the time they were back on the road, Joe had rejoined them. He sat astride Ranger, gazing down at her.

"Good job, Miss Weaver."

"Thank you. You too."

"What if they don't leave?" her mother asked.

"Then you wait at my house while I tear into Austin and bring back the sheriff and a posse."

"Tonight?"

"If I have to, ma'am."

"Please, it's Emma, and my daughter is Molly."

Molly frowned a little but didn't say anything. She wasn't at all sure she wanted to be on a first-name basis with this rough ranchman. But then, who stood on ceremony in the Wild West? She'd just shouted an insult at a hooligan and fired a warning shot. Maybe she didn't deserve to be called Miss Weaver.

Joe swung down from the saddle. "Thought I'd leave Ranger with you and go back to where I can see the cabin door. If they don't come out real soon, we might have to apply more pressure."

"Is there a back door?" Molly asked.

"Nope. There's one window on the back, but I doubt that big fella could squeeze through it." Joe tied Ranger's reins to the tailboard and gave Molly and her mother a lazy salute.

"I wonder if he was in the army," Ma said.

Molly watched him walk down the dirt road at an easy but quick pace. Most men Joe's age had been soldiers in the war, but not all. How had things been way out here? She recalled vaguely that some battles had taken place west of the Mississippi River, but she hadn't heard much about Texas—other than not being able to travel directly there by railroad. Wasn't it a Confederate state? And she had an idea they grew cotton down near the coast.

Joe went out of sight, and she sighed.

"He seems like a good-hearted man," Ma said.

"I guess."

36

"What? You don't like him?"

Molly shrugged. "Hard to say, at this point. He lied to them, Ma."

"Well, yes, there is that. I'm sure he felt it was the best way to dislodge them."

Molly couldn't help smiling at that. Ma had been a schoolteacher before she married Pa, and she sounded like one. "Don't get me wrong," she said. "I'm grateful he turned up when he did, and that he's willing to help us."

"He seems to like Andrew, and he's willing to stick his neck out for his friend's family." Ma stared steadily down the road.

"That's true. I'd just hate to see us become too ... indebted to Joe Noyes. We don't know anything about him."

Ma's gaze sharpened. "On the contrary, I'd say we know quite a lot about him. His character, I mean."

Did they really? Molly clamped her lips together. She could think of several reasons why a man like Joe might want to get those squatters out. Did he know more than he was telling about Andrew's absence? Maybe he hoped to get Andrew's land for himself.

She heard a faint shout and stood up so she could see better.

"Stay down until we know it's safe." Ma tugged at her skirt.

Molly thumped down on the wagon seat. Would they ever truly know they were safe again?

5

Joe watched Andrew's house intently. What were the squatters up to? Would they just stay inside and guzzle a jug or two and laugh about scaring off Joe and the women? He glanced up the road, but he couldn't see Mrs. Weaver and her daughter, or the horses and wagon.

The door of the little house creaked open, and he snapped his attention toward it. The burly man came out into the yard holding his gun, with a sack slung over his shoulder. Behind him came a second man. He had a saddle resting on his left arm. A gun barrel glinted in his right hand.

Joe stayed out of sight but continued to observe as they traipsed to the corral and caught their horses. They saddled up and slung their packs with their bedrolls. When they mounted and turned toward the road, Joe stood but didn't relax. The two men talked back and forth as they walked their horses toward the road, discussing where to go next.

As they gained the roadway, Joe stepped out, pointing his revolver in their general direction. He didn't want them heading toward where the two women waited.

"You boys have a nice ride now, y'hear?" he said.

The nearest horse jumped, and both men swung their heads toward him.

"Now, don't get excited," Joe said. "I expect the good folks in Austin will welcome you."

They scowled at him and muttered curses, but they rode on toward Austin, and Joe let out his pent-up breath.

Darkness had descended, and he couldn't see very far down the road, but he listened carefully to make sure the hoofbeats kept going. When they were well away, he walked swiftly toward the wagon. As soon as he could make out Molly Weaver's form on the wagon seat, he waved his hat and whistled.

"They're gone," he said when he was close enough. "Let's get you ladies settled." He strode to the rear of the wagon, untied Ranger, and leaped into the saddle.

Riding ahead, he reached the house and led his horse into the corral. "It's only for a few minutes, boy," he promised. "I know you're hungry."

Molly halted the wagon as close to the house as she could get it. Joe helped her mother down, and Molly hopped down unaided on the other side.

"Let me take a look inside," Joe said. "Andrew usually keeps a lantern hanging by the door."

The lantern wasn't in its spot. Faint embers glowed in the box stove, and he took the last twig from Andrew's kindling box and coaxed a flame on its end. It didn't take him long to find the lantern on the table and light it.

Molly entered immediately, as the light flared and he set the glass chimney in place.

Joe looked around. "Looks like they've been here at least a couple of days."

"How can you tell?" Molly's lip curled as she surveyed the room.

"Because Andrew keeps his place neat. It looks like those fellas ate all his food and dirtied all his dishes." He shook his head. "I'm sorry. I should have checked every day."

"No, you have your own ranch to tend," Emma said from the doorway. "If you can just help us bring in the trunks, we'll clean up here and get settled."

Joe eyed the older woman with new respect. "Are you sure you want to stay here tonight, ma'am?"

"Of course. This is my son's house. In the morning, Molly and I will set to work and make it ready for his homecoming."

Joe nodded slowly. "I have to go home and feed my stock after we unload your luggage, but I could come back and sleep here."

"We'll be fine," Molly said, setting her pistol on the table. She began to stack the used dishes that lay there.

"Yes, we will be." Emma smiled at him. "We do so appreciate your help, Joe."

He nodded and went out to the wagon to fetch their luggage. When he'd taken in the smaller bags, Molly joined him in the front yard.

"I'll help with the trunks," she said.

"Obliged."

The first one wasn't too bad, and they carried it into the main room. Emma had explored the small bedroom off the main room of the cabin, and she came to the doorway.

"Molly, I'll get some clean sheets out of my trunk, and we can make the bed up fresh."

Joe set down his end of the trunk. "Are you sure—"

"We'll do nicely, thank you." Emma knelt and unfastened the latches on the trunk.

"Let's get the other one in," Molly said. "I need to put the horse up."

Joe followed her out to the wagon. "I'll take care of the horse for you. But won't you need to take the rig back to Austin?"

"The liveryman said to bring it tomorrow." She hesitated. "I may have to buy a horse. I'm not sure I want it to be this one, though. He's a little sluggish."

"You want a riding horse?" Joe asked.

She nodded. "Eventually, Ma will want a wagon of our own, I'm sure. I was hoping Andrew had one."

"He's got a buckboard. It's probably around back."

"That's a relief. I'll scout around in the morning. I suppose Andrew only had one horse."

"Yeah. He was hoping to get an extra next spring."

"Maybe if I buy one tomorrow, it will be enough. Let's get this last trunk."

The wooden chest was heavier than the last.

"Is this full of books?" Joe asked with a grunt after they'd lowered it to the ground.

"Books, dishes, lead shot, you name it," Molly said with a smile. "And my Sunday clothes."

He grinned. "Sounds like a practical inventory. Ready?"

When they had the trunk in Andrew's kitchen at last, he stood and stretched his aching back. Molly pulled off her hat and wiped a sleeve across her brow. The lantern light glinted on her rich, golden hair. Joe looked away quickly. He didn't want her to think he was ogling her.

A second lantern was burning in the bedroom, and Emma called out, "Is everything in now?"

"Yes, Ma," Molly said.

Emma came to the doorway. "We appreciate all your help, Joe."

He nodded. "No problem, ma'am. I'll unhitch your horse and put him in the corral. I saw you had a small sack of feed in the wagon bed. Want me to give him a ration?"

Emma smiled. "Thank you."

"I'll water him from the rain barrel and leave the harness under the wagon seat. Do you have anything to eat?"

"I believe we'll get by for tonight."

Joe still hesitated. He felt responsible in a measure for their situation, and he couldn't be sure those two squatters or some other no-good wouldn't come along in the night to steal the horse. Besides, Andrew *was* his friend, and he felt he owed it to him to watch out for his womenfolk. But how, if they didn't want him to?

"I'll come by in the morning. Your daughter said she needs to return the horse and maybe buy another. I could go along if you like."

"It would make my mind easier," Mrs. Weaver said.

"Good. I'll come over after breakfast, then. You ladies be sure to bar the door tonight, now won't you?"

"Of course," Emma said.

He looked at Molly.

"Thanks again," she told him.

He nodded and headed outside. Even though they'd made arrangements, he felt a bit uneasy. What if those roughnecks came back? The women had guns, and he'd seen proof of Molly's skill. He couldn't insist they let him keep watch.

WHEN RANGER HAD JOGGED off toward Joe's ranch, Molly shut the door. The locks on the inside consisted of a wooden bar that slipped into a slot, and a metal hasp near the top that fitted over a staple. A wooden peg slid into the staple. Not enough to stop a large, determined man, but it would slow one down long enough for Molly to grab a gun.

"Need help with the bed?" she asked her mother.

"It's done. I wish we could air out the bedding that's here, but frankly, I'm exhausted. You must be too."

"I am." Molly walked over to the small window by the table. On the wall hung two wooden shutters that would meet in the middle. She closed them and fastened the catch. At least no one could peer in at them from outside. "Is there a window in the bedroom?"

"Yes, a small one like that." Ma looked around. "We'll scrub this place down tomorrow. Or rather, I will while you go to Austin."

"I'm not sure I like the thought of leaving you here alone."

Her mother smothered a yawn. "Let's get some rest and see how things look in the morning."

That seemed reasonable, so they ate a meager supper of apples, crackers, and cheese they'd bought after getting off the stagecoach that morning. When they'd finished, Molly turned out the lamp on the table, grabbed her leather satchel, and carried it into the other room. Ma came in her wake and closed the door.

The room was so tiny, they could barely move without jostling each other. Somehow they managed to change into their nightclothes. Molly took her hair down but skipped her usual ritual of brushing it.

Ma had insisted on bringing one of the quilts she'd pieced in the long Ohio winters. It now covered the bed, and a crumpled pile of used bedding lay in one corner. Trust Ma to insist on a clean blanket, not the one those filthy squatters had likely used. Molly eased down onto the straw tick, a poor excuse for a mattress. How did Andrew stand sleeping on this night after night?

Still, it was better than sleeping on the floor. A wooden box served as a night table. She laid her revolver on it beside the lamp. Ma had opted for the far side of the bed, and Molly was glad. If someone burst through the door, she wanted to be between the intruder and her mother.

At first she thought she wouldn't sleep, or couldn't. She refused to allow herself to think about bedbugs and other critters, but the evening's bizarre events wound through her mind over and over. If she were back home, she'd have risen, dressed, and gone out for a walk. But this wasn't home.

A whole new wave of painful questions flooded her thoughts. Would this rundown cabin really be their new home? How long would it take to feel that way? And what if Andrew never came back? Could she and her mother build a new life here, or should they go back north, where at least they knew some people?

She pondered about the money. Half was safe in the Austin bank. But then, if Texas was overrun with criminals, as the rumors and their experience that day seemed to indicate, was it really safe in the bank? And what about the rest of the money? Most of it was in Ma's handbag. She'd insisted Molly carry some of it, so that if one part was stolen or lost, they might be able to save the rest. They needed to find a place to stash the money, to protect against potential thieves and marauders.

Two women setting out alone with all that money. They'd acted foolishly. So far, thank heaven, they hadn't run up against thieves. Ma wanted to give Andrew most of the proceeds from the store to help him establish his ranch and buy good livestock. But what they'd seen of the ranch so far would need a whole lot more than what they'd brought to make it a thriving success.

She jerked awake when her mother rolled over. The bed was too narrow for both of them, and Molly lay on the extreme edge. A gleam of light at the joining of the shutters surprised her. Was it daylight? She must have slept after all. Cautiously, she pushed aside the sheet and quilt.

As she sat up slowly, Ma said, "What is it?"

"I think it's morning."

Ma gave the softest of moans then sat up. "We have a lot to do."

Molly felt her way to the window and fumbled with the latch. The shutters swung open, and she looked out at grass, a rough fence, a few trees, and in the distance, hills. Not so bad. She must be getting the view from the back of the house. Were those treetops? The stream must be back there somewhere.

"Looks like a good day."

Ma shuffled to her side and peered out. "Hmm. Good day for laundry. Let's hope your brother has a clothesline."

Molly hastened into her traveling dress and sturdy shoes. She took the revolver from the crate. "I'll see if I can find where he gets water."

"Good idea," Ma said.

Joe mentioned a rain barrel last night, and Andrew had written that he hoped to get a well dug before fall. He must be hauling water from the stream for now.

She paused in the larger room to open the shutter there. The sunlight poured in, and the wagon sat reassuringly in its place outside. The livery's horse stood placidly in the corral, twitching its tail. One more anxiety lifted.

The kitchen consisted of a workbench with an enameled dishpan, a table, a smallish box stove, two stools, and a short bench. The shelves were practically bare. When she took the horse to Austin, she'd have to stock up on food. She spotted a bucket tipped over on the floor near the workbench and seized it.

When she'd unbarred and unhooked the door, she swung it inward. Glorious sunshine bathed her. Maybe this place was not as bad as she'd feared. They wouldn't have to deal with frozen winters. She stepped outside with the bucket in one hand and her revolver in the other. The hired horse pricked up its ears and gave a soft whinny. She'd have to feed the horse.

Water first.

A small, three-sided shelter stood at the end of the corral farthest from the road. Beneath its sloping roof, she found a well-worn harness hanging from a wall post. Beyond that hung an extra bridle, a few tools, and several ropes. A metal bin stood at the back, and a quick peek under its heavy lid told her Andrew had left it half full of oats. Joe had nestled the small sack of feed they'd bought on top of Andrew's supply.

Beside the bin was a substantial stack of firewood, and just outside the shelter stood a wooden barrel with a few inches of water in the bottom.

Molly scooped some oats from the bin and took them to the horse. She spilled them into a small, square wooden container on the ground, and the horse immediately stuck his nose in and began to munch. She managed to get half a bucket of water for the horse too.

Turning back toward the cabin, she spotted another barrel at the corner, under the eaves. Andrew's rain barrel, no doubt. She went to it and looked in. Only an inch of water lay in the bottom. Molly frowned and went back to the barrel inside the shed. With a lot of stretching and gasping, she managed to tilt it and get a third of a bucket of water.

"It looks like Andrew goes somewhere to get water in barrels," she told her mother a minute later. "There's a rain barrel, but there's hardly anything in it, and another barrel at the shed. I think there's a stream out back, beyond the field."

"We'll have to ask Joe about that." Ma looked up from the sack she was rummaging through. "I think I could manage biscuits if we had an oven."

"Pancakes?"

"Yes, if you can find enough wood for a fire in the stove. We'll need it anyway, to heat wash water."

"Oh, there's some wood in a shelter near the corral. Oats too. I fed the horse. But hardly any water."

Molly brought in an armful of split logs and kindling and started a small fire in the woodstove. If they were going to live here, Ma would need a cookstove.

"There's a clothesline between the shed and the house," she told her mother. "I can take Andrew's bedding out to air. There's not enough water for laundry."

While Ma puttered about the kitchen, Molly headed outside. After slinging the sheets and blanket over the line, she sauntered about, looking for any sticks or dead trees near the house. She soon surmised that Andrew had picked the place clean of burnables long ago.

She found the buckboard Joe had mentioned behind the house. Beyond it was the fence she'd seen from the window, enclosing a large, grassy area, bigger than the corral out front.

This must be where he planned to put the cattle he'd gone to buy. He may have figured that was more urgent than improving the cabin. Molly went to the wooden gate, unlatched it, and pushed it open.

The open area beckoned her, and she ambled across. In the distance, she could see the treetops. That seemed a logical place to find some firewood. After ducking through the fence rails on the far side of the field, she walked down a bank and entered a copse, watching for suitable sticks. Not much lay on the ground, and she decided Andrew had again been frugal and cleaned up the debris nearest his house.

The sound of running water drew her to a healthy stream that flowed beyond the trees, and she could see a wagon trail leading to it. Water problem solved. He must have to go farther to get his fuel. Probably he didn't cook much, but every man would make coffee, wouldn't he, and a few flapjacks and eggs?

Turning back, she spotted something near the fence. She stepped closer to a large rock protruding from the ground. Several smaller stones lay beside it. Closest to the big rock was a flat one about eight inches across, with a smaller one on top. Her heartbeat quickened as she turned over the top stone. An *X* was scratched on the underside. Close examination told her the ground under the small stones had been recently disturbed.

Molly's heart thumped. She and Andrew had used this method to mark a cache they'd made as youngsters, when the family left Brooklyn and moved to Ohio. They hadn't been able to take everything they wanted with them in the wagon, so their father had suggested they put a few things into a lard pail and bury it. If they ever came back to New York, they could dig up their treasures. Or someone else might find them and have a nice surprise.

Of course, they took their favorite toys on the journey, but Andrew had contributed a small pouch of marbles and a handful of brass buckles he'd collected from various finds. Molly had put in a small ragdoll and a roughly carved horse.

She agonized when they buried the pail, almost unable to part with her bits.

Their "treasure" wasn't worth much, and it wasn't large. In fact, they probably could have fit those things into the baggage they took. She suspected now that their father suggested it to keep them busy and out from underfoot while he and Ma packed. Probably the stones that marked the cache in the back yard had been kicked out of place long ago, and the ragdoll had likely crumbled to dust.

She and Andrew had very few toys as children, but she'd kept the one doll she owned that had a head and hands of composition, and Andrew had a small cast-iron dog. Her mother had let them keep a picture book. In Ohio, after the mercantile became successful, they'd received more toys and gifts, but the oldest ones meant the most to Molly and were now in her trunk.

Raising her hand to her throat, she touched the small item she wore as a necklace—a small, round coin with odd symbols on it and a square hole in the middle. She'd asked Ma once where it came from, and Ma had replied rather vaguely that a friend had given it to her when she was a baby. Molly knew she'd had it before the move from New York, so it hadn't come into the till at the mercantile. It was an odd thing. She liked it, though, and so she kept it.

She ran back to the cabin with the scant handful of sticks she'd found.

"Ma, Andrew left a cache!"

Her mother looked up from the flapjacks she was cooking on the stovetop.

"What are you talking about? Cash money?"

"No, a cache. You know, a hiding place. I found a spot where he's buried something in the ground. Do you think we should dig it up?"

"I don't know." Ma frowned and handed Molly a plate. "What do you suppose it is?"

"No idea. But probably something he wanted to keep safe in

case someone like those squatters came along." Molly noticed that Ma had done a great deal of cleaning up and now had clean dishes draining on the sideboard. All the trash had been cleared away, and the floor swept. "You've been working hard, and I've been off exploring. I didn't find much extra wood, either, but I found the stream. Maybe we can get water later."

"We'll ask Joe about the wood."

Hoofbeats sounded outside as Molly finished her second pancake, and she ran to the window. "Speaking of whom, he just rode in."

Joe ground tied Ranger and left him standing there with his saddle and bridle on while he sauntered to the front door. She opened it before he could knock.

"Morning," he said with a grin.

"Good morning." Molly stepped back to let him enter. Something deep down made her want to smile back and act as if she was glad to see him, but she wasn't ready to be Joe's pal.

"Hello, Joe," Ma said warmly.

"I've been thinking about when we go into Austin." Joe pulled out a stool and sat down by the table as though he was used to making himself at home in the cabin. "You'll want supplies."

"We brought a few things," Ma said, "but if we're going to stay here more than a day, we'll definitely need more food. I think those men cleaned Andrew out."

Joe leaned with his elbows on the table. "He told me he was going to stash away some staples, and maybe some extra cartridges. I don't know where he hid that stuff, though."

"I think I do," Molly said.

Joe gazed at her. "You do?"

"I found a place where I think Andrew hid something. He marked it in a way we used as children. Sort of a secret sign."

"I see."

"I haven't looked in it yet, though. Wasn't sure I should." Molly looked toward her mother.

"Maybe we should see what's there." Ma wiped her hands on a dishtowel Molly recognized from back home.

Joe shrugged. "I doubt he hid any money. He'd been saving up for a long time, and I think he took it all with him to pay for the cattle. I gave him a little bit, too, to see if he could find a couple of good cows for me."

Molly hesitated. Why hadn't Joe told them from the start that he had money invested in Andrew's journey too? Could he be lying about that to gain their sympathy? She wanted to believe him. He was very polite and kind to her mother, and he did chores for them without being asked. Still, Andrew hadn't confided in him about where he'd made his cache. She didn't want Joe to see where Andrew had hidden things. But she did want to know what was there.

"Maybe I'll dig it up after we get home from town," she said.

Ma shook her head. "I think you should do it now. We may learn something important. At least we'll know if there's something we don't need to buy."

"All right. I think I saw a spade out in the shed."

Joe grinned and stood. "Andrew calls that his barn. I'll go with you."

"I ... I think I'd rather do it alone."

His brow furrowed. "All right. Let me know if it's more than you can handle."

"I will."

"Meanwhile," Ma said, "Joe can tell me where we can get wood and how we haul water. And maybe he can help me decide if it's safe for us all to leave here and go into town."

"That would probably be better than you staying here alone." Joe shot a glance Molly's way. "Up until yesterday, I wouldn't have thought it was too dangerous for you to wait here, ma'am, but now I don't know."

"It was quiet last night. Do you think those two will come back?"

"I sure hope not. But there's a lot of other drifters in these parts since the war ended."

"Is there a way to lock the cabin?" Molly asked.

"I don't think so. Not from the outside."

Molly let out a long, slow breath. "All right, I'll go dig up Andrew's cache. You two figure it out. Whatever you think, Ma."

She went to the bedroom first and put the money she'd been entrusted with in her pocket, along with a pencil and a page from the small notepad in Ma's handbag. Then she fetched the spade and carried it across the fenced field. Several times she glanced back to see if anyone watched her, but she saw no sign of life near the house or at the back window.

Sweat rolled down her face by the time she'd dug a foot or more finally hit a metal container. It took a lot of work to uncover the top and remove enough dirt so she could open it.

The square box was about eighteen inches long and half as wide and as deep. Inside were small sacks of beans and cornmeal, a smaller one of coffee beans, a couple of tins of peaches, and two boxes of ammunition. Emergency supplies, Molly decided. If he came home and his cabin was stripped or burned flat, he'd at least have a meal or two and some cartridges for his guns.

She thought about it for a moment and then replaced everything. She and Ma didn't want to use up the supplies he might need badly one day. From her pocket, she took the paper and pencil and used the flat rock as a desk to write on.

Andrew,

Ma and I were here. I found this spot. We're hoping you come back soon.

Molly

She folded it carefully around a five-dollar bill and tucked it between two of the small sacks. If Andrew returned to find someone had stolen everything he owned from his house, he'd have a bit to help get started again.

And if they lost what her ma was carrying, they'd have this besides what she'd left in the bank. It might not be much, but five dollars seemed like a lot to put in the ground, and she hesitated to leave it. She reasoned that if someone else found it, it wouldn't send her family to the poorhouse.

After shutting the metal box securely, she shoveled the dirt back into the hole, taking extra care to clean up around it. Sweeping away extra soil, she tried to hide the evidence of her work, in case anyone else stumbled on this spot. Last of all, she replaced the stones exactly as she'd found them and paused at the fence to look around for a long moment before heading across the open ground carrying the spade.

When she got back to the cabin, she entered the main room. Joe sat at the table, drinking coffee. The bedroom door was open, and Molly could hear her mother moving around in there.

Joe smiled at her. "Find it?"

"Yes. He left some food and cartridges. No money, as you thought."

"Right. Your ma and I think we should all head into Austin. We discussed if I should head out for the Hewitt ranch, where Andrew said he was going, but Mrs. Weaver thinks we should all go to town."

"We can check at the post office and ask around, I guess."

He nodded. "She said if there's no word from Andrew, you two might go with me tomorrow when I head out to look for him. I figure to at least find this Hewitt fellow and see if Andrew's been there."

That was a surprise, but Molly liked the idea. "Would we slow you down?"

"Emma says we can all go on horseback. I wasn't sure how you'd feel about that—how well your mother would hold up. It would be a rough trip, and we'd be camping at night. You know your mother. Think she's up to it?"

"She's tired from the trip here, but worrying about Andrew is wearing on her. I think she'd hate being left here alone."

"But, if you were here with her—"

"Oh, I'm going." The decision was final. With or without Ma, Molly was going with Joe, and Ma would never, ever let her go on an extended trip alone with a man.

Joe nodded slowly. "All right, then. The three of us need to pack bedrolls and supplies for the trail. Just what we can carry on our horses. You can rent two riding horses in Austin."

Or buy them, Molly thought. She'd have to discuss that with Ma. She didn't want to clue Joe in on the fact that they could afford mounts. Could they really trust him?

They'd have to. She and Ma were about to head off into wild country with him. She still wondered if Joe knew more than he was letting on.

"We'll see what we find out in Austin and get you ladies whatever you think you need for the trail—but I warn you, we want to travel light."

"Sure."

"And we can ask the sheriff to send a deputy out here once or twice in the next week to keep an eye on my place and Andrew's."

"What about your livestock?"

"My cattle are fine for a few days. My extra horse—well, I was going to say I'd turn her out, but I don't know as I want to do that after your run-in with squatters. Maybe you or Emma could ride her on our trip. That would save you a little money."

"Is that what you want?"

"I admit I'd feel a mite easier if both my horses were where I could keep an eye on them."

Ma came from the other room. "There you are, Molly. What did you find?"

"A little food and some cartridges, Ma. Nothing wonderful or worrisome. We'll all go to town now, if you're ready, and tomorrow we'll set out to find Andrew."

"We're all going then?" Ma looked from her to Joe.

"If you're sure," Joe said.

Ma smiled. "Maybe we'll meet Andrew on the way."

"Could be, but maybe we'll miss him too."

"Then we should leave him a note explaining where we've gone."

Molly said nothing about the message she'd left in the cache. She watched Joe's face. He seemed to be holding something back.

"What is it?" she asked.

"Well, it shouldn't have taken him more than a few days to get there. Less than a week."

"And the same coming back," Molly said slowly.

"Maybe more, with cattle."

"What do you suppose has delayed him?" Ma frowned as she untied her apron strings.

"I don't know. The cattle could have got away from him, but the most likely thing would be that Hewitt didn't have the stock he wanted, and he had to go someplace else."

Molly's heart sank. They'd thought their quest was ended when they arrived here, but it could drag on and on. If Pa were here ... but he wasn't. Pa would never be here again to take care of them. When he'd died, they'd expected to rely on Andrew, or perhaps Molly would marry a husband who would look out for both her and her mother. That was the usual way.

It was up to Molly now. She was the only one who truly cared about Ma. She had to decide what was best. She wanted to find Andrew, but what danger would she and Ma go into if they went looking for him? Ma mustn't really want to traipse off into wild country full of cutthroats.

She took a deep breath. "Ma and I might be safer to stay here and wait for him to come back."

"You might." Joe settled his hat on his head. "I can go by myself and check with the rancher. But you still have to settle up at the livery."

"I think we should get a couple of saddle horses and go with Joe tomorrow." Ma's voice had that stubborn edge Molly had heard when she and Pa used to wrangle over ordering inventory for the mercantile. They would go back and forth— "I think we should order more hardware." "But more women are coming in for yard goods. I think we should order a wider variety of cloth and yarns." Sometimes they spent days settling on what they would order.

"It could be dangerous, Ma."

Her mother's eyebrows quirked. "You think I don't know that, child? But this is your brother we're talking about. I know you want to go after him. If it's me you're worried about, quit that. I know we won't be very comfortable, but it's worth it for Andrew."

It all came down to that. Andrew had been gone a month. What if he never came back? Molly didn't like the idea of having to take care of herself for the rest of her life, but she wasn't sure whether she liked the thought of depending on some man, either. Someone like Joe Noyes? She still wasn't sure about him. He was a proven liar, if nothing else.

With Ma watching her keenly, Molly felt the burden of making the decision. If she insisted, Ma would give up the idea of tracking Andrew down. On the other hand, their best chance of learning what happened to him probably lay in this expedition.

She raised her chin. "Let's get moving."

"I can harness your horse. And we'll stop at my place to pick up Firefly so you can ride her home after you turn in the wagon." Joe opened the door with obvious relief that the issue was settled.

"Thank you," Molly said. "We'll be right along."

The horse was harnessed when they went outside.

"You've got your money?" Ma asked.

What's left of it. "Yes. I won't ask if you do."

Ma chuckled. Molly climbed to the wagon seat and gathered

the reins. Joe rode along ahead of them, and their horse seemed willing to keep a steady pace with Ranger leading them. All the way to Austin, Ma dithered over the list of supplies she thought they should take on the trip, and Molly mostly let her go on, only once reminding her of Joe's admonition to travel light.

6

"That's the only sidesaddle I've got." The stable owner shook his head regretfully.

"We'll take it," Ma said. "It's a start."

"There's one other livery, on the other side of town, but I doubt he's got a sidesaddle to sell."

"I can ride astride," Molly said.

"Not modestly." Ma's dark glance brooked no argument.

"Begging your pardon, ma'am," the liveryman said, "but my niece is a dressmaker. She might fix you up with a split skirt if you tell her Uncle Harry sent you."

He gave them directions, and Molly went off to find the shop while Ma and Joe haggled with Harry for a dependable horse for her mother.

To her surprise, the niece offered to pause in the project she'd been working on and help Molly out.

"I've made this kind of skirt a couple of times before," Carrie, the dressmaker, said. "The ranching wives find it very serviceable. It's frowned upon in town, but I can make it look like a normal skirt when you're standing still. Just don't let any so-called gentlemen see you when you mount."

Molly smiled. "I understand. How much would it cost?"

Her price was higher than Molly would have paid back in Ohio, but after all, it was a rush job.

"Where's the skirt you want altered?" asked Carrie.

"Oh." Molly winced. "I didn't bring an extra skirt."

"Hmm." Carrie eyed her figure. "You could buy a plain skirt ready-made at one of the stores for me to alter, or I could split the one you're wearing if you'd rather. It's full enough."

"Really? That might be the best solution, but—"

"Do you have more shopping to do?" Carrie asked.

"Well, yes. My mother's in town with me. We have several errands to run."

"Perfect." Carrie walked to a closet and returned with a gray cotton skirt slung over her arm. "Go in that room over there and put this on. It should fit you, or near enough. When you're done with your shopping, come back for your altered skirt."

Molly had never heard of such an outrageous way to shop for clothing, but it seemed practical.

"Thank you so much."

"It's nothing. But let me measure you to be sure, and then give me at least two hours."

They got home late, with Molly riding Joe's reddish mare, Firefly, in her newly configured riding skirt and Ma on a docile gelding they'd bought.

Their purchases loaded down their saddlebags, but Ma had exercised restraint. Molly helped carry everything inside, including the saddle she was borrowing from Joe and the one they'd bought from the livery. "Let's pack."

Ma smiled. "I did mine this morning while you were outside."

"Then you write the note we'll leave for Andrew while I pack. Keep in mind that strangers might come in while we're gone and read it."

She hurried into the little bedroom and saw Ma's bedroll lying on the bed. One blanket, no doubt with a few clothes curled up inside. The only other blanket they knew was clean was the quilt they'd brought along and used last night. Molly picked it up and went to the doorway.

"Do you want me to use this?"

Ma was gathering a few pans. "I expect there's nothing else. Andrew didn't leave much, and we haven't had a chance to do laundry."

"I'd hate to ruin it."

"Well, the only other choice is to use the one we found here. Oh!" Ma glanced toward the door. "We need to bring in Andrew's bedding."

"I'll get it."

"No, you do your packing. We want to be ready to ride when Joe gets here in the morning."

Molly quickly chose her most utilitarian clothing, and not too much. Only one complete change, with extra stockings. She only took along an extra dress in case her split skirt met with tragedy.

She added the revolver, shotgun, and cartridges. Ma had left more money at the Austin bank today, but she would carry a large enough sum to pay for a few nights' lodging or other unexpected needs. Molly had a few dollars and some coins left, which she shoved into a pouch she could pin inside her waistband to hang beneath her skirt.

Although Ma had been a bit scandalized when she saw Molly wearing the split skirt, Joe had assured her that a few women were adopting the fashion on the range here in Texas. He'd even met one woman who wore a pair of her husband's trousers under her skirt during a roundup. Ma had shivered and let out a tense breath, but from that moment on, she'd seemed to accept her daughter's odd attire.

But she'd made Molly promise to take that extra dress in case they had to enter a town.

"I won't have my girl looking like a hoyden," she'd said.

Molly went to the kitchen and found Ma seated at the table,

composing her note to Andrew. The empty coffeepot and frypan and two lumpy sacks sat next to her.

"I thought we'd take some basic dishes for camping." She glanced up. "I added the food we bought."

Molly nodded. They'd taken Joe's advice on provisions for the trail. They wouldn't feast, but they could get by for at least a week on what they'd selected. Along the way, they should find places to replenish their supplies.

"Do you think we should leave the rest of our stuff at Joe's ranch?" Ma asked.

"We already took the wagon back." Molly supposed they could try harnessing Firefly or the new gelding—Harry, Ma had named him, after the stable owner—and use Andrew's buckboard. But she shook her head. "Joe's place wouldn't be any more secure than this one."

"I suppose you're right."

"I wondered about the quilt," Molly said. "We'll want it tonight. I can't make my bedroll until we get up."

"All right. Be sure you take your coat."

"Ma, next week it will be August."

"It might get cold at night."

"I'm not riding all over Texas in high summer wearing a coat."

Ma blinked. "I guess not. We'll want bonnets at the least, and some kind of jacket or overshirt." She smiled. "I know. You can wear the extra shirt I made for Andrew over your dress."

"No, Ma, I've got the jacket I used to wear for chores in my trunk."

"Well, I don't want to leave the new shirt here. More squatters might come and take it."

Molly let out a big sigh. "It's a risk. We're risking everything to do this."

Slowly, Ma nodded. "I guess you're right."

"If you roll it up small, maybe I could fit it into the box at his cache."

"Out there, away from the house?"

"It's not dark yet," Molly said, patting her arm. "I'll be careful. And I'm thinking I should leave Andrew a longer note there, too, in case something happens to the one we leave on the table."

Ma caught her breath. "Do you think it's dangerous to leave Andrew a note? If someone like those squatters comes in and sees it, they'll know the place is unprotected."

Molly frowned. "You might be right. Let me see what you've written." Only a few lines graced the paper in her mother's neat handwriting. "Go ahead and finish, but don't say where we're going. Tell him there's a message in his private spot. I think he'll know what that means."

"I'm not sure ..."

"I'm not either, to be honest, but I don't have a better idea."

"All right." Ma glanced at the window. "Write your message and get it out there before dark. And take the shirt too."

Molly hurried to fetch the new shirt and her pencil. She borrowed another piece of paper from Ma and pondered for a moment over what to write.

"I'm going," she said a minute later. "I'll be quick."

Before Ma could fret and fuss over her, she dashed out the door. After a good look around, she fetched the spade and ran across the pasture toward the trees. The cache was as she'd left it. She dug as fast as she could, panting as she worked. When she'd uncovered the lid of the metal box, she didn't try to lift it out, but opened it in the hole.

Wiping her hands on her skirt, she hoped she wouldn't get dirt on the precious new shirt her mother had stitched for Andrew. She rolled it into a tight little stick and laid it in on top of her previous note. The new note went on the very top. With a quick prayer, she closed the box and stood to shovel dirt over the cache once more and replace the rock.

When she got back to the house, Ma had lit the lantern and was pacing the main room.

"It's all right," Molly assured her. "I don't know about you, but I'm tired. Let's go to bed and get some rest."

"Oh, I forgot the things on the clothesline."

"I'll get them."

Molly stepped outside and was surprised how quickly night was falling. Stars pricked the dark sky, and she took a deep breath. Sometimes Ma nearly drove her batty with her fussing over details. Overall, she supposed they'd benefit from having an organized person along on the journey. Molly hadn't expected to have to look out for Ma, though. This past month or two, everything had turned topsy-turvy.

If only they had set out today. Every hour, every minute, might make a difference in finding her brother.

She strode to the clothesline and took down the bedding, folding each piece as she went. Drawing in a deep breath, she took a last look out over the moonlit field toward where Andrew's cache lay. Texas was so big. It was beautiful in its own way. Not Ohio beautiful, but it would do. She turned and plodded back toward the cabin, her arms full of her brother's laundry.

THEY WERE right to leave early in the morning, Molly decided as she and Ma ate a hasty breakfast and cleaned up the leavings.

She reached for her bonnet and the coffeepot. "Should I dump what's left?"

"I'll take it." Ma held out her cup.

Molly poured the last of the coffee into it. Ma didn't like to waste anything. Around the corner of the house, she dumped out the grounds and then tied the empty coffeepot to the back of her saddle with her bedroll.

She and Ma carried out the rest of the gear Ma deemed essential. Molly had convinced her not to take much beyond what Joe recommended, and they'd compared lists with him, so they didn't end up with two coffeepots or two frypans when they only needed one of each.

The sun had been up an hour, and the temperature was pleasant, but they would probably be baking in a few hours. Ma came out the cabin door and closed it with an air of finality.

"Ready?" Molly asked.

Ma nodded and walked to Harry, the patient gelding. "I put a small paring knife in my handbag."

"Good." Molly untied Firefly and stowed the lead rope in her saddlebag—Joe's saddlebag. She liked the plain stock saddle he'd loaned her with the mare. She didn't tell Ma she also had a knife in her pocket. She'd bought it at the general store while waiting for her skirt to be altered.

Ma knew about the revolver, and the shotgun was sheathed by Ma's sidesaddle. They'd debated whether or not Molly should carry both their guns with her on Firefly, but Ma knew how to use the shotgun, and it seemed sensible for each of them to have access to a firearm. Ma looked less vulnerable with its stock resting near her right knee.

Hesitating for a moment, Molly watched her mother mount unassisted. Satisfied, she hopped up on Firefly's back, pleased with the freedom she felt in her new attire. With a good horse under her, she could go anywhere she liked.

"I guess this is it," Ma said.

They'd arranged to meet at Joe's house. They wouldn't ride to Austin again but would turn off and go southward at a crossroads a few miles away. Firefly set off eagerly, headed toward her home and master. She might not be so enthusiastic when she realized they weren't going to stay at the Noyes ranch.

When they arrived at Joe's place, Molly looked over the snug little house and spacious corral. Ranger stood at a hitching rail outside the front door, fully saddled and carrying plump leather saddlebags. Joe's bedroll was tied behind his saddle.

He came out of the house grinning, carrying a rifle and a sack. His handgun was strapped around his waist in a formidable holster. Joe could pass for a gunslinger, Molly thought—at least, according to her limited knowledge of them. But he'd assured her most everyone wore a gun out here. You never knew when you'd need it. She shivered. They'd come prepared, and yet this land was so different from what she knew that she couldn't suppress a few ripples of fear.

"Heard you ride up." He hefted the sack. "I've got my share of the grub packed."

He proceeded to slide the rifle into a scabbard at Ranger's side and swung easily into the saddle. He gathered his reins and smiled over at them. "All set?"

"We are if you are," Ma said with a broad smile.

Molly picked up the reins with a stirring of excitement and a bit of trepidation.

JOE LED THE WAY, keeping Ranger at a steady jog. They were a bit later getting started than he liked, and Mrs. Weaver had packed a little more than was needful. Still, for two women, they seemed to be efficient and logical in most of their choices. He'd paid a short visit to the sheriff's office yesterday, while the ladies were at the dressmaker's, and asked him to look in at both his place and Andrew's over the next few days.

If all went well, they'd be back in ten days or so. He hoped. Already he was planning in his mind how to get the ladies to come back home and let him journey on alone if they didn't find Andrew soon.

He paused and looked over his shoulder. Molly was keeping her mother between her horse and his. That was probably best. Emma was the weak link, older and riding sidesaddle. He sure hoped she could keep up on this jaunt, but he couldn't exactly refuse to have her along.

After a couple of hours, he stopped to give the horses and the women a rest. Emma dismounted stiffly and winced when she hit the ground. As he'd feared, she wasn't used to much riding. But there was no way to ease into a trip like this and not lose precious time.

He tended the horses to give the ladies a chance to freshen up. After giving the animals a few minutes to graze, they mounted up again. He pretended not to notice that Molly had to help her ma get into the saddle.

By the end of the day, their routine was established. They stopped an hour for nooning and then went on. Emma never complained once, but Joe caught a few grimaces on her face as she moved.

"I'm sorry it's so harsh, ma'am," he said when they halted for the night a half hour before sunset.

"Don't worry about me," Emma said firmly. "Finding Andrew is the only thing that's important now."

TRAVELING day and night did not appeal to Ryland. At least the stagecoach kept moving most of the time, and that was more than he'd be able to do on horseback or in a wagon.

He was always glad when the passengers included a woman or two. The men were generally more civil then, and he felt marginally more secure from pickpockets and schemers. His sword cane was always close at hand, and his new knife was hidden in his jacket pocket. Even so, he never slept deeply while they were rolling. Maybe after a couple of days, he'd get used to the sway and bump of the ride.

At every stop, he inquired discreetly about Ben Cooper. So far, he'd heard nothing about the man since the railroad supervisor's caution. That didn't mean Cooper hadn't come this way, only that he hadn't called attention to himself.

On the second day, the stage made an hourlong stop for dinner at a home station, one where the agent and his family lived and provided quarters for the drivers waiting for their return coach. Ryland got permission to go out behind the agent's barn and practice his knife throwing.

For some reason, he was afraid he'd be less skillful without Quincy's guidance, but his aim was as good as before. When one of the tenders yelled for the passengers to board, he concealed the knife and hurried around to the yard.

Two ladies—sisters in their forties—joined them for the next leg of the trip. Ryland enjoyed a few minutes of pleasant conversation and then settled back, feeling more relaxed than he had in days. Maybe he could catch a nap this afternoon.

AFTER FOUR ROUGH days on the road, Joe was surprised and pleased to learn they were only a few miles from the Hewitt ranch, Andrew's destination when he left the month before. He wished they could go on and arrive that evening, but he didn't want to approach the ranch after dark. Besides, Emma was about played out.

When he'd finished staking out the horses, Molly wandered slowly about the campsite, alternately searching the ground, probably for something to burn, and gazing at the setting sun in the west. Emma was busy getting out dishes.

"Let me help you," Joe said, walking toward Molly.

"There's not much burnable here."

"No, and this is a dry campsite. We'll have to watch for a stream tomorrow or fill our waterbags at the ranch."

"You think we'll be there tomorrow?" Her face lit with hope.

"Pretty sure. Maybe in the first hour."

"Why not go on then?"

"It's better to approach a stranger in daylight. We don't know what we'll find."

"Of course. One more night then."

Joe pointed the way they'd come. "There's some brush a little ways back on the trail. I'll go get some. We don't need to keep a fire all night, but I think I can find enough to make coffee."

"There's still a few sticks in Ma's saddlebags." Molly turned and looked toward her mother. "We hate to use the last of the wood, but ..."

"I know. We'll see if we can't restock tomorrow."

"How will we do that? I've heard the wagon train people burned buffalo chips, but I haven't seen any buffalo."

Joe laughed. "Right. They're not so plentiful as they used to be, and I'm not sure they ever came this far south. Anyway, I figure to ask the rancher. We should be able to get water, and I'll ask him where we can find some fuel." The sun was hitting the horizon. "It'll be dark soon. I'd best move if I want to find some brush."

He'd had a lot of thinking time during this ride. Every day he'd hoped to spot Andrew moving toward them with a small herd of cattle. Every minute that passed seemed to make that less likely. Joe was starting to fret about what would become of Emma and Molly if Andrew never returned.

They had more spunk than he'd expected. That Molly was unstoppable. And she was determined to make things easier for her mother, though not much was easy on a trip like this. At least Emma seemed to have gotten over her saddle soreness. She was tired, though, he could tell. And Molly could tell too. Her anxiety showed on her face whenever she knew her mother wasn't looking.

Her very lovely face.

Joe scowled at himself. Where did that come from?

All right, it was true. He'd been attracted to Molly Weaver since the first time he'd seen her driving that wagon Harry'd rented them, along with a poor excuse for a harness horse. He'd made sure Emma got a good mount for her money, and that Harry gave her a good deal on it.

But Molly, she was something else. She wasn't an expert rider, but she passed muster. He didn't think she'd done a lot of riding in Ohio, but enough for her to know which end of a horse was which.

And the way she could shoot! Andrew had never told him about teaching his little sister to shoot, but Molly claimed her brother was her mentor in that regard. He grinned, remembering how proud she'd sounded when she told him she could outshoot Andrew now. Joe believed it. She'd do all right in Texas.

But would Emma? Although she was a lady, she was used to hard work. She might adapt to the heat and the loneliness. Not all women could.

A half-moon was rising, showing him where the bushes grew. He worked carefully, making sure he didn't disturb any snakes before he started harvesting brush. It wasn't dry, but he could make it burn. He'd get Emma enough to heat up their beans and coffee tonight. Breakfast would probably have to be canned peaches, but they wouldn't mind since they were so close to their goal.

The Weavers were good company, all of them. Unused to isolation, Joe had been a mite lonely on his ranch before Andrew bought the ramshackle place next door. His new neighbor didn't have a lot of money, and he'd settled for the small ranch and rundown cabin. He planned to turn it into a profitable working ranch and maybe buy more land. He'd made some improvements already. Joe hoped he found the cattle he needed, and that he made a go of it.

Joe liked Andrew. They'd become friends the first time they met, on the range between their ranches. Having him for a neighbor was almost like having a brother again.

A little way off the trail, he saw a couple of pine trees. He might get a few dry twigs from under their lower branches. His thoughts turned back to Molly as he worked.

THE NEXT MORNING, they broke camp early. All of them felt the excitement, the possibility that they'd find Andrew today. The ranch they sought was indeed close by, and in about an hour, they approached the house.

Molly and her mother stayed in the saddle as Joe dismounted and went to the door. It was opened by a tanned, middle-aged man in worn work clothes and scuffed boots.

"Mr. Hewitt?"

"No, I'm Fred Allison."

"Oh." Joe frowned. "We understood Mr. Hewitt owned this property."

"He did. Sold up last spring and moved on. I own it now."

"I see." Joe looked over his shoulder at the two women behind him.

"Andrew," Molly mouthed.

Joe cleared his throat and faced the rancher. "I don't suppose a fellow named Andrew Weaver has been by here within the last month? He'd heard Mr. Hewitt had cattle to sell ..."

Allison shrugged. "There's been quite a few come here looking to buy stock, but I'm not selling any of mine."

"I see. Do you happen to recall Andrew Weaver? He's about twenty and has a gray horse with a black mane and tail."

Allison's face crunched up. "Might have been here."

"And if he did come here, what would you have told him?" Joe asked.

"Same as I told all of 'em. I couldn't help 'em, but there might be someone down New Braunfels way. If not there, it's not too much farther to San Antonio."

"Thank you kindly. Oh, and would it be all right for us to get some water?"

Hewitt nodded toward a stone-rimmed well with a trough beside it. "Help yourselves. Water your horses if you want."

Molly tried not to show her disappointment. She swung down off Firefly's back and hurried to the well with Joe's army canteen and one of the water bags they'd bought in Austin. Ma dismounted a little stiffly, arched her back, and then removed the waterbag from her saddle. After all their drinking containers were full, they drew up buckets full for the animals.

Joe remained silent while they watered the horses. Molly wished he'd say something. Finally all the animals seemed satisfied. Allison had long since retreated into his house. Joe gave a wave toward the empty front window, and they led their mounts toward the road.

"So?" Molly said. "What now?"

"That's up to you ladies." Joe eyed her mother as he spoke. "We can go back and wait for word, or—"

"No." Ma looked at him fiercely. "Enough waiting at home. We go on. What is this New—this place he mentioned?"

"New Braunfels? It's a town settled by Germans back before the war."

"They have ranches?"

"I expect so. There's farms and ranches all over, just not many towns."

"Then we go there."

"Ma, are you sure?" Molly asked. It was what she wanted, but she didn't want to exhaust her mother.

"Of course I'm sure. We can't give up now."

"But we don't know if Andrew went there, or even if he came to this place for certain."

Joe stopped walking and swung around so that Ranger was out of his way. "I could keep going, and you two could head home."

Molly hated the idea, but she could almost read his thoughts. Camping out was hard enough for him alone. He could go a lot faster without them. Still, he wouldn't want to send two women off without a man to lend an air of security, would he?

He gritted his teeth. "Whatever you think, ma'am."

"We're not doing that," Ma said.

Joe looked at Molly, and she nodded. "We may slow you

down, but we can cover more ground together. Ma and I can ask at one house while you go on to the next."

"All right, then. We forge on toward New Braunfels, but we ask along the way."

They fell into a routine. When they spotted a house or a ranch gate, one of them would veer off to speak to the landowners while the other two pushed onward. They kept their inquires short and hastened to catch up when they were sure the residents hadn't talked to Andrew.

The territory was less wild now. The houses were closer together, and they met several wagons and horsemen along the road. They questioned each one, but by noon had no leads on Andrew.

"He might have gone straight through to this other town," Emma said, dabbing at her brow with a handkerchief.

"Maybe." Joe glanced at the sun. "I think we should stop and eat something."

"There's another house up there." Molly pointed ahead. "Maybe we could sit in the shade of that tree in their yard."

"It won't hurt to ask."

Their horses plodded toward it with Joe in the lead. Molly prayed silently for some news. In her black dress and bonnet, Ma was wilting in the relentless sun. Maybe they should have gone back.

She straightened her spine, reminding herself that it was Ma who insisted they keep going. *Lord, give us something. Anything.*

7

R yland squeezed into the corner of the stagecoach seat and
tried to relax, but it was difficult.

The driver had promised him they'd reach Texas tomorrow.
Fort Worth the next day if he was lucky, but it was still a long
way from there to Austin, the nearest town of any size within
striking distance of where Andrew Weaver lived. If he had no
further delays and the teams ran day and night, another day or
two beyond Fort Worth might do it.

He didn't dare speculate closer than that. If only his mind
could let go of his surroundings and let him drift into sleep.

The coach hit a rut, and they all jerked forward. Ryland
grabbed for the leather strap hanging beside him and righted
himself while the drummer across from him swore.

That was the trouble with stages—it wasn't just the road that
kept him awake. It was the other passengers. Eight of them were
jammed into the coach, and another man was lying on the roof
with the luggage.

Ryland was glad he hadn't left his money or his weapons in
his suitcase. He patted his chest and felt the comforting shape of
his wallet over his heart. His knife lay in his side pocket, out of
sight. He still had occasional regrets that he hadn't purchased a

revolver, but he'd need some training with that, and it could present more problems than benefits. Besides, it would be a major expense he wasn't sure Mr. Turner would cover.

His sword cane had fallen to the floor when they were jostled, and he retrieved it and lodged it between his knee and the outside wall. He almost wished he didn't have that along. It was mostly in the way.

After another uncomfortable hour, the driver pulled the coach in to a way station. "Twenty minutes," he yelled. As the tenders led out the fresh team, he hopped down and headed around the back of the building.

Ryland climbed out stiffly and went inside the station.

"Got anything quick?" he asked the woman near the long table. No doubt her husband was out helping switch out the horses.

"I've got meat pies," she said. "Fifty cents for two." She nodded toward a dish on the table, where a dozen half-moon pastries nestled, giving off a lovely fragrance of beef and piecrust.

"Done." Ryland fished two quarters out of his pocket. "And a drink?"

"You'll have to drink it fast." She poured a mug full of coffee. "Blake doesn't wait for stragglers."

Ryland sat down and took a bite of his first pie. "Delicious."

"Thank you." The woman hurried to serve two other passengers and the driver, who'd come in through a back door.

A minute later, she was back at his side. The driver was eating with relish, so Ryland decided to risk an extra minute before going out to the necessary.

"I don't s'pose a man named Cooper's been through here?" He hadn't heard any more about Ben Cooper since Kansas City, but he always asked, just in case. Maybe he'd lost him.

Her face skewed in displeasure. "There was an oaf by the name of Cooper here two days ago. Made a big fuss when we wouldn't give him strong drink."

"What happened?" Ryland met her troubled gaze.

"The tenders tossed him out, but not before he made a big ruckus and upset the lady passengers. Knocked some dishes on the floor, he did."

"Heavens."

"Yes, it was shocking. Not the first time we've had an unruly customer, but it doesn't happen often. Most folks are glad to get some good, quick food while they wait."

Ryland stood and pressed another quarter into her hand. "I'll snatch another scrumptious pie, if you don't mind, and take it with me."

She smiled, etching lines into the skin on each side of her mouth. She probably didn't get many reasons to smile out here. Ryland wrapped the extra pastry in his handkerchief and slipped it into his pocket before hurrying out and around to the back.

Not for two more days did he receive more news of Cooper. The stagecoach stopped in a small town, but one big enough to have a local jail and a post office inside a dry goods store. Allowed an hour to eat and walk around, Ryland dashed off a note to Mr. Turner and gave it to the postmaster.

"I'm on the stagecoach," he told the man behind the counter. "Is there a place where I can get a good, quick meal?"

"Boardinghouse across the street," the postmaster said.

"Thank you. Has there been a man named Cooper in here? He may have been on the last stagecoach."

"Cooper, you say?"

"That's right."

The postmaster frowned. "Seems like that might be the fella that made a ruckus over to the Blackbird."

Ryland arched his eyebrows.

"Saloon, you know."

"Oh, I see. I suppose he got back on the stagecoach?"

"Not that day, he didn't. Sheriff Adderly kept him overnight."

His heartbeat quickening, Ryland asked carefully, "Is he still in jail?"

"Don't think so, but you can ask the sheriff. He's probably down to his office or at the boardinghouse eatin' dinner."

"Thank you." Ryland hurried out. Since the boardinghouse was close by, he marched across the street. If the sheriff wasn't there, he'd grab a bite and then seek out the lawman if he had time. He mustn't miss his stagecoach, or he'd be stranded here for at least a day.

Inside, twilight shrouded the dining room. Several of his fellow passengers and the coach driver were partaking of the luncheon special. After a moment's study, Ryland spotted the sheriff and managed to get a seat directly across the table from him.

"Sheriff Adderly?"

"That's me." The man went on eating but threw quick glances at Ryland between bites.

"You want the special, mister?" An aproned woman stood at his elbow.

"Yes, thank you," Ryland said.

"Two bits."

He pulled out a quarter and placed it in her hand. Her prices were low, compared to some along the stage line. She probably had competition in town, whereas the way stations had none.

She went away, and Ryland turned his attention back to Adderly. "I was told you arrested a man off the stagecoach a couple days ago."

"That's right. He a friend of yours? Because if he is, you can just keep on moving, mister."

"No, no. I've never met the man. But I was curious. Was his name Ben Cooper?"

The sheriff eyed him in silence for a moment then reached for his coffee mug. "What are you, a bounty hunter or something?"

"No, sir, nothing like that. I'm employed by a lawyer, and I'm looking into some matters for him concerning a client. Not

Cooper, but someone he might be connected to. I'm told you detained him overnight?"

"I did. Let him get on the stage next morning—yesterday."

"I see. May I ask if he made inquiries about anyone in your fair town?"

"He asked about someone named Weaver. You know anything about that? Is he up to no good? 'Cause I couldn't find anything that said I should hold him longer. He busted up a saloon down the street—that's all I know."

The serving woman placed a dish of stew and a plate of biscuits in front of Ryland, and he took a bite before telling the sheriff, "I'm afraid Cooper might be planning something against the Weaver family. A widow and her daughter are traveling to Texas, hoping to locate the widow's son. I'm not sure why Cooper is trailing them, but I've heard he inquired about them along his journey, as far back as Kansas City."

"Hmm." The sheriff took a swig of coffee and set down the mug. "Well, if I was a woman alone—and a decent woman—I surely wouldn't want to meet up with that one, that Cooper." He took a large bite of beef stew on his spoon and shoved it into his mouth.

"I see. Well, I can assure you that I have only the best interests of Mrs. Weaver and her daughter in mind. Did you meet the ladies?"

"Can't say I had the pleasure."

Ryland nodded. "They are, indeed, ladies, in case you've been wondering. And I fear you are right about Cooper. He has designs. I'm sure of it."

The sheriff's eyes narrowed. "You're tracking the Weavers, I take it."

"Yes, sir. My employer has some news for them, and I hope to find them soon."

"You'd best get on the stagecoach, then."

"Good grief, yes." Ryland pulled out his watch. "I seem to have five minutes."

Sheriff Adderly rose. "Finish up. I'll make sure they don't leave without you. But don't dawdle."

"Thank you, sir!" Ryland attacked his meal, which was surprisingly good.

"Pie, mister?" the aproned woman was back.

"No, thank you. I have to catch the stage."

"Thought so." She smiled, revealing a gap where one of her canine teeth was missing, and held out a fragrant brown lump of dough wrapped in a napkin. "Apple fritter for a nickel. Take it with you."

"Oh, I say. Well, yes, thank you." Ryland yanked a nickel and a mostly clean handkerchief out of his pocket and handed her the nickel. Sometime he'd have to find a place to get his laundry done.

She quickly transferred the fritter to his handkerchief, and Ryland dashed out onto the street.

The driver and shotgun rider were already in their places on the stagecoach box, and he ran for the door. Sheriff Adderly opened it, and Ryland dove in. The sheriff shut him in with the other six passengers and said briskly, "Safe travels."

Ryland waved out the window as the stagecoach jerked into motion.

MOLLY STOOD STILL, watching Joe. What was he doing? She frowned and looked in the direction Joe was looking, but she didn't see anything unusual.

He stood with one wrist against a tree trunk, at chin level, and he was either staring off to the east or ... was it possible he had his eyes closed? Maybe this was all getting to him. Well, fine. If Joe wanted to quit, she and Ma could go on alone. She strode toward him.

"Joe? What are you doing?"

He jerked toward her, and his creased face smoothed into a smile.

"Honestly?"

"Yes, honestly. If you think it's useless to go on ..."

"No, that's not it." He cocked his head to one side. "Truth is, I was prayin'."

She hadn't expected that. Trying to school her features and knowing she failed miserably, she swallowed hard. "So, you do think it's useless."

He shook his head. "I didn't say that. But I'm at a loss as to what we ought to do now."

Molly straightened her shoulders. "That fella we met a few days ago saw Andrew. Spoke to him."

Joe's lips tightened. "It could have been Andrew. I want to think it was. But we really don't know, do we? A rider stopped and asked him if he knew where he could buy some stock, and Allison said he didn't know. That's all. Could have been anyone."

"Seems like nobody's selling cattle right now. Everyone's buying."

"Yeah. Trying to build up their herds, or rebuild them. A lot of cattle got lost or butchered during the war, when there weren't enough men to keep an eye on them. And there's a whole lot of fellas drifting around now. Some are troublemakers. Some just haven't got any place to go home to since the war."

Molly blew out a breath. "Ma and I are praying too. But we haven't got any answers yet. Have you?"

"I'm thinking ... thinking I could go faster and quieter if I was alone."

Outrage swept over Molly, and she clenched her fists. "We told you—"

Joe held up his hands, palms toward her. "Now, hear me out. You and your ma could ride hard and be back to Andrew's in two days."

"No. That would be harder on Ma, and more dangerous without you."

Joe nodded. "I have to agree. But what if we find a rancher with a wife? They might be willing to take in you two as boarders for a few days. I could go on ahead and really scour the area."

He sounded determined to shed himself of their company. Molly said, "You really think you could do it quicker than the three of us?"

"I don't know, not for sure. But ..."

"But you're always having to wait for us and worry about where we've got to."

He shrugged. "I admit, it makes me uneasy to send a woman —or even two women together—off into unknown territory to talk to strangers. We're getting into places where the ranches are far apart again. Some of the men we've met are tough customers. Let me try it on my own, Molly. Just for a few days. It would give you and your mother a rest."

"I don't need to rest until I've found my brother."

His smile was back, sadder this time. "I know, but your ma does. She's tired, Molly. Now, Emma Weaver is made of stern stuff. But face it, this past week—month, even, if you count the journey down from Ohio—has been hard on her."

The sun beat down on her, though it hadn't been up for more than an hour. Molly wished she'd put on her bonnet. She hadn't been able to keep strict track of the days, but they might be into August now. It must be two months since Pa died.

And Joe was right. Her mother should be sitting in a rocking chair somewhere, not tearing around this simmering wilderness and sleeping on the ground where there were vile creatures like scorpions and rattlesnakes.

"Mo-o-o-lly!"

She turned back toward camp. Her mother stood flapping her apron and holding up the coffeepot.

"Looks like breakfast is ready," Joe said.

Molly waved and walked toward the campfire. Guilt, a frequent companion, returned. She was supposed to be looking for fuel while Ma saw to their meal.

"Can we ask her?" Joe studied her face as he walked beside her.

"I ..." They were nearly there, and Molly dropped her voice. "I'm afraid she'll think we're giving up. She won't ever give up, Joe."

He sighed. "Andrew could be back at his cabin, waiting on us."

She pressed her lips tightly together. The thought had crossed her mind more than once. "We might be able to send a telegram in one of the towns up ahead."

"Could be. But who would you send it to?"

"The county sheriff in Austin?"

Joe's forehead wrinkled, and he nodded slowly. "That's a big if, though."

"And I can send Andrew a letter from any post office. We should be near one of those in the next couple of days. When we ask people about Andrew, we can find out where they mail their letters."

"How would we know if he got it? We're not staying put long enough to hear back from him, even if he's there."

"What's this?" Ma asked. "Letters?"

"We were just discussing how we could contact Andrew if he was already home," Joe said, "or at least let him know we're out here looking for him."

Emma smiled. "If he's there and he got the messages we left him, he could send us a wire at the next big town ahead."

"That's a thought." Molly looked eagerly at Joe.

He pushed his hat back. "Might be a good idea. Whyn't you write a letter and tell him if he's home to send us a telegram to New Braunfels?"

"We don't know yet if they've got telegraph service there," Molly said.

"Hmm. Right. I guess we'd better start asking about that too."

As they ate, they continued to discuss their options. When

Joe went to bring up the horses, Emma rose to clean up and pack their dishes.

"Ma," Molly said. "I don't want to sit somewhere while Joe hunts for Andrew."

"I know." Her mother laid a hand on her shoulder and leaned over to pick up the frying pan. "You want to be doing something."

"Yes."

"Then help get ready to move on. And pray as you work."

Molly considered the flitting idea of leaving Ma somewhere safe and continuing the search with Joe. But Ma would never stand for that. She sighed and lumbered to her feet. Praying and doing chores didn't seem like enough.

8

F inally—Austin. Ryland eased down from the stagecoach and unfolded his long legs, stretching and looking around. He considered his best options for finding Molly Weaver, and after claiming his bag, he walked into the depot.

The station agent was busy issuing tickets and answering travelers' questions. When he finally came out from behind his counter, Ryland approached him.

"Pardon me. I'm looking for some passengers who may have come through here in the last few days."

"Can you wait? I've got to see this stage off again."

Ryland nodded with an inward sigh. The agent took another ten minutes to make sure everything went smoothly in switching the teams and loading all the luggage and passengers for the next stop. Finally he came back inside and blinked at Ryland as if surprised to see him.

"Oh, yes. How can I help you?"

In his travels, Ryland had learned that he got more information in some situations if he presented his credentials, so he introduced himself and offered the letter Mr. Turner had given him to assure people he was telling the truth about his employment.

"And you're here to find someone for this lawyer?" The agent pushed the letter back into his hand after scanning it.

"Yes. A Mrs. Weaver and her daughter. It would probably be several days ago now." He hoped he was gaining on them, but he couldn't be sure.

The man frowned. "We get a lot of people through here."

"I know." When the agent began straightening things on his desk, Ryland decided to try another tack. "Also, there's a man who I believe came in on yesterday's stage. One Benjamin Cooper."

The agent shook his head. "I don't usually take people's names. What did he look like?"

Ryland gave him what details he'd gleaned from the sheriff who detained Cooper. "And he probably inquired about Mrs. and Miss Weaver."

"These ladies are popular, I take it."

"Well ..." Ryland decided to take the plunge. "This Cooper was in trouble up the line. Do you know Sheriff Adderly?"

"I know of him."

"He arrested Cooper for being disorderly and held him overnight in his jail."

The agent's eyes narrowed. "There was a fella came through yesterday with a rough kind of look. Hung over, if you ask me. Maybe you should check with the county sheriff's office on Oak Street."

"I'll do that, thank you."

The sheriff himself was out, but a deputy was more than willing to speak to Ryland.

"Yep, Adderly notified us about him. He hasn't turned up in any sort of fracas here, though. Not yet, that is."

"Wait a minute," Ryland said. "That town doesn't have a telegraph office."

"No, he sent a note with the stage driver. We've been looking out for Cooper, but I think he must have moved on. You could ask at the livery."

That seemed like sound advice. "And what about a family named Weaver?"

"Weaver? Nothing comes to mind. Got a first name?"

"Andrew, a young man with a ranch not far from town. I believe his mother and sister came in by stagecoach a few days ago, hoping to visit him."

"Huh. Well, if they aren't in some kind of trouble, we probably wouldn't know about them. You could stop back later and ask the sheriff, but personally, I don't know anything about those people."

"Thank you." Ryland got directions for the nearest livery and stepped outside. On his way to the stable, he spotted a post office and hurried there.

"Why, yes," the woman sorting mail told him. "Andrew Weaver's lived out the Hill Road for the past several months. Perhaps a year, but I don't think it's been that long. And his mother was in here just a few days ago."

"His mother? Mrs. Emma Weaver?"

The woman looked up and smiled. "Yes. Lovely woman. You know her?"

"We've never met," Ryland said, "but I'd dearly like to find her and her daughter, Molly."

"Hmm. She left her name and Molly's, so they can receive mail here. Gave the address as her son's ranch."

"Wonderful," Ryland said. "Could you direct me to the ranch?"

Her eyes clouded. "I really shouldn't."

"I assure you, I have only good intentions, ma'am." Ryland took out his credentials.

The woman eyed Mr. Turner's letter, frowning. "Well, that looks all right, but it's easy enough to forge a letter."

"True, but I can assure you that I'm representing myself and my employer truthfully."

Still, she hesitated. "There was another fella here yesterday, asking about the Weavers."

Ryland's back stiffened. "Benjamin Cooper?"

"He didn't give his name, just kept asking questions. I didn't tell him anything."

"Nothing?"

"I said it was private, and we weren't supposed to tell if people lived in Austin or not, nor where to find them. It's part of the post office rules."

"I see. Good for you."

"I didn't like his looks." She shrugged. "I expect he found out someplace else."

"Yes. I'm headed to the livery stable myself, hoping to ride out to Andrew's ranch. I believe it's on the Hill Road?"

She flushed, realizing she'd let that slip earlier. "That's correct, but please don't say you heard it here. And I promise, I didn't tell that other man anything." Her nose wrinkled. "Smelled of beer."

Ryland got directions to the local telegraph office and the livery. He lifted his hat for a moment. "Thank you, ma'am. I'm sure you're doing a good job."

He hurried out and down the street. A quick telegram to Mr. Turner was in order.

ARRIVED AUSTIN, HEADING TO RANCH.

Abby should get at least a postal card, but he didn't dare take the time. He needed a horse. Mrs. Weaver and Molly were probably sitting in Andrew's kitchen right now. Of course, Ben Cooper had probably found them by this time. Although he couldn't see any way he could have beaten Cooper to their goal, he kicked himself mentally. No time to lose.

At the livery stable, he strode inside and walked the aisle between stalls where eight horses were tied, head in. A man in overalls and an undershirt was shoveling manure near the back of the barn, and Ryland approached him, carefully avoiding waste on the floor.

The man leaned on his shovel and looked at him. "You need a horse?"

"Yes, Mr.—"

"Harry."

"I'd like a good riding horse and some direction."

Twenty minutes later, Ryland had a horse he felt confident would serve him well. He'd tried to remember everything his friend Mory had taught him about picking horseflesh, and this one looked good. Well fleshed out, but not fat. Harry assured him the seven-year-old gelding was healthy and had good feet. That was the most important part of the horse, Mory had said. Too bad his friend wasn't along on this trip.

Of course, Ryland had to buy the saddle and bridle as well, but Harry assured him he'd buy them back at full price if Ryland brought them back within a month. He certainly hoped he wouldn't need the animal or his gear that long. He hadn't ridden much lately, and he wasn't looking forward to a twenty-mile jaunt to Andrew's ranch. He'd be sore tomorrow for certain. But if all went well, he wouldn't need to ride much after that.

"Funny," Harry said as he saddled the faded gold horse for Ryland. "Mrs. Weaver bought herself a riding horse from me a week or so ago. That surprised me. She took the only sidesaddle I had."

"That is odd," Ryland said. "What about her daughter? Did Miss Weaver buy a horse as well?"

"Nope, she had one. The gentleman with them was loaning her one, I dare say."

Ryland perked up at that. "You mean Andrew Weaver? He was with them?"

Harry shook his head. "Naw, his neighbor, Joe Somethin'. He told me they were goin' on the trail for several days, and he needed a reliable mount for Mrs. Weaver."

Ryland puzzled over that. He didn't like the mention of going on the trail. "And no sign of her son?"

"Nope. But now it seems everybody and his brother wants to find him. Or at least, wants to find the Weavers."

"What do you mean?"

"Yesterday. Fella came in—long drinka water—asking after Mrs. Weaver and her brood. Sold him a horse too." Harry looked around his stable. "Yep, I've got to get me more stock. Pretty soon I'll be down to nothin' but harness horses and mules."

"This man you sold the horse to yesterday—was his name Cooper?"

Harry frowned. "Hmm, sounds about right. Not sure. I reckon he rode straight out to Weaver's ranch yesterday afternoon." He looked up with a gleam in his eyes. "But I can tell you what the horse looks like."

"Yes, please."

"Bay gelding, on the thin side, with a white strip on its nose. White sock on the left hind foot."

ANDREW PULLED his horse to a stop and stood in the stirrups. He clenched his teeth as pain lanced through his shoulder and ribcage. Weariness overtook him, as it had each day since his accident.

He'd left home optimistic, but after learning Hewitt was no longer offering cattle for sale—in fact, was no longer living in the area—he'd lost heart. For two solid weeks after that, he'd gone from ranch to ranch, asking where he could buy a few cattle. He'd just about made up his mind to return home emptyhanded and wait until it was roundup time in the fall—surely some of the cowmen would sell him and Joe a few head then—when his horse, Blinker, had stumbled.

Blinker had always been surefooted, if not the quickest cow pony. That was the main reason Andrew kept him, though he might need a better trained cutting horse once he got a start on his herd.

He'd huddled over his campfire for several days, not strong enough to saddle up and ride for help. Finally, two ranchmen had stumbled on him when they saw the smoke from the fire he coaxed, heating his last bit of grub.

After a painful ten-mile ride with those men on each side of Andrew to make sure he didn't fall off Blinker again, they'd reached their boss's ranch. For the next week, he'd rested in their cramped bunkhouse, nursing his injury. He must have broken a couple of ribs. They didn't have a doctor within fifty miles, but the foreman had wrapped him up with strips of cloth.

His ribs still hurt every time he mounted, dismounted, or made any sudden move. His shoulder still pained him each time he raised his arm. But he was able to move on.

The rancher hadn't let him pay for his board, but he hadn't sold him any beeves either. Everyone was trying to rebuild their herds now that the war was over. A recommendation was the best he could do. He'd heard that a fellow farther on might have a few extra head. As soon as he speculated he could stay in the saddle a whole day at a time, Andrew had set out.

He saw some cattle grazing along a hillside in the sweltering heat. Half a mile farther on, he spotted a small house and a corral, back from the road. This must be the place. It had to be. He didn't think he could last much longer without a respite.

Andrew hesitated. Once he got down off Blinker, it would be hard to mount again. He'd best hunt out a boulder or something else he could climb on first. And there was the matter of the money. He considered himself lucky—blessed, his mother would have said—to have made it this far without being robbed.

He'd left home confident that he'd be back in a couple weeks with the livestock he and Joe needed. Now he wondered if he'd ever get home, let alone with either cattle or the cash in his pocket. He rubbed his chin. What would his pa do? Pa was a shrewd man. He dickered a lot at his store, but he never let anyone get the better of him. And right now, Andrew could almost hear him warning him to be cautious. He wasn't fully recovered, and he was carrying a lot of money.

Pushing Blinker with his legs, Andrew hunted around for a good place to dismount. Finally he saw a rock that stuck up a foot or more out of the ground. He sidled the gelding next to it and slowly swung his right leg over the back of the saddle. Even though his foot landed on the rock, the drop jarred him, and he had to hold on to the saddle for a minute and breathe carefully. He dropped the reins, eased his left foot from the stirrup, and climbed the rest of the way down.

Blinker was good at ground tying, if nothing else. At once, he began to nuzzle about and clip off mouthfuls of drying grass.

Andrew gathered a few stones and started digging. He didn't have a shovel, and he didn't want to dull his knife, so he used a mostly flat stone with a pointed end. It didn't take him long to scoop out a shallow hole near the rock he'd stood on.

After taking a good, hard look around, he slipped the leather pouch that held his money out of his pocket, removed two dollars and pocketed them, and then put the pouch into the hole. He filled in the depression and positioned a stone about five inches wide on top of it. He wished he could have found a better one, but this would have to do. On a smaller rock, he used his digger to scratch an X on the flattest side and set it on top of the other small rock.

With a sigh, he stepped back, one hand pressed to his side, pushing on the place that hurt the most. He looked around to make sure he was still unobserved and then made note of the landmarks he could use to find this spot again. He wished it was farther from the road, and farther from the ranch house, but it would have to do.

Climbing back into the saddle would be too hard. It just wasn't worth the pain. He walked along slowly, leading Blinker. As they ambled down the dusty lane together, Andrew assessed the ranch. The small house looked to be in good repair. Several cattle grazed nearby, rather thin ones.

By the time he reached the stoop, exhaustion threatened him. He let go of Blinker's reins and winced as he mounted the flat rock that served as a step. He knocked and then waited. He could hear soft movements inside, so someone was at home, even if no horses were in the corral.

The door opened, and he found himself face-to-face with a woman scarcely older than himself. She blinked her brown eyes and then peered past him, as if expecting someone else. Her dark hair was caught up in a bun, but the thing he noticed most was the blue and purple bruise across her left cheek, reaching up to her eye.

Andrew stepped back and down off the doorstone. "I beg your pardon, ma'am. Is this the Nolan place?"

She gazed at him for a couple of seconds then nodded.

"A fella up the road a few miles told me Mr. Nolan might have a few cattle to sell."

After another pause, she said, "He might."

At least it wasn't a flat-out no. Andrew cleared his throat. "Is he in? I'd like to talk to him."

"He'll be back soon for lunch."

Andrew thought about that. "If he's working about the place, maybe I could go find him."

It was almost a question, and she shook her head. "Best if you wait. He shouldn't be too long. But wait out there."

"Yes, ma'am." He supposed any woman in such an isolated place would hesitate to invite a strange man into her home. "All right if I water my horse?"

"Surely. The well's there." She pointed to the enclosed well he'd already spotted. "You can put him in the corral if you want, or turn him out to graze."

The choice wasn't difficult. The corral was a bare patch of dirt that had been much pawed and scuffed. The grass outside it didn't look very good, but Blinker could put something in his belly, which was better than nothing. The door closed softly behind him.

He led Blinker to the well and drew water to pour into the trough. The water level was low, far down in the bottom of the well, but he didn't know if that was unusual. It was probably always this way in high summer. He winced and slowly cranked up the bucket.

Someday he'd get a well dug on his place, so he wouldn't have to keep hauling water from the creek. When he did, he'd put a pump on top and not have to pull up dozens of buckets every day. How long had the Nolans been doing it the hard way?

He took hobbles from a saddlebag and attached them to Blinker's forelegs. The saddle and bridle came off next, and he hung the saddle on the corral fence, with the bridle draped over it. Rubbing his ribcage, he considered finding a clean patch of grass to stretch out on, but then he heard the thud of hoofbeats. A thin chestnut horse jogged wearily around the corner of the house.

"Howdy." Andrew stepped forward.

The rider eyed him darkly from beneath the brim of his hat and rode to the corral gate. He swung down and pulled off the saddle then turned the horse into the enclosure. Last of all, he slid the bridle off over the chestnut's nose.

Andrew stepped closer as he shut the gate.

"Mr. Nolan?"

"Who are you?"

"My name's Andrew Weaver, sir. I'm looking for a few head of cattle. A fella down the way said you might have some to sell."

Nolan looked toward the house. The door stood open six inches, and his wife hovered just inside.

"Git dinner on, Sophie," Nolan yelled.

She shut the door quickly.

He turned back toward Andrew. "Where do you live?"

"East of Austin, sir."

"You had a long ride."

"Yeah, I thought I could get some stock closer to home, but

94

it seems everyone's trying to rebuild their herds, and nobody's selling much right now."

Nolan looked out toward where his steers cropped grass. "It's hard times. I might let go a few, but I got to eat first."

"Of course." Andrew stepped back.

"I suppose you're hungry." The words came out grudgingly.

Andrew shrugged. "I can't say I'm not, but you don't need to feed me."

Nolan grunted and walked toward the house. Andrew followed a few paces behind, not sure if he was welcome or not. His host walked into the house without shutting the door, so Andrew went in too.

"Give this man some coffee," Nolan said.

Andrew noticed that the table was already set for three. Unless they had a child or a hired hand, he guessed Mrs. Nolan had done that for him.

"Sit right here, sir." The woman touched the back of a chair then turned toward the stove.

Andrew sat, and Nolan took the other chair with a back. Mrs. Nolan would have to sit on a stool, and Andrew felt guilty that she'd given him her chair. As she poured coffee for him and then her husband, Nolan studied him.

"You got cash?"

Andrew swallowed hard. "Yes, sir, if we reach an agreement."

"What'd you say your name was?"

"Weaver. Andrew Weaver."

"You sound like a Yankee."

"I did move here from Ohio last year. Is that a problem?" Andrew made an unconscious decision to drop the "sir." He didn't want to sour the transaction, but Nolan's rudeness struck a nerve. He wouldn't be cowed into a bad deal.

Sophie brought over an iron kettle and a pan of biscuits. Ma would have put the food into pretty serving dishes, but Andrew wouldn't complain. The Nolans probably didn't have fancy dishes. Anyway, it smelled good.

Nolan scooped a large helping from the kettle onto his plate without offering to serve the guest. Sophie came with a saltshaker in one hand and a dish of butter in the other and sat down on the stool.

"Won't you help yourself, Mr. Weaver?" Her gaze would be kind and even sweet if she'd smile a bit, but her sober expression and the bruise robbed her of appeal.

Andrew swallowed hard. "Thank you, ma'am." He ladled out a medium-sized portion—less than Nolan had claimed, or that he would take for himself if he were alone. He made sure he didn't take more than half what was left.

Nolan put two biscuits on the edge of his plate and made no move to pass the pan to Andrew. Sophie picked it up and held it out to him.

"Biscuit?"

"Thank you. Everything sure smells good, ma'am."

A smile flickered on her lips for just a moment, but then she darted a glance Nolan's way and retreated behind her blank expression again.

They ate in near silence, except for Nolan's curt, "More coffee" to his wife.

She rose and went to the stove for the coffeepot. Her shoulders drooped, and she gingerly touched her bruised cheek for a moment.

Nolan was staring at him. Andrew quickly turned his attention back to his dinner.

After he'd finished his meal, Nolan shoved back his chair and stood. Andrew rose more slowly, fighting not to grimace at the pain in his ribs. Without meaning to, he put a hand to his side and inhaled carefully.

Nolan was nearly out the door when his wife said softly, "You all right, Mr. Weaver?"

He nodded. "Thank you for that very nice dinner, ma'am."

He followed Nolan outside and found him at the corral.

"We'll ride out and take a look at the stock," his host said.

Andrew turned away from the rancher when he hefted the saddle onto Blinker's back. He eased upward into the saddle, hoping Nolan didn't notice how slowly he moved. The chestnut was already jogging away, and Andrew squeezed Blinker, urging him to catch up. They trotted out past the steers he'd seen earlier.

"These here are ones I'm keepin'," Nolan said.

They topped a slope and paused, looking out over a long downgrade that led to a sluggish stream. Only two or three feet wide, it trickled along a sandy bed.

"You have good water here?" Andrew asked.

"Mostly."

He didn't elaborate, but the stream looked as though it might dry up to nothing soon. Andrew was betting August would be a dry-as-a-bone month in these parts.

They rode down the hill, and Nolan stopped where they could view about two dozen cattle grazing on the other side of the stream, scattered across the range.

"These here are the ones I'd let go, if the price is right."

Andrew swallowed hard and pulled back on his reins. Blinker stopped, and they sat for a long moment, looking at the sorriest cattle he'd ever seen. But still, they were beeves. He could fatten them up once he got them home—if they made it home.

"What's the right price?" he asked.

Nolan eyed him keenly. "What are you willing to pay?"

Andrew shook his head, recalling his father's lessons in sharp dealing at the mercantile. "If you've got a price in mind, tell me. But those steers look mighty spare, so I warn you, I'm not paying top dollar."

Nolan scowled. He named a price that was a bit higher than Andrew had hoped, but not as much as he'd feared. Maybe Nolan wanted to sell off most of his herd before the water dried up.

"Most of them don't seem to have a brand," Andrew noted.

Nolan's jaw tightened. "Mostly they're strays. They's been

quite a few roaming the plains since the war. Nobody can rightly claim 'em, which means anybody can. I been roundin' 'em up to sell."

Andrew knew it was true. Joe had told him how he'd acquired three cows the same way, but the strays were mostly taken now in their area. He wished he knew more about Nolan. Had he been involved in the war? Maybe he'd come back recently. Or had he moved here after the armistice? The rancher didn't seem to welcome questions. It might be better not to raise them. He surveyed the cattle.

"I count twenty-two head," Andrew said. Then he named a sum he would give for all of them.

Nolan frowned. Was he doing arithmetic in his head?

"It's fifty cents less per head than you offered," Andrew said. "But I'll take them all off your hands tomorrow morning if you agree."

"Tomorrow?"

"I don't have the money on me. But I'll be back with it at sunup if we agree."

Nolan lifted his chin and eyed Andrew as if he were a bug. The steely, cold eyes made Andrew shiver.

"All right," Nolan said at last. "Be here early. I'll deal with you right after breakfast."

If Andrew had ever heard one, that was a warning not to expect another free meal.

"I'll be here shortly after sunup, then."

"You do that."

Nolan wheeled his chestnut and set him into a lope, back toward the house. Andrew followed at a leisurely pace. He didn't see Nolan or his horse near the house or corral when he arrived. Mrs. Nolan peered at him through the front window. Andrew touched his hat brim and rode on, back the way he'd come.

He rode past the rocks hiding his cache and kept going for a mile, in case Nolan had eyes on him. He found himself a place to camp, off among some trees. Glad he'd replenished his water supply, he set about making coffee and lay down to wait for darkness.

When he went to get the money by moonlight, he moved slowly. He was sore all over, but mostly along his ribcage. And his stomach roiled. Had he got some sort of infection from his injuries? Or maybe there was something wrong with the can of beans he'd eaten for his supper. He collected his money and started to cover the hole but stopped.

The amount he'd brought was more than he'd promised Nolan. He'd hoped to find a larger herd than Nolan was ready to sell him. In fact, he would only be paying a little more than half what he'd carried with him. And he wasn't sure he completely trusted Nolan.

He peeled off enough bills to pay for the steers and put it in his pocket. The rest of the money went into a can he'd washed out, and he put that in the cache. He filled the hole carefully and replaced the rocks that were his markers.

Back at his campsite, he rolled tight in his blanket with the bulk of the cash inside his shirt and his revolver close at hand. If he wasn't able to fetch it, would anyone find the money he'd left in the can before it rotted away? Even so, he felt better not approaching the Nolan ranch again with that much on him.

For some reason, he thought of Ma and Pa and Molly, back in Ohio. If he died out here alone, how would they ever know? He hadn't wanted to worry his family, but now he wished he'd sent them, or at least his friend Joe Noyes, details about his journey. But he'd kept thinking he'd be back to his ranch soon. With a groan, he rolled over and closed his eyes.

THIS HAD to be the right place. Ryland halted his horse and studied the little house for a long moment. The place looked to be in fairly good repair. But if this was Andrew Weaver's ranch, why weren't the horses Emma and Molly had ridden, not to mention Andrew's own mount, in the corral out front? The liveryman had said they were planning a trip. Had they left already?

He rode slowly toward the dwelling, dismounted, and looked around for a place to tie the horse. "Can't have you hightailin' it back to Austin without me, now can we?" He wrapped the ends of the reins around the top rail of the corral fence, stepped up to the door, and knocked. He listened hard, but he couldn't hear any movement inside.

Maybe he had the wrong place after all. But, no. He went over Harry's directions in his head, and this had to be it. He mulled over the livery owner's words. Emma Weaver had bought a horse, and the neighbor who escorted her and Molly to the stable said they were taking a horseback trip of several days. Several questions came to mind. First, who was "they"? Was the neighbor, Noyes, going with the ladies? Surely Emma and Molly wouldn't set out alone on such a jaunt.

And did Andrew accompany them? If so, why had Noyes brought the women to the livery stable? It was all very confusing.

No keyhole graced the door. Ryland reached out and tried the latch. The door swung open. Hesitantly, he stepped over the threshold.

"Hello?"

Only silence greeted him. He walked slowly around the main room. No food was stored on the shelves or in the cupboard, and that struck him as odd. The only thing on the table was a coffee mug.

Wasn't Andrew Weaver living here? He peered through a doorway and saw a bed made up with sheets but no blankets. No luggage, except for two trunks that stood against the wall.

Ryland's pulse throbbed. He knew from conversations he'd had with various stagecoach tenders that the Weaver women had traveled with trunks and smaller bags. He walked over and ran his hand along the top of one of the trunks. Its brass fittings told him it wasn't a cheap piece of luggage. But then, Mr. Weaver had owned a mercantile store. His wife would have good merchandise.

He couldn't bring himself to open the trunks. A tag tied to one's handle assured him it belonged to Emma Weaver. What good would pawing through her wardrobe do him? He flushed just thinking about handling ladies' undergarments and turned away.

Maybe the neighbor, Joe, was at his ranch. Ryland would stop and see, and then what? Go back to Austin? That wouldn't do him much good. The stagecoach agent had told him the Weaver women ended their stage journey there. And they'd bought mounts and said they were going off on horseback.

Frustrated, he walked outside. A small shed stood behind the corral. With a sense of futility, Ryland walked over to the three-sided structure. A rain barrel stood below the corner of the slanting roof. Inside were a small supply of firewood and an oat bin. A harness and an old bridle hung on the back wall, along with a hammer, a shovel, and a bow saw. No sidesaddle. No saddle at all, in fact.

Not much help. Might as well go see if the neighbor was home, but he had a feeling he'd be disappointed again.

Behind him, the horse whinnied.

"What's the matter, fella?" Ryland smiled and turned toward him. In a blur of motion, something smacked the side of his head. He put out his hands to cushion his fall.

9

"Weaver, you say?" Ed Swanson, the owner of one of the more prosperous-looking ranches they'd approached, shoved his hat back and gazed off into the distance. "Yup. He came through here."

Molly and Emma crowded closer on their horses.

"How long ago?" Joe asked.

"Three or four days. I told him I wasn't selling cattle right now, but to come back if he didn't find anything and I'd let him buy a couple of steers. Can't really let go of more right now. I'm working to build a good herd, and it's mighty hard."

Joe didn't doubt it. The man had one sleeve pinned up, where his right arm was missing below the elbow.

"Where'd you serve?"

Swanson sighed. "Louisiana and Mississippi mostly."

Joe met his gaze. "I was in Pennsylvania. And other places."

"Gettysburg?"

Joe gave a curt nod. He'd had a slight wound, and they'd let him go home after Gettysburg. His enlistment was about up anyway. That was when he'd headed for Texas.

"I'm Andrew Weaver's mother," Emma said, squeezing her

gelding closer to the rancher. "We're worried about my son. He should have been home weeks ago."

Swanson frowned. "He did look a little peaked when he was here. I'm sorry, ma'am, but I don't know exactly where he went. He was headed south, though. He seemed a decent sort, and if he hadn't said he had his own place, I'd have offered him a job. My wife's ... well, she can't ride right now, and we're struggling. I've only been home from the army a few months, and we want to make this work, but ..." He shook his head.

Joe glanced at Emma. She seemed agreeable, so he spoke up. "I had a mind to settle Mrs. Weaver and her daughter for a few days, so I could ride around a little faster myself and ask after Andrew. Do you know of anyone who'd board a couple of women for a short time?"

Swanson's brow furrowed. "Well, my wife might welcome some company. She can't do heavy work, but—"

"We could help her with the housework," Emma said quickly.

"Ma," Molly murmured.

Joe could almost read her mind. Now that they had word Andrew had passed through here, she didn't want to stop.

"It wouldn't be for long," Joe said. "I just want to get some solid information on where he's at. Then I'll come back for the ladies." He glanced at Molly. "I promise."

Molly didn't agree until they met Mrs. Swanson. Even Joe could tell she was expecting a baby. She seemed overwhelmed at first, when her husband suggested she might board the Weavers. When Joe explained that he wasn't staying, just the ladies, she looked relieved and admitted she would be glad to have someone to talk to.

Emma assured her that she and Molly could make up the bed they would share and would help her with the cooking and housework.

"Oh," Mrs. Swanson said. "That would be lovely."

"And we'd pay you fifty cents a night besides," Emma added.

Joe thought Mrs. Swanson might cry.

Molly's eyes met his. She nodded, her face sober.

Joe rode away with an invisible burden weighing him down. Molly had agreed to stay, for Emma's sake and maybe for Mrs. Swanson's too. But she didn't like it. Not only had he made Molly peevish, but he realized he'd taken on a huge responsibility for the entire Weaver family. And Molly was a young woman he didn't want to peeve.

She had spunk. Sometimes she might not look far enough down the road, but she was a smart woman, and determined. Add to that her intriguing face and her glistening hair. Her ma was handsome, too, but not nearly so pretty as Molly. In fact, they didn't look much alike at all. Emma had dark hair with a few strands of gray, and soft brown eyes. Molly's eyes were blue like the Texas sky.

At least he'd gotten a lead, or he thought so. Ed Swanson's recollection was the first definite news they had of Andrew. Since his conversation with Fred Allison, he'd feared they might never find his friend. Now he had a spark of hope.

SOMEONE HAD BUSHWHACKED HIM. Ryland had learned the term on a previous journey west, when he'd been searching for Matt Anderson. He'd found Matt on a ranch in Colorado. Now he was hunting Matt's sister, and it seemed this quest wouldn't be any easier than the earlier one.

Smells of earth and horse manure helped clear his mind. He sat up, his head spinning. How long had he been out, lying under this rickety roof?

The sun was sinking. He'd never been good at telling time by the sun, so he felt in his pocket for his watch. It wasn't there. He held back an oath and put his hand gingerly to his head. The sorest place seemed to be on the left side of his skull, behind his ear. The pain made him jerk away from his own fingertips. They'd got him good.

But still, by the time he'd ridden out of Austin, it had been midafternoon. The ride had taken two hours or more, maybe closer to three. It couldn't be later than six o'clock now. Maybe a couple hours of daylight left?

He looked around. The small cabin—Andrew Weaver's cabin —sat close by. The corral before him was empty, and his spine stiffened. He'd left his horse tied to that fence, he was sure of it.

Ryland closed his eyes for a moment then popped them open and glanced around. Whoever brained him could still be lurking about.

His head still swam, but he managed to put together a few coherent thoughts. Someone had ambushed him and stolen his horse and his watch. He patted his pockets and swore aloud.

"Sorry, Lord." He glanced skyward. For the past couple of years, he'd tried to swear less and pray more. This would be a good time for prayer.

"All right, Lord, it's me. I'm praying with my eyes open, if it's all the same to you. I've got no horse and no money. At least he didn't take my letter from Mr. Turner, but I have no idea what to do now."

He found he could walk without stumbling, and he made his way slowly toward the little house. A bed was inside. Maybe he should rest. Stay here overnight and start walking in the morning.

He'd have to go back to Austin and telegraph Mr. Turner for more money. Much as he hated the thought, it would be necessary. That hike would take most of a day, especially if his head was still pounding. Maybe he'd be lucky and some farmer would come along in a wagon and give him a ride.

As he walked toward the door, he heard a faint whinny and stopped in his tracks. He whipped his head around toward the road, which was a mistake. The pain and lightheadedness that followed almost took him to his knees. With his hands holding his temples, he looked toward the road but didn't see any horses. Had he imagined it?

A glance toward the corral brought further confusion, and he walked slowly toward the fence. In the exact spot where he'd tied the horse, a leather strap was hanging. A bridle rein? Had his horse broken free?

Another whinny came, louder this time. He turned slowly. It was coming from behind the house. Carefully, he walked along the end wall. A wide expanse of grass lay between the cabin and some trees, enclosed by a rough rail fence with an open gate. At the far side, near the tree line, his faded palomino horse was grazing. The horse lifted its head, looked at him for a moment, and neighed.

"Yes! Thank You, Lord!" Now, if the horse would just come to him. He tried to whistle, but his mouth was too dry.

The gelding went back to cropping the grass, and Ryland sighed. Headache or no headache, he was going to have to chase a horse. He walked grimly across the pasture. About halfway to his goal, he caught his breath. One rein trailed from the bridle, and his saddle was still there. It had slid down the horse's side, until it was almost under its belly. Whoever had attacked him hadn't gotten the horse, but just as important, he hadn't gotten the saddle or the saddlebags.

If the thief hadn't rifled those saddlebags before he left, there was a chance Ryland still had a bit of money and extra clothing.

"Good horse," he murmured as he approached. "You're a good horse, yes, sir. You got away, didn't you?" His small satchel was still tied behind the cantle, and it surely looked as if the saddlebags were untouched. Ryland smiled.

Catching the horse was easier than he'd expected. When he bent for the end of the rein, the animal jerked its head up.

"Easy, now." Ryland slowly edged closer and took hold of the bridle's cheek strap. He stroked the horse's neck. "Are you all right, fella?" He looked carefully at the gelding's mouth. On the side with the broken rein, a small cut was evident in the corner of its lips.

"Had to pull pretty hard to break that rein, didn't you, boy?

I'm sorry." Ryland stroked the horse's face and scratched beneath its forelock. "But you got away. I could kiss you. In fact ..." He laughed and planted a big smack on the horse's long nose. "You're a prince, that's what you are. Yeah. I'm going to call you that. What do you say, Prince? Should we head on back to Austin? We might not get there till after dark, but I'm sure you can find the way."

He adjusted the saddle but didn't want to mount the animal until he had somehow fixed the second rein and made sure the bit wasn't hurting Prince's mouth too badly. He'd lead him back, that was all. He wanted to check the saddlebags, but he couldn't do that easily while holding on to the bridle. Ryland eyed the fence. No, he couldn't hitch poor Prince to a fence again just yet. Bad memories might cause the horse to panic.

Ryland was about to turn back toward the cabin when he spotted some rocks outside the fence. A large one stuck up from the earth, but it was the two smaller rocks that held his attention. One about the size of his fist lay on top of a bigger, flatter rock. But the oddest thing was that the dirt near them looked as if something had dug under the rock. Loose bits of darker dirt lay close to the stones.

It was nothing, he was sure. Maybe a prairie dog had been busy there. But the way the small rock was centered on the flat one niggled at him.

"Come here, fella." Gently, he urged Prince closer to the fence and reached through the rails. He picked up the small rock and examined it. To his surprise, when he turned it in his hand, he found an X scratched into the bottom surface. No prairie dog did that.

Again he looked around. A gentle breeze ruffled his hair, but all was peaceful. Ryland hopped over the fence, leaving Prince to enjoy the grass for a few more minutes. With the help of a stick, he soon uncovered a metal box. His heart raced. Treasure? Somehow he doubted it.

He set the box on the biggest rock and levered the top open.

The first thing he saw inside was a folded piece of paper. He pulled it out and opened it.

Andrew,

Ma and I got here and you were gone. Joe Noyes told us you're gone to the Hewitt ranch to buy cattle, but you're late getting back. We've decided to go with Joe and look for you. If you get home and we're not here, ask at the post office to see if we've sent you a message. I'm not taking any of your stuff from this box, as you may need it later. Some squatters used up most of your supplies in the house.

Praying we'll see you soon,
Molly.

Well. That answered several questions. Ryland smiled. This Molly—or Jane—was quite a girl. Next he took out a tightly rolled item of clothing. He laid it aside and reached for another piece of paper. To his surprise, when he unfolded it, a five-dollar bill fell to the ground. He snatched it up before it could blow away and read the second note.

Andrew,

Ma and I were here. I found this spot. We're hoping you come back soon.

Molly

After thinking about it, Ryland decided the shorter note was written first. Molly had left the money in case her brother was in need. After that, she and her mother had decided to go looking for him. Maybe she'd been in a hurry the last time she visited the hiding place, or she was working in darkness. That would explain why the hole wasn't hidden as carefully as it should have been.

He read the longer note again and sighed. At least he knew asking the neighbor wouldn't be an option. Noyes had gone with the women on their quest. He recalled the livery owner telling him they'd bought a horse for Emma and were going on the trail. They were following Andrew. He was glad they had a man with them.

Ryland folded Molly's money in the note the way he'd found it and then put everything back in the box and covered it carefully. The rocks went back on top of the spot, just as he'd found them. With his hand, he brushed away loose bits of dirt until he was reasonably sure a passerby wouldn't notice this place the way he had.

Now he just had to figure out where this Hewitt ranch was. Oh, and fix the rein on his horse's bridle. He'd seen a few tools in the shed where he'd been attacked. If he couldn't fix it himself, he was sure another bridle hung on the wall in there.

Ryland climbed back over the fence and patted the horse. "Come on, Prince. We've got work to do."

IN THE MORNING, Andrew had all he could do to saddle Blinker and stow his gear. Only by climbing on the rock that had marked his cache was he able to mount, and by the time he walked his horse into Nolan's yard, he felt he might tumble from the saddle.

Mrs. Nolan opened the door and peered out at him. "Albert's gone to town. He said you were late and you probably weren't coming back."

Andrew clenched his teeth. "I'm back. I was just moving a little slow this morning."

Her gaze sharpened. "Are you all right? I thought yesterday you were a bit poorly."

"I've been better." Andrew grimaced at a twinge of pain.

"Look, I've brought the money for your husband. Is it all right if I just give it to you and take the steers we agreed on?"

She hesitated. "I'm not sure. He's particular about what I do."

Andrew thought about that, though his brain seemed to be floating somewhere above the compact house.

"Are you sure you could ride out there and get the steers, even if I took the money?" she asked. "You don't look good."

"I—" Andrew clutched his fiery side and bent over the saddle horn. "I feel sick."

"You'd best get down from there." Mrs. Nolan came out on the stoop, her face drawn tight.

Carefully, Andrew swung his right leg over the saddle and lowered himself. He fell the last foot, and his legs buckled on him. He ended up in the dirt, staring up at his stirrup as Blinker edged nervously away. The blazing sun seared his vision, and he squeezed his eyes shut.

"Here, what's wrong?"

She was kneeling beside him. Andrew reached out a weak hand.

"Sorry." He turned his head and managed not to retch on her dress or shoes.

She jumped up and backward. "Oh, my. You need to see a doctor, Mr. Weaver."

"I can't ... I'm sorry."

"Now, you quit saying that." She glanced anxiously toward her house. "I can't have you inside when Albert comes back, even if you're sick."

Andrew tried to speak, but nothing came out, so he just shook his head.

"There's some straw in the shed. I'll get your bedroll, and you can lie down there until he gets home. And I'll put your horse in the corral."

10

"Sophie says you're likely to die."

Andrew forced his eyes open and squinted up at the bearded man. Nolan stood just outside the shed, peering in at him.

"What kind of sick are you?"

"Not sick," Andrew managed. "I was hurt a couple weeks ago. Fell. I think I busted some ribs or something." He coughed and grimaced at the pain that brought on.

Nolan gazed down at him through narrowed eyes. "Didn't think you'd come back for them steers. You got the money?"

"I got it." He was helpless now. The rancher could rob him here and now. Andrew struggled to sit up and fell back on the straw. "Just let me rest for today, then I'll move on."

Nolan frowned. "Sophie thinks you oughta be in the house. Rain's coming, and this roof's like a colander."

Rain. That would be a relief from the heat. The sky had darkened, it was true. Had the air cooled? Andrew still felt hot, but he suspected he was feverish.

"I don't mean to inconvenience you, sir."

"See that you don't. I'll tell her you can put up in the

storeroom. Don't you be extra work for her." It was the most consideration he'd shown for Sophie.

"I'll do my best. Thank you."

"Shoot." Nolan scowled and stepped toward him. "Come on. I don't reckon you can get yourself inside, and I don't want you laying hands on my wife."

"I wouldn't."

"Huh."

Nolan bent over him and held out a hand. Andrew took it and tugged, letting out an involuntary moan. The rancher sighed and shoved one arm around Andrew's back and hauled him upward. The pain made everything reel and whirl. Andrew tried not to let out a sound, but he knew that was him groaning.

"Oh, come on." Nolan stepped forward, and Andrew did his best to keep up, but he was more dragged along than led into the house.

Mrs. Nolan was waiting and opened the door. "I've put down some quilts in the storeroom."

Nolan got him into the room and lowered him onto the waiting bedding. It wasn't as soft as a featherbed, but Andrew was sure he had several blankets folded beneath him, and it wasn't too bad. Much better than the straw-covered dirt floor in the shed. As he lay back, his head sank onto a mound of folded cloth. The heavy drumming of rain clattered on the roof above him.

WHEN HE AWOKE, Mrs. Nolan crouched beside him. Andrew struggled to sit up.

"There. Let's see if you can take this soup now." She put an arm under his neck to boost him a little, while she shoved a pillow under his head. From a steaming bowl on the floor, she scooped a spoonful of broth with a chunk of carrot in it. Andrew leaned forward, suppressing a moan. He'd never once thought about how far apart doctors could be when he moved to Texas.

The broth was good, nice and warm and beefy. He sank back onto the feather pillow, something he hadn't been privileged to use for at least a month. "Thank you, ma'am."

She smiled. "It's Sophie. Ready for more?"

Five minutes later, she gathered the dishes and stood. In the small space between shelves, kegs, and crates, she barely had room. She must have rearranged their stores to make room for his pallet.

"There, you get some rest now, you hear? I'll be right out in the front room if you need anything."

Andrew closed his eyes. He might have fallen asleep if Nolan hadn't snarled, "You gave him your pillow?"

"Only so's he could eat better," Sophie replied, so low Andrew could barely hear her.

"Oh, and where is it now?"

"I—I guess I left it in there."

Smack!

Andrew's eyes flew open. He lay rigid, listening with dread, his heart pounding. Had Nolan struck her?

The front door slammed. A moment later, he heard a chair scrape on the floor and then a sob.

Andrew made himself breathe slowly. Each intake of air was painful. He wanted to take short, shallow breaths, but he forced his muscles to relax and counted mentally to four before allowing himself to exhale.

What had he brought into this house? Surely Nolan couldn't be jealous of him. He remembered the bruise Sophie had borne yesterday, the first time he saw her. Maybe he treated her this way all the time. But this time, the blow had come because of him.

Andrew felt his muscles tighten and again lay still, willing himself to relax. He would rest today and get out of here first thing in the morning. And when it came time for him to use the necessary, he would somehow get himself up and out back. He would not depend on either Sophie or her husband for help.

When he awoke, the room was dark. It took him a moment, but when he shifted, the pillow beneath his head reminded him of where he was. He'd noted the small storage area had no window. Had Sophie closed the door? It couldn't be nighttime. He made the excruciating effort to roll himself toward the door and saw a glimmer of light through the crack at the bottom.

Lying still, he listened hard and heard a pan rattling. A bit of smoke wafted in. Then came the unmistakable *thunk* of a stove lid being replaced, and a few minutes later, the scent of coffee. She was cooking Nolan's breakfast. Had to be.

Now was the time. He pushed himself upward and managed to get to his knees. He groped in the darkness for something to hold on to, to lever himself to his feet.

A light tap came at the door. It opened and she stood there with a candle in her hand.

"Mr. Weaver, are you all right?"

"Yes. I thought—thought I'd go out back ..."

"Let me help you."

"I can make it on my own, if you'll just help me up."

She set the candle on a shelf and came to his side. "Push on my shoulder." She seemed to know better than to grasp his torso.

Andrew pushed with his legs. A groan escaped him, but he was on his feet.

"Easy," she said. "It might take a minute to get your legs under you."

He panted from the effort. After slowing his breathing, he stepped shakily forward. "I'm all right," he whispered. On stumps of legs, he took one step at a time, into the large room that was mostly kitchen. A lamp burned on the table, and he made for the door as quickly as he could without pitching headlong.

At last he reached it and lifted the latch. The hinges creaked as the door swung toward him.

"I'll get it," Sophie whispered near his ear. "And I'll bring you something to eat before I wake my husband."

Grateful, he clung to the jamb as he lowered himself to the doorstone. She shut the door softly behind him. Andrew stepped off the stone and leaned against the wall for a moment. He set off unsteadily, with one hand trailing along the boards to guide him and assure him he would stay upright.

He'd thought he was on the mend when he'd left the ranch where he'd been allowed to rest. But now his pain was as bad as it had been right after his fall. What was wrong? He supposed he shouldn't have resumed his journey so quickly. All the jostling and jogging, mounting and dismounting had probably aggravated his injuries.

A good fifteen minutes later, he returned to the house. He was proud of his unassisted journey, but he felt as weak as a newborn kitten. Carefully he worked the latch and swung the door open. Nolan sat at the table eating. He didn't so much as glance Andrew's way.

"Mr. Weaver." Sophie sounded as though she forced cheerfulness into her voice with a hammer. "I can bring you some breakfast, or if you feel up to it, you're welcome to join us at the table."

Welcome by whom, Andrew wondered, but his stomach cried out for food. He didn't want to anger Nolan, but it would be easier for Sophie if he ate out here.

"I ... maybe just a bit." He staggered to the nearest chair and lowered himself into it gingerly.

"Feeling better today?" Nolan asked.

"I ... yes, I think so."

"Up to riding?"

Andrew hesitated. "Maybe."

Nolan grunted and continued forking pancakes into his mouth.

Sophie brought him a plate and fork. "Help yourself." She

nodded at the platter in the middle of the table and went back for the coffeepot and a mug.

Andrew cleared his throat. "I hope you'll let me give you a little something for the meals, ma'am."

"Don't think of it. It's not much." She poured his mug full and refilled her husband's. Taking the platter away, she left the two men alone for a minute, while she fetched more flapjacks from the stove. Then she sat down at the far side of the table, on a rickety stool.

Andrew moved slowly. Even cutting into a pancake hurt, but he didn't want Nolan to see that, or to think he wanted to stay on longer.

The rancher took one last swallow of coffee and shoved his chair back. "Soon's you're ready, come out to the corral. I'll saddle your horse."

"Yes, sir. Thank you."

Sophie drew in a quick breath.

"What?" Nolan glared at her.

"Nothing."

After Nolan clapped on his hat and left the room, Andrew let out a big sigh. He realized Sophie did the same. "Sorry, ma'am."

"No need to apologize. Albert has that effect on people." She gave him a wan smile. "I'd hoped you wouldn't need to face him yet. You need another day of rest, so you can mend."

"I'll manage, ma'am."

"Please, call me Sophie."

Andrew nodded. In the candlelight earlier, he hadn't been able to see her clearly, and he hadn't dared to look closely while Nolan was in the room. Now he studied her face. Her left cheek was swollen, and he would swear the bruise was worse.

"Is there anything I can do to help you?" He hadn't meant to say anything, but the words were out, hanging between them.

She met his gaze, startled, and a flush crept up her face. "You mustn't mind Albert. He's ... different since the war."

"I think you said he was in the army?"

"Yes. The Confederate Army."

"I see. Were you here alone while he was away?"

"No, I—we lived in Arkansas before, and I stayed with my family while he was in the army. But when he came home, he wanted to come farther west."

"How long have you been here?"

"Only since last fall. Albert heard there were a lot of cattle running loose, and he thought he could earn some money catching them and selling them to people who wanted to ranch."

Andrew nodded. "Guess I'd best get out there."

She half rose in her chair and peered out the window. The sun was up now, and her face was drawn with anxiety. "He's mounting up. Looks like your horse is tied to the fence, but he's heading out. You can catch up with him. Of course, you mustn't wait too long." Her blush was back.

"I don't like to mention it," Andrew said, "but Mr. Nolan seems to treat you poorly. Are you safe here with him?" If Pa knew a man was beating his wife, he'd tell the law and have him arrested. Even so, Andrew knew there were men who ruled their families by brute force and thought it was their right.

She looked away. "I'm fine." She took a careful sip of her coffee then set down the mug.

"Are you sure?"

She met his gaze then. "The truth is, I'm frightened, but I can't do much about it. As I said, he's different since the war. In the old days, he never would have acted this way."

Andrew thought about that. "Have you considered leaving?"

She pulled in a slow breath. "I've thought about it, but it's not an option. We had a hired man, you see. He didn't like the way Albert treated him either, and he tried to leave."

"Tried to?"

She pressed her lips together.

"What happened?" Andrew asked.

"He's buried out back."

He swallowed hard. He could disappear easily out here.

"I'd best go find him and pay him for the cattle."

Sophie blinked a couple of times. "You be careful, Mr. Weaver. Watch your back."

"I will." He tried to rise as decisively as Nolan had, but he had to wait a few seconds for the pain to recede. He fished in his pocket and brought out a few coins, which he placed on the table. She nodded and looked away.

Slowly he walked to the door. Behind him, he heard Sophie push her stool back and stack the dishes.

He made it to the corral, where Blinker waited patiently. Before mounting, he patted his pockets to be sure the cattle price was safe, then he untied the lead rope and brought Blinker close to the fence. The girth was loose, and he untied the cinch strap. Tightening the saddle took all his energy and lanced his side with a sharp pain.

After climbing onto the bottom rail, he tried to get his foot in the stirrup. The first two times, he failed. Looking up, he saw Sophie's white face at the window, and he made sure he got a good toe hold the next time. The wrenching of his ribs nearly sent him to the ground, but he held on to the saddle, thankful he'd been able to tighten the girth. It stayed in place as he slowly raised himself. Getting his right foot over Blinker's back was the worst. Then it was done.

He looked toward the window and touched his hat. Sophie waved and turned away.

"Up, son." Blinker started moving hesitantly in the direction they were pointed. Andrew put his heels to the horse's sides, wincing but determined, and guided the chestnut toward where he'd assessed the cattle the day before. He should have just told Nolan yesterday that he wasn't interested. Then he could have ridden away, found a place to hole up, and let his body recover. Now he had to drive cattle by himself for several days. Was he unhinged?

Topping the rise, he spotted his host. Only half a dozen

steers lingered near the stream this morning. Great. They'd have to round up the rest. And what he really wanted was cows.

He pushed Blinker onward, anticipating an exhausting day. He was within ten yards of Nolan when four riders burst from a cluster of trees on the far side of the stream and galloped toward them screeching.

"Run!" Nolan spurred his horse toward his house.

Andrew pivoted Blinker as Nolan passed him and followed. A shot rang out behind them, and he expected to feel the tear of a bullet, but it didn't come. He reached the top of the rise and barreled down it behind Nolan.

11

"**M**y horse is hit." Nolan had charged to the corral gate and flung himself off his chestnut. Now he was examining the animal's right flank.

Andrew rode closer. "Is it bad?" Blood ran down the horse's haunch and dripped onto his hock.

"Not really. We need to get inside. Come on." Nolan led the gelding into the corral and dropped the reins. "Put your horse in here. Move!"

Andrew clenched his teeth and swung down from the saddle. "If we leave the horses here, they might kill them or steal them."

"Can't help it."

Pounding hooves sounded on the hillside.

"Come on," Nolan snarled.

Andrew pushed Blinker into the corral and let go of the reins. Nolan was already tearing toward the house, leaving the gate open. Andrew swung it closed and ran.

Gunfire broke out as he reached the doorstone. Sophie nearly pulled him inside and locked the door. Andrew stood panting, letting his eyes adjust to the dimness inside. Nolan already had a rifle at the ready and was watching from a post at one side of the front window and swearing a steady stream.

"Are you hurt?" Sophie asked.

"No, but there's at least four riders shooting at us."

"Do you have a gun?"

Andrew's stomach gave a sickening drop. He'd left his rifle in his saddle scabbard. He pulled his revolver. "You'd best take cover in the storeroom. Stay low, between some of those boxes." The board walls and the barrels and crates in the storeroom wouldn't stop all the bullets, but that was her best chance. He swallowed hard. In Austin, he'd heard of gunfights and standoffs, but the Wild West had remained a tall tale in his mind. Until now.

Losing no time, Sophie grabbed a carving knife from her worktable, dashed into the storeroom, and slammed the door.

Edging up to the window on the side opposite Nolan, Andrew peered out. Three of the riders sat in view, their horses sidestepping and pawing while the horsemen reloaded their guns.

"Where's the other one?" Andrew asked.

"Probably sneaking around back."

Andrew gulped and flattened himself against the wall between the window frame and the door. Then he turned sideways. Those walls were none too thick, and he knew from his practice sessions that a rifle ball could rip through them. A sensible man would present as small a target as possible.

Everything seemed to move slower than normal, and dizziness threatened to haul him to the floor. His father had taught him how to drive a hard bargain and how to take care of animals and how to stack merchandise neatly and efficiently on the store shelves. Nobody had taught him what to do in a gunfight. Was he crazy to come out here?

Two gunshots boomed and the window glass shattered inward. He and Nolan both turned away. When Andrew looked back, Nolan had already thrust the barrel of his rifle out through the broken glass. He fired a shot, and the report hurt Andrew's ears. He stared dumbly at Nolan for a moment. When the rancher drew back and crouched to reload, he realized it was now his turn.

"Don't shoot their horses," Nolan growled.

Andrew could barely hear him over the shock to his ears, but it made sense. If they shot the outlaws' horses, they couldn't ride away unless they stole his or Nolan's.

He'd never shot at a human being. Andrew peeked around the window casing. Now or never. He started to raise the revolver when the something whizzed past his ear and more glass fragments sprayed him. At nearly the same instant, a report assaulted his battered hearing. It wasn't as loud as before. Jerking back from the window, Andrew wondered if he'd be somewhat deaf for the rest of his life.

After a few seconds of silence, a thud and the clink of shattering glass came from the bedroom.

"He's coming in the back window." Nolan strode toward the open doorway. Another deafening report sounded as he let off a round.

Andrew's heart stopped then galloped on. He stared at Nolan's back.

The rancher called over his shoulder, "Got him."

Andrew turned toward the front of the house and leaned a little to get a glimpse outside the front window. Movement caught his eye. He ducked back then chanced another peek, his pistol aimed straight ahead. A bearded man was taking aim at the house from behind the corral gate. His horse and Nolan's trotted nervously about the far end of the enclosure. Andrew made sure the horses weren't in his line of fire, pulled the trigger, and jerked back behind the window frame.

One of the few remaining glass panes shattered, and a shard lodged in the back of his hand. He yanked it out, and blood spurted through the skin. He fumbled to pull off his neckerchief.

Nolan was back, on the other side of the window. "You hit?"

"Just glass." Andrew wrapped the cloth around his hand and tucked in the end.

"Hey, they're moving out."

"You sure?"

"Yeah. Looks like one of 'em's hurt bad."

Andrew bent toward the window, flinching at a pang in his ribcage. One of the intruders was boosting another clumsily into his saddle. The third was already mounted and charged around the corner of the house.

"Did you hit that one?" Nolan asked.

"I might've clipped him at the last."

Nolan nodded.

"They didn't take our horses," Andrew said.

"Nope."

"Sophie—"

"She can take care of herself," Nolan growled and strode to the bedroom.

Andrew pushed hard on the bandana, hoping he could stop the bleeding. His mind raced. How could the man not worry about his wife?

Exhaustion overtook him, and he stood still, willing strength into his body. After a moment, he tottered to the storeroom door and cracked it open. "Miz Nolan? Sophie?"

In the dim, windowless room, he could barely see her, but she rose from where she had crouched between piles of supplies.

"Are they gone?"

"I think so." Andrew looked toward the bedroom door. "Best stay in there till we're sure."

"All right."

He closed the door and walked to the other doorway. Nolan was leaning out through the frame of the broken window. He turned as Andrew entered.

"They're gone. Didn't pick up their friend."

"Is he alive?" Andrew asked.

"Don't think so." Nolan gave him a ghoulish grin. "He was climbing in the window, but he fell back outside. I plugged him right in the face."

Fighting nausea, Andrew swallowed hard. "What do we do now?"

"We'll have to move him, and I'll need to board up the window. But I'm not going out there until we're good and sure they're gone."

"We killed one and wounded another. You think they'll come back?"

Nolan scowled. "You never know. If they're mad enough, they might want revenge. We need to keep watch, even in the night."

Andrew's legs felt wobbly. He longed to sit down, but he didn't want to show his weakness in front of Nolan. Staying here another night was the last thing he wanted. On the other hand, he didn't want to ride out of here alone now.

"I guess I'd better stay. At least for today."

Nolan nodded soberly. "I'd say so. You can help me bury that renegade."

"But not yet," Andrew said.

"Right." Nolan looked out the window. "Well, wha'd'ya know? They didn't get his horse." A wolfish smile curved his lips. "Payment for damages, the way I see it."

Andrew stepped up next to him, crunching broken glass underfoot.

"It's yonder." Nolan pointed.

Andrew saw the horse then, a scrubby dun. Its head hung down as it cropped the grass fifty yards away. Every few seconds, it raised its head and looked about, snorted, and went back to eating.

"Looks to be in decent shape," Nolan said. "And it's got a saddle too."

Andrew felt a little sick. He didn't look down directly beneath the window, not wanting to see the dead outlaw's battered corpse.

"Albert, are they gone?" Sophie asked from the bedroom doorway.

Both men turned toward her.

"I think so," her husband said. "One of 'em's layin' right under the winder, where I dropped him."

She swallowed hard.

"If they don't come back within the next hour, Weaver and I will move him," Nolan said. "And catch the horse they left behind. It's our bonus."

His wife stared at him. "Who are they?"

"How should I know?" Nolan seemed annoyed that she'd asked. "My guess is rustlers."

"Those men could be wanted," Andrew said.

Nolan's eyebrows shot up. "You think there's a reward?"

"Could be."

The rancher frowned. "It's too far to bother with taking him in. I think we'll just bury him."

Andrew wondered if he was afraid he'd lose the windfall horse if he transported the dead man to the nearest sheriff or marshal's office.

"I'll need to tend my horse as soon as we think it's safe," Nolan said. "I don't think he's hurt that bad, but we'll see."

Sophie stared at the wreckage beyond him. "The whole window frame's busted."

"Yeah, yeah. We'll board it up for now. Don't know if it's worth buying more glass." Nolan scowled at her. "Fix us somethin' to eat, woman."

Sophie said nothing, but turned away.

Andrew followed her into the big room. "Your husband thinks I should stay another night, in case those outlaws come back."

She paused in arranging her cooking utensils. "I guess we'd appreciate that. Will you take the cattle tomorrow?"

"I don't know." That task looked more daunting now than before. Andrew glanced back, but Nolan hadn't come into the room. "He seems to think they took some of his cattle, or at least scattered them. And to be truthful, they're mighty poor-looking animals."

She swallowed hard. "I expect you're right. Have you paid him?"

"Not yet."

She nodded and picked up a wooden spoon. "Make sure you don't before you've got your stock rounded up—that is, if you decide to go ahead with the transaction."

Andrew opened his mouth, but Nolan came in and he kept quiet. The man wouldn't want to hear his wife advising his customer on how to get a fair deal out of him.

JOE RODE HARD for several hours, stopping only to water and rest his horse. A couple of hours past noon, he approached an isolated ranch. He'd heard a hint that the owner might sell some steers—nothing definite, but a possibility. When he saw the roofline of a small house off to his right, he pulled Ranger down to a walk and patted his neck.

"Almost there, boy."

He'd also heard there were ruffians in the area. Remembering the squatters at Andrew's ranch, he ground tied Ranger behind some trees and dismounted, rifle in hand. As he crept closer to the house, he kept a sharp eye out for movement.

A small corral lay to one side of the building, and three horses milled about in it with nothing to feed on. Joe darted a few yards to take cover behind a scraggly bush. Lying on his stomach, he studied the horses carefully. A chestnut so thin he could count its ribs, a small, tough-looking dun, and a lanky gray. After a couple of minutes, he was sure. The gray was Andrew's Blinker.

He walked back to where Ranger waited patiently and hoisted himself into the saddle.

"Come on, boy. We're going to get some answers." Blinker's presence wasn't positive proof that Andrew was here, but it was a good indication he'd at least been to this ranch. He was glad

Emma and Molly weren't with him, on the chance that he would soon hear bad news.

He turned Ranger in at the narrow lane and trotted briskly toward the ranch house. Emma would be so thrilled if he could bring her son to her tomorrow, but he wasn't banking on it yet.

A gunshot sounded, and he focused on the house's front window. The glass was broken, and a gun muzzle poked through the hole where the pane had been.

Whirling his horse, he hightailed it back the way he'd come. Ranger needed no urging. No sense sticking around to find out why they were shooting at him.

A quarter mile down the road, Joe slowed and turned his horse. Nobody followed him. He frowned and tried to make sense of what had just happened, absently stroking Ranger's withers.

No way would he leave here without knowing what was going on. He couldn't face Emma if he did. His own curiosity and desire to help his friend burned in his chest.

"So, Ranger, what now?"

Joe realized he was talking to the wrong being. He glanced up at the sky. "Sorry, Lord. I get used to talkin' to my horse. You know what's going on. I'm not always the smartest person, but if you give me a little help, I might be able to work this out. Andrew wouldn't give up his horse without a fight. He loves that gray nag. So either he's in that house, or he's been hurt or killed. That's the way I see it. If I'm wrong, you steer me different."

He waited in silence for a moment. Ranger tossed his head and stretched against the reins, wanting to reach a clump of grass a yard away. Joe drew in a deep breath.

"All right. How am I going to find out what that shooter's got against me?" He pushed his hat back and scratched his head. That window had to be already broken before he arrived. Somebody inside was on guard, watching for trouble. He pondered for another moment then shook his head. "It's beyond me."

Taking quick mental stock of what he had in his gear, Joe dismounted and opened a saddlebag. He didn't wear white shirts —no ranchman would be that silly. But he had a tan one that would do. He had to hunt for several minutes before he found a four-foot stick. He could use his rifle for a flagpole, but that might defeat his purpose.

After tying the shirt by its sleeves to one end of the stick, he checked his revolver to make sure it was fully loaded then did the same with his rifle.

"All right, Ranger, you stay here. I'll be back." Ranger wasn't fond of gunfire, but Joe was pretty certain he wouldn't run off if he heard it from this distance. He gave the bay's flank an extra pat. "You hear me?"

Ranger's ears flickered, but he kept on grazing.

"Right." Joe took his flag in his left hand and the rifle in his right and walked cautiously toward the ranch house.

At the top of the lane, he stopped on the verge of the road and peered toward the small dwelling. Everything looked the same. The three horses still shuffled each other in the enclosure.

Joe hauled in a deep breath and stepped forward, waving the shirt flag over his head.

"Don't shoot!"

Before the words had left his mouth, another shot rang out, and Joe ran.

12

When Nolan let off another blast, Andrew's heart pounded. He looked out the bedroom window, but nothing moved behind the house.

"What's going on?" he yelled to Nolan, who held the post at the front window. Sophie had been banished once more to the storeroom.

"Some fool," Nolan said. "First he rode up, then he came back on foot."

Andrew heard him going through the motions of reloading.

"Did you shoot his horse?"

"Nah."

"What if it's not them? It could be somebody else."

"Can't risk it."

His heart skittering, Andrew took another look through the gaping window hole and went to the bedroom doorway. "There's nobody out back."

"Good." Nolan scowled at his guest. "We need to think of a better way to keep those horses safe tonight. Somebody could sneak in and steal them out of the corral."

Especially if Nolan had hit the man's horse with his first round. Andrew wasn't convinced he'd told the truth about that.

But what outlaw would come back on foot after his mount was injured?

"If there's bandits lurking about ..."

"I know. I didn't see nobody when we went out earlier to see to the horses."

Andrew didn't like any of the options that came to mind. "We could take turns tonight, keeping watch out there in the shed. "

"Or you could just sleep out there," Nolan said, still staring out the front window.

Andrew didn't dare to speak.

From behind him, Sophie said, "It's too dangerous, Albert. I don't want either one of you out there in the dark, with cutthroats trying to get at our stock."

After a moment's silence, Andrew asked, "Do you think he's still out there?"

"No way to tell."

Andrew frowned. He didn't want to lose Blinker. Even more, he didn't want to be stuck here in this man's house.

In the heat of that morning's battle, he'd almost forgotten about his earlier injuries. He was sore now, but the pain in his ribs seemed much less severe than it had been when he got up. Maybe he'd just needed to move around a bit. Still, he didn't want to stay in a place targeted by outlaws.

"Have you got anything we can secure that back window with?"

"No." Nolan didn't even look at him but kept staring out the shattered window.

"There are crates in the storeroom," Sophie said. "We could take them apart."

"The pieces wouldn't be long enough," Nolan snapped.

"Maybe I could piece them together," Andrew said. "If you don't mind me trying." He waited several tense seconds.

Nolan swung toward him. "They'd be flimsy. And anyway, my hammer's out in the shed."

"It would be better than nothing," Sophie said.

Andrew nodded. "I reckon I can find something to pound with. If nothing else, it would give you warning if someone was trying to get in. You'd hear them at the window if it was boarded up."

Nolan's jaw flexed. "Do what you want. And Sophie, get me some coffee."

"YOU'RE positive it's Andrew's horse?" Molly asked.

"Oh, it's Blinker all right. But something's not right there." Joe looked from her to Emma.

"We'll get packed," Emma said at once.

"It's already late," Joe said. "It would probably be best if we was to stay here and set out in the morning." He'd arrived back at Swanson's ranch as they were about to sit down to the evening meal, since Ed Swanson had come in late from checking his cattle on the range.

"You said something's not right. We shouldn't wait." Emma looked at Molly.

Under most circumstances, Molly would have agreed with her. But Joe had been shot at in broad daylight. It probably wouldn't be wise to approach the ranch in the middle of the night.

"Ma, remember the squatters." She held her mother's gaze.

Emma let out a little sigh. "I guess you're right, but I hate to think Andrew might need us and we delayed several hours."

"Tell you what," Joe said. "We'll set out before sunup. We could get there before noon. We'll all go together. They surely wouldn't shoot at women. What do you say?"

"I think it's the best we can do," Molly said. The squatters in Andrew's cabin hadn't hesitated to shoot at her and her mother. She turned to look at her hosts. "Is there a lawman near here, Ed?"

Swanson had come to the door when Joe rode up, and now he hovered with his wife at the far end of the room.

"Not in fifty miles," he replied. "You're welcome to stay tonight. Joe, you can sleep by the fireplace."

"Oh, I'll sling my bedroll outside." Joe grinned. "I'm used to it."

Mrs. Swanson looked relieved and said, "At least eat some supper with us. Emma's got stew cooking, and Molly makes fine biscuits."

That was true, but Molly avoided Joe's gaze. She didn't want him to think she was proud of her cooking skills. And anyway, he'd already tasted her biscuits and flapjacks during their journey.

"It would be my pleasure." Joe's spirits rose, knowing he hadn't missed their supper. "So, Ed, I need to put my horse up. Then I can help you with any chores you need to do tonight."

The two men headed outside, and the parlor seemed larger after they were gone.

"Ma, we're close. We'll find out something tomorrow morning."

"I pray you're right." Her mother smiled at Mrs. Swanson. "Ginny, if you'll excuse us, I think I'll stir up some extra biscuits."

"I'll help you," Mrs. Swanson said. "I'm glad I thought a dried apple pie would go down well tonight. It's probably ready to come out of the oven."

The three women went to work. Molly could tell her mother was encouraged. She thought they'd be reunited with Andrew tomorrow. But what kind of person would shoot at a man who appeared in his dooryard? What if Blinker's presence meant her brother no longer needed his horse? She determined not to raise the question in her mother's presence.

Emma measured out flour and baking soda while Molly laid an extra place setting on the table. "Ginny, is there a bank hereabouts?"

"No, not short of New Braunfels." Ginny hesitated. "If you need to get funds ..."

"Nothing like that." Emma smiled. "Oh, and we'll pay you for Joe's board tonight too."

"No need. He's not even going to sleep in the house."

"Even so, you're feeding him, and mighty good meals we've been having too." She smiled at Molly, who took that as a signal.

"Yes, the food here has been excellent." Molly took an extra napkin from a drawer and folded it.

"Guess I'll whip some cream." Ginny carried a deep mixing bowl to her worktable and eased down onto a stool. "To be honest, I'm embarrassed to take your money, Emma."

"Well, don't be. We asked for a safe place to stay, and we got it. And good company. The money's not a problem for us."

Ginny nodded, and the topic was closed.

Later, as they settled in for their last night at the Swansons', Molly whispered to her mother, "Are you worried about our money?"

Emma sighed. "We have plenty. But we don't know what will happen when we go to that place tomorrow. Perhaps we should leave some of it here with the Swansons."

"What if we don't come back this way?" Molly turned around so her mother could unbutton her dress. "We could take it with us, and when we get close to that place where Joe saw Andrew's horse, we could bury it in a can or something."

"Maybe."

"I'll ask Joe about it after we leave here in the morning. He can find us a good place. And I'll see if I can fetch an empty can from the trash before we go."

The money was the least of Molly's worries at the moment. Andrew was in trouble. She was sure of it. Was he even still alive? If he was, he might not survive without their intervention.

"Oh, wait," Emma said. "I forgot to bring in those few things off the clothesline."

Ma's underthings. She'd be mortified if they left those behind.

"I'll get them," Molly said. "Button me up." As she made her way out to the line, she prayed silently for her brother.

Her fingers flew as she plucked her mother's laundry off the line. It was so dark outside the Swansons' house that she could barely see the black stockings swaying in the breeze. She shoved each clothespin she removed into her pocket. She didn't want to lose any of those. Mrs. Swanson would need them soon for diapers. She was almost sorry they wouldn't be here to see the new baby and help with the extra work that would bring.

Something rustled, and she stiffened. Peering around, she listened but heard nothing. Only two more things left on the line —Ma's petticoat and her own spare blouse. She had the last of the clothespins in her hand and the laundry draped over her arm when the form of a man emerged from the shadow of the woodshed. Molly caught her breath. Mr. Swanson? No. And certainly not Joe with that city slicker hat.

"Hello."

She didn't recognize the voice.

"Who are you?" She backed toward the house.

"Easy, now. I'm not going to hurt you."

Molly wasn't so sure about that. "Are you here to see Mr. Swanson?"

"No, Mary Weaver. I'm here to see you."

She froze, clutching the clothes to her chest. "I don't know you."

"You haven't seen me in a long, long time."

She stared at him. Light spilled out of the windows behind her, but it didn't reach his face. He was tall, she could see that. A short beard blurred his face in the darkness.

"Who are you?"

"My name's Cooper. Benjamin Cooper. Does that mean anything to you?"

Molly shook her head. She'd never seen this man before in

her life. She couldn't be certain, of course. She'd seen hundreds of people in her father's store over the years, and it was possible she'd met this man but didn't remember the occasion.

"No. Should it?"

Now she could see his white teeth as his smile broadened. "Well, I was hoping."

Something about the way he spoke snagged her attention. His words were accented in a way Molly couldn't quite place. In fact, he sounded a little like Pa had. Something about his inflections ...

"How do you know my name?"

"Well, now, that's a long story. Could we talk for a few minutes? Maybe you'd invite me inside."

"No. I don't want to talk to you. Leave me alone." Molly's heart raced as she turned and ran to the door. She fumbled with the latch, almost dropping the laundry. When the door swung open, she tumbled inside, tripping over Ma's trailing petticoat.

"Molly!" Ed Swanson stood from where he and Joe were sitting near the stove. "Are you all right?"

"There's a man," she gasped. "Out there." She pointed.

Joe jumped up and reached for his rifle. Mr. Swanson strode across the room and, with his good arm, reached for his revolver that hung in its holster by the door.

"Where?" Joe asked.

"I was at the clothesline."

"Stay here," Joe said.

Both men hurried outside. She closed the door all but a crack and stood peering out into the night. She heard their quiet voices and their footsteps.

"Molly?"

She whirled around. Her mother stood in the doorway to the room they were sharing.

"Ma! There—there was a man outside."

"Who?"

"I didn't know him, but he said he knew me. He knew my name."

Emma's face paled. "What did he want?"

"I—I don't know. I was so scared."

"Maybe he knows something about Andrew."

Molly tried to swallow the huge lump in her throat. "Then why didn't he come knock on the door? He didn't say anything about Andrew."

The door opened, and Joe and Ed came in.

"Did you see him?" Molly asked.

"No, but we heard hoofbeats going away." Instead of returning his revolver to its peg, Ed laid it on the table.

"Molly, did you get a good look at him?" Joe asked.

"Not really. It was dark. He had a beard."

"Here, sit down," Ed said gently, guiding her to a chair.

The other bedroom's door opened and Ginny Swanson peeked out at them. "Is everything all right?"

"It's fine," Ed said.

"You're sure?"

Ed sighed and went to her, shutting the bedroom door behind them.

"How old was he?" Joe asked Molly, crouching beside her.

She shook her head. "I'm not sure. Older than me. Yes, and older than you, I think. Forty, maybe. But it was so dark. He was as tall as you. I think."

Joe sighed. "Was there anything else about him that stood out?"

"His hat. It wasn't like the ones you and Ed wear. Not a working hat, if you know what I mean. At least, not a rancher's hat. More of an in-town hat." She looked toward her mother. "Like Pa's Sunday hat."

Emma pressed her lips together and nodded. She'd given the hat to their minister after Pa died. Molly regretted mentioning it.

"Sorry, Ma." She reached out and clasped her mother's hand.

"What did he want?" Joe asked.

"He said he wanted to talk. I told him to leave me alone, and I ran inside."

Emma scowled at Joe. "If he was a decent man, he'd have come up to the door and knocked, instead of riding off in the dark."

"I think you're right." Joe stood. "Did he say anything else?"

"Wait. He told me his name."

Joe started to speak then closed his mouth. Molly almost felt he was going to rebuke her, the way her brother would do when she did something silly. She should have told them this first.

"Cooper. He said his name was Cooper and asked me if it meant anything to me."

"Does it?" Joe asked.

She shook her head and looked up at her mother. "Does it to you, Ma?"

"No, I don't think so."

"I wondered if it could be someone who used to come into the mercantile," Molly said.

"But ... why would somebody from Ohio be way down here?" Ma looked helplessly at Joe.

"He said I hadn't seen him in a long time," Molly said slowly, trying to reconstruct the conversation in her mind. "A very long time."

Emma shook her head. "I have no idea ... but you said he knew your name."

"Yes. He called me Mary Weaver."

Emma's head jerked up.

Joe looked from her to Molly. "He called you Mary?"

"It's the name on her birth certificate," her mother said. "But we've never called her that. She's been Molly since ... since she was a wee babe."

Ed came out into the main room. "Everything all right?"

Joe gave a half shrug. "Does the name Cooper mean anything to you?"

Ed frowned. "Seems like there used to be a Miss Cooper who taught school when I was a boy back in Virginia. I don't know anyone out here by that name."

"If it was someone who knew you, Ed, he'd have asked for you, not Molly," Emma said.

As usual, Ma's was the voice of reason. Molly pulled in a deep breath. "Well, he's gone now, anyway."

Joe looked at Ed. "I'm thinking we ought to take turns sitting up, just to be on the safe side."

Ed nodded.

"I'll take the first turn," Joe said. "I was going to sleep outside anyway. I'll sit up in here, if you don't mind."

"Fine by me."

"Do you think we should check on the livestock?"

Ed took an extra lantern from a hook near the door and set it on the table to light it. "I'll go check around the barn and the near pasture. You stay here with the women."

"If you need help," Joe began.

"I'll fire off a round." Ed picked up his gun and went out.

Joe clapped his hands together lightly. "So, ladies, off to bed. We've got a long ride ahead of us in the morning."

"I won't sleep until Ed comes in," Ma said.

"Me either." Molly stood and faced Joe alongside her mother.

"Well, go get settled, at least. When Ed comes back, I'll knock on your door and tell you everything's all right."

In the bedroom, Molly made sure the curtains completely covered the window before she let her mother unbutton her dress once more. She'd be wearing her riding skirt tomorrow, so she folded the dress and put it in her pack. She'd be glad to ride again, though she would miss Ginny and Ed. They'd treated her and her mother wonderfully. Maybe they'd come back this way after they found Andrew. She hoped they could see the baby, but it would probably be too soon.

They had just blown out their lamp and nestled in on the featherbed when three soft knocks came on the door.

"It's me," Joe said. "Ed's back, and nothing's amiss."

"Thank you," Ma called.

"Goodnight, Joe." Molly nestled into the feather pillow. Her mind whirled for a long time. Joe was a good man. Her feelings toward him went beyond gratitude. She knew that now. Whether good or bad news met them tomorrow, Joe would stand by them.

Finally, she heard her mother's slow, even breathing. Molly rolled over and determined to pray for Andrew until she, too, was able to rest.

13

"They'll be back," Nolan said grimly from his stance beside the window.

"If that's true, you'd better give me some more ammunition," Andrew said.

Nolan shifted his feet. After a moment, he said, "In the storeroom. Sophie, show him."

She lit a lantern and took him into the windowless room. "Yonder."

Andrew walked to the shelf she indicated and chose a box of cartridges that would fit both his rifle and his revolver. Although he'd expected the rifle to be stolen off his saddle, it wasn't. When Nolan had finally ventured out to tend his injured horse, he returned with it. But he hadn't retrieved Andrew's cartridge box, and the rifle only took one at a time.

He frowned at the box he took from the shelf. Several more were left, and he was glad Nolan had stocked up.

"Did your husband get this ammunition when he was in the army?"

"I don't know where he got it. I think he bought a supply before we came here. He wanted to be prepared in case anything happened on the way."

That made sense, but Andrew still wondered about Nolan's military service. Why was he discharged six months or more before the end of the war? Of course, Joe had left the army before the war was over, but he'd been soldiering for two years and was due to be discharged. Even so ...

"He wasn't wounded in battle, was he?"

"No. Why do you ask?"

"Just curious. I heard our army wouldn't let the men go toward the last of it. You said he came home last fall."

"No, we got here in the fall. Albert came home in June last year."

"Oh. I guess his enlistment was up."

She started to speak, then closed her lips. Her brown eyes avoided his gaze.

"Well, thank you." He held up the box of cartridges and headed for the kitchen.

He sat down at the table, and Sophie followed and blew out the lantern. Carefully, Andrew checked over his guns and filled the revolver's cylinder. He pocketed several rounds for it and the rifle.

A mug of steaming coffee appeared at his elbow.

"Thank you, ma'am," he murmured.

Nolan looked over with a scowl.

"We need to work together," Andrew said. "You can't defend this place alone."

Nolan turned back to the window.

Probably stewing about his cattle, Andrew thought. But the bandits hadn't tried to take the horses. Maybe they were waiting for dark. He fully expected them to come back for their friend's horse, if nothing else.

He shuddered, remembering the body Nolan had dragged away. The marauders hadn't returned by dark, and they'd buried the dead man in a shallow grave behind the shed. Nolan had done most of the heavy work. Andrew had managed to close up the gaping hole where the bedroom window had been just fine.

He used slats from the crates, as Sophie had suggested. Then they'd slept in shifts.

Andrew laid his revolver on the table and picked up the mug. Sophie Nolan knew how to make good coffee. Even so, he couldn't wait to leave this place behind.

RYLAND GUIDED Prince across a wide-open space toward where two men were driving half a dozen cattle.

"Hello," he called. He hated to keep stopping and asking people if they'd seen Cooper or the Weavers, but he had to be sure he was still on their trail. After leaving Andrew's ranch, he'd ridden hard to the former Hewitt ranch. After being turned away there, he'd headed on south, assured that both Mrs. Weaver's party and Cooper were ahead of him.

One of the riders hung back while the other rode on, keeping the cattle together and moving them away from the road.

"Help you, mister?" the man asked.

Quickly, Ryland described the people he was looking for.

"Nope, haven't seen 'em, but we just brought those steers down from the hills."

"All right, thank you." Ryland turned away. Next time he'd stop at a house, but he was almost certain he was on the right track. Last night he'd learned Cooper had ridden this way and made inquiries only twelve hours before him.

He patted Prince's withers. "One more place, boy. Then we'll stop for a bit and you can rest."

Prince snuffled and broke into a lope.

AFTER A QUIET NIGHT, Molly rode out early, as planned, with her mother and Joe. At Joe's advice, Molly carried her revolver in the saddlebag on Firefly's right side, where she could reach it more easily than if she concealed it in her pack behind the saddle.

Although Joe had dark smudges under his eyes, he led them confidently along the dusty road at a jog. As the sun climbed, so did the heat, but Molly didn't complain. They were getting closer to Andrew.

They'd been traveling for an hour when hoofbeats drummed on the road behind them. Molly turned Firefly and gazed at their back trail. "Joe, someone's coming."

He wheeled Ranger and pushed him up past Emma, beside Firefly. The sun had fully risen, so they could see clearly. A horse came loping around a corner a hundred yards back and kept on steadily toward them.

"You and Emma get behind me," Joe said.

"You think that's necessary?" Molly asked.

"Just a precaution."

"You think it's Cooper?"

"Do you?" Joe met her gaze, but Molly wasn't sure, and she lifted her shoulders in helplessness.

"Get back," Joe said again, and she took Firefly a few steps behind him but turned beside her mother's horse to face the newcomer.

The horse barreled toward them—a dark bay with a white strip. The rider leaned low over the saddle horn. On seeing them, he slowed his mount and trotted up to within five yards of Joe and Ranger.

"Mornin', folks."

Molly stiffened. It was Cooper, all right. He sounded smooth, like a salesman coming into the mercantile to sell her father a big order of merchandise. His clothes seemed a bit out of place too. Molly didn't know how the average Texan dressed, but Joe's work clothes were sturdy and practical. His trousers and plain cotton shirt were well worn, but he could probably wear those for another year or so while he worked around his ranch.

The stranger, on the other hand, wore a white shirt, with

black trousers that might be the bottom half of a suit. Close inspection showed his shirt's cuffs were frayed. The fancy hat sat atop his head. He wasn't a cowhand, that was for sure. Although he did sit his horse comfortably.

"Howdy," Joe said.

The man looked past him at Molly and Emma. "Uh, I made Miss Weaver's acquaintance last evening, and I'd like to speak to her and Mrs. Weaver."

Emma let out a little gasp.

His gaze homed in on Molly, and he gave her a little nod. Molly shuddered.

"I'm Mrs. Weaver," her mother said, and Molly wished she hadn't. She wasn't sure quite why.

"Well, now." He eased his bay toward them, grinning at her mother. "I'm delighted to meet you, ma'am. And this is your daughter, I believe."

"Yes," Ma said. "And may I inquire as to who you are, sir?"

"Name's Cooper." His eyes narrowed, and he watched Emma keenly.

"What business do you have with Mrs. Weaver?" Joe's voice had a hard edge to it.

"Do you have news of my son?" Emma asked.

"I ... no, I'm afraid not. Actually, I wanted to have a word with Miss Weaver, with your permission."

Molly's heart pounded. What could this stranger possibly want with her?

"Do you know this man?" Joe called without turning his head.

In the harsh morning light, Molly couldn't place the horseman. "No, I don't."

"Mrs. Weaver?" Joe asked.

"I—no, I don't think so."

Joe's hand hovered near the butt of his revolver. "Explain yourself now, mister."

Cooper smiled. "Easy there, fella. Maybe we could hop down and make some coffee and talk things over."

"Not happening," Joe said. "Talk. Now."

Cooper's appraising glance ran over Joe. Molly had to admit, Joe looked tough. He was a former soldier and a cattleman. If Cooper had bad intentions, he'd have to answer to one hardened rancher.

He smiled at Joe. "Well, now, it's a delicate matter. I'd really rather sit down with Miss Weaver and her ... mother and discuss it."

"We're on an urgent errand, sir," Ma said firmly. "We don't want to be delayed."

"I believe you're searching for your son," Cooper said.

Ma hesitated. "Yes. It's very important that we get on our way."

"Perhaps I could help you out."

"What do you mean?" Joe asked. "You said you don't know where Andrew is."

"I just meant that an extra pair of eyes might be useful to you. If I ride along with you and help you find him, maybe then we can relax and talk things over."

Molly didn't like his suggestion, and she could tell Joe didn't either. His back stayed stiff as a flagpole.

"I can't stop you from riding wherever you want to, mister," he said, "but we don't really want your company, and we don't need your help."

"I see." The smooth smile was back. "I assure you, I didn't mean to intrude, or to delay you. Please, go on with your errand, by all means."

Joe sat still for a moment then wheeled Ranger to face the women. "Let's go. Keep ahead of me."

Molly turned Firefly. Her mother came alongside her as they started their horses jogging.

Ma's face was troubled. "Molly ..."

"What?" Molly threw a quick glance over her shoulder. Joe

and Ranger trotted a few yards behind them. Cooper and his mount stayed where they'd left them.

"I don't like that man, but it seems as if he knows something."

Molly nodded grimly. "I agree. Ma, do you think he's got a ... I don't know, maybe a New York accent?"

Emma's eyebrows nearly met in the center of her forehead. "Now that you say it, yes. He sounds as if he comes from Brooklyn."

"I thought he sounded a little like Pa. Not his voice, but the way he says things. Didn't we used to live in Brooklyn? Before we moved to Ohio?"

"Yes." Emma's frown deepened, cutting little lines at the corners of her mouth. "Maybe he knew your father there."

Molly considered that. "I wonder if he knows Pa is dead?"

After they'd ridden a few more strides in silence, Emma said, "He must. How could he have found us if he hadn't talked to people who know us?"

"That's true. We're not exactly in the middle of civilization." Molly looked back. Joe was still right behind them, scowling as he rode. Behind him came the bay. "He's following us, Ma. He's keeping back a ways, but he is definitely following us."

"Come on." Emma drove her heels into Harry's sides and urged the gelding into a lope. Firefly leaped forward to keep pace with him.

Joe kept up with them. The stranger fell back a little but stayed within a quarter mile. When they topped a rise and were momentarily out of his sight, Molly slowed Firefly.

"Joe, what are you thinking?"

"I don't like it, but what can we do? It's a public road."

Ma circled her horse and moved in closer. "That fellow's got me a little worried. Does he know something about Andrew?"

"I don't think so," Molly said.

"But the first thing he told us was that he wanted to talk to us."

"Maybe there's some news from back home?" Joe said tentatively.

"Oh, I doubt it." Emma sent Molly a worried glance. "We don't have any family left in Ohio. I do still have a cousin in Brooklyn and a sister near Rochester, and I wrote them both that we were moving down to Texas. I think I sent them both Andrew's address, but still ..."

Molly crinkled her brow. "How does he even know about us? And how did he know my real name is Mary? I never use that. Ever. Even in school, I put 'Molly' on my papers."

"I'd think he was just out looking for a mark if he hadn't mentioned your name first," Joe mused.

Her mother frowned. "You mean, he's a swindler?"

"Could be. He might have snooped around and learned enough about you to try to gain your confidence."

"Maybe he stopped at the Swansons' this morning," Molly said. "I'll bet he chatted up Ginny or Ed and heard about us from them."

"He'd have to have gone there mighty early this morning. And besides, Ed was alert. He wouldn't tell him anything personal, especially after last night." Joe looked behind him. "Oops, here he comes. What do you want to do?"

Emma heaved a sigh. "I don't think I'll feel easy until we settle this. I hate to delay for even a minute, but he's obviously not giving up."

Molly clamped her jaws shut. A minute could make a crucial difference to Andrew. If he needed their help, she wanted to give it to him now.

The horseman rode closer. "You folks ready to talk?"

"Reckon so," Joe said and dismounted.

Ma looked over at Molly. "There's some trees over there. Why don't you see if you can find enough sticks for a fire? We'll make some coffee."

"Coffee?" Molly whispered in shock. "You want to make coffee now?"

"Relax, honey. Let Joe and me find out what this man wants."

Now she got it. Ma had come up with an excuse to get her out of earshot for a few minutes. And here she'd thought she was the one protecting Ma. No, her mother still saw her as her baby girl.

Molly didn't like it one bit, but she did as her mother asked. As she ambled among the small trees and plucked up a stick here and there, she threw frequent glances back toward where Emma and Joe were in earnest conversation with the stranger. After a few minutes, she saw her mother reach out toward Cooper and then sway. Joe put an arm around her and eased her down to sit on the ground.

Molly clutched the half dozen sticks she'd collected to her chest and ran back to them.

"What happened? Ma, are you all right?"

Her mother looked up at her and blinked. "I ... yes."

"Here." Joe took the sticks from Molly.

Molly turned on Cooper. "What did you say to her? Tell me!"

A slow smile crossed Cooper's face. "Why, just the truth. I've been looking for you and your brothers for quite some time now."

"Brothers? I only have one."

Cooper's smile tightened, and he glanced away. "Well, that's not exactly true, is it, Mrs. Weaver?"

Emma stared up at him. She opened her mouth but said nothing.

After placing the sticks in a pile on the ground, Joe came to Molly's side and placed a hand on her shoulder. "Molly, this fella —well, he claims he knew you when you were a baby."

"What?" She frowned at Joe, then at Cooper. "So?"

"Truth is, Janie," Cooper said, with that feral smile, "I'm your pa. Your real pa. Your name's Jane Cooper."

Molly had never fainted in her life, and she wasn't about to start now, but she grabbed Joe's arm and hung on with all her strength.

Joe winced and patted her hand. "Easy, now. Let's sit down and talk about this. I'll get the coffee going."

"But—Ma—Andrew—" Molly huffed out a breath and turned on Cooper. "You're talking nonsense, mister. My pa is Simeon Weaver. Was. He's dead now."

Cooper's face drooped into exaggerated sympathy. "I am so sorry, my dear. I know that must have been a big blow for you and for Miz Weaver. But that man wasn't your real daddy. I am. And I don't know about this Andrew you're looking for. He could be one of your real brothers. If the Weavers adopted him, too, that is. But the word I got from the orphanage—"

"Stop!" Molly held up both hands as if she could stem his words. "You don't know what you're talking about. I am not adopted. Tell him, Ma." She turned to plead with her mother, and her throat constricted.

Emma's eyes streamed tears, and her mouth worked, but nothing came out.

"Ma?" Molly croaked. Drawing a breath seemed an enormous effort, as though her lungs were being squeezed. She sank to the ground and put her arm around her mother. "What's going on, Ma?"

"Oh, Molly, can you ever forgive me?"

14

Molly's heart wrenched. "Forgive you for what?"

"Your father didn't want you to know. We ..." Ma's face twisted, and she sobbed. "We adopted you when you were just a tiny little thing."

"Adopted?"

"Yes."

Molly sat in silence for a long moment, vaguely aware of Joe puttering with the sticks to build a fire, and Cooper standing a couple of yards away, watching her like a buzzard.

Molly swallowed hard and nodded slightly toward Cooper. "Is he ... what he said? My real—" She couldn't make herself say it. Simeon Weaver was her pa, and he always would be. She gazed deeply into her mother's eyes and met anguish.

"Why should we believe you?" Molly lurched to her feet and glared at Cooper. She wanted to throw something at him.

"Because it's the truth." Cooper's steely eyes didn't waver.

"Ma?" Molly looked back to her mother. "Is it?"

"I don't know." Ma pulled a black-edged handkerchief from her sleeve and wiped her face. "We weren't told your birth parents' names."

"But ... there must be a birth certificate. You mentioned it last night."

"They issued a new one with Simeon's and my names on it. They said it was standard practice, and that it would save you a lot of problems later on. We ... we agreed, but we really didn't have a choice. Simeon and I asked about your family, but they wouldn't tell us anything except that your mother was dead and you'd been abandoned by your father."

Cooper's mouth tightened.

Molly's heart clenched. Everything was wrong. She didn't know how to feel. She sucked in a ragged breath and strode over to Cooper.

"What about that part? Did you abandon me after my mother died?"

He looked away first. "I ... it was a lot. I left you with a neighbor. She said she'd look after you for a few days. But when I came back, you were gone."

"Gone where?"

"I ... I was told you were taken to an orphanage in White Plains. New York, that is."

"I knew it." She whirled on her mother. "I told you he was from New York."

Emma nodded mutely.

Molly took a step closer to Cooper. "So, assuming that's true, why didn't you come get me from the orphanage?"

"You were gone by the time I got there. You'd been adopted, and they wouldn't tell me who took you."

Joe let out a little scoffing sound and stood. "I'm no expert, but that sounds fishy to me. People don't pass a kid along that fast."

"Well, they did this time." Cooper glared back at Joe.

"How long?" Emma's voice quavered. "How long was she at the orphanage before you got there?"

"I ...I don't know. A few days, I guess."

"And how long was she with the neighbor before that?"

Cooper waved his arms in protest. "How should I know? A day, maybe? Two?"

Emma struggled to her feet, and Joe hurried to support her. She raised her chin.

"Mr. Cooper, we were told Molly's mother died in childbirth, or soon after."

"No, no. It was a while. A month, at least."

"But Molly was three months old when we adopted her."

"According to who?"

"The birth certificate they gave us, and the doctor's report from the orphanage."

Molly tried to sort that in her mind. Her chest ached, but she made herself inhale slowly. "Mr. Cooper, if you are indeed my father, you waited two months or more before you came looking for me."

"No, I don't think ... it couldn't have been that long."

"It was." Emma's voice was hard now, and her brown eyes were cold. Molly sensed the strength she'd always known her mother possessed returning. "You left your daughter for months, and no one thought you were ever going back for her. So they found her a home where she'd be cared for."

"You've got it wrong! I cared about those kids, but I was distraught."

"Kids?" Joe barked. "Just how many kids are we talking about?"

Cooper looked away, his face scarlet. After a long moment, he said, "Three."

Molly gasped. "There were more? You're saying I wasn't an only child?"

"There were two boys, Zeb and Elijah. Older than you, of course."

"And did they go to the orphanage too?" Molly demanded.

He hesitated then nodded.

"Where are they now?" Emma asked.

"I don't know."

"Why weren't we told this when we adopted Molly? If she had brothers ..." Emma staggered to Molly's side and touched her shoulder. "Dear Molly, I'm so sorry. We had no idea."

"Maybe they were adopted first," Joe said.

Molly's parched throat ached with each breath. "Excuse me." She went to the horses and took the canteen from Joe's saddle. She tipped it up and took several swallows of water and then put the canteen back. She stood staring at the tooled oak leaves on Ranger's stirrup leather. When she felt she could walk without stumbling, she didn't go back to the group. Instead, she walked away, into the long grass.

No one followed her, but she imagined Emma and Joe were keeping an eye on her. Grasshoppers flew up ahead of her footsteps. After she'd gone fifty yards or so, she sank to her knees.

"Lord, You've got to make sense of this, because I can't."

Emma and Simeon Weaver were godly people. Yet they'd lied to her for twenty years. And what about Andrew? Did he know? Or was he adopted too?

The sudden notion that Andrew might be one of her real brothers crossed her mind, but she discarded that. Her mother had seemed surprised, too, when Cooper mentioned his sons. And Andrew had brown eyes, like their parents. She'd often wondered why she had blue eyes and the rest of the family's were brown. Emma simply said odd things like that happened sometimes, and she thought maybe her grandmother had blue eyes, but she wasn't sure.

Andrew was three years older than Molly. When they found him, she could ask him if he remembered when she was born. But he'd been so young, he probably didn't have any suspicions when a baby sister suddenly appeared.

She heard footsteps and looked up. Cooper was coming toward her. Molly scrambled to her feet. "I don't want to talk to you."

"Don't you have questions? Questions a father could answer?"

"Oh, I've got questions all right, but I'm not sure you're the one to ask."

He cocked his head to one side. "I could tell you things about your family. Your *real* family."

She eyed him sharply. "How did you find me way out here?"

He smiled, and the shrewd gleam in his eye made Molly wish she hadn't given him the satisfaction of asking one question. She looked past him, toward where the horses stood in a bunch. Joe had planted himself near the dusty road, hands on his hips, staring out at them. Knowing Joe was looking out for her made her feel a little better, but she wished he hadn't let this scary man come out here to talk to her.

"I went back to New York and sniffed around," Cooper said.

"Back from where?"

He ignored her query. "I talked to everyone I could find who'd been around when your mother and I lived there. It took a while. The Pruitts, where I'd dropped you off for a bit, were gone. But I finally found another old neighbor who said you kids went to the orphanage. I tell you, if I ever meet up with those Pruitts, they'll have to answer to me."

"For going off and leaving us? The way you did?"

He didn't answer.

"Tell me, when did you speak to the people at the orphanage?" Molly asked.

"Long time ago now."

"How long? Because I intend to write to them about this, and if their story doesn't match up with yours, mister, you'll be in trouble." She had no such intention—the idea had just popped into her head. But it seemed to make him uneasy.

"Been over a year now."

"Ha! You didn't even start looking for your children for almost twenty years? You said you went to the orphanage when I'd only been there a few days. I'll tell you what I think. I think you're a liar! You made up this whole thing."

His eyes flickered, and she wondered if she was anywhere near the truth.

She wished he *had* made it up, but how could it be? Ma had admitted that she and Pa had adopted her. If Cooper was a confidence artist, he wouldn't pick someone at random and accuse them of adopting his own true child. He'd make sure he knew something about them first.

That had to be it. Someone told him this family had adopted a child, and he looked into it with the intention of defrauding them. Pa's sale of the prosperous mercantile was common knowledge. Cooper might be after the proceeds. They hadn't had a chance to hide the money Ma had brought along yet. Molly clenched her teeth.

"Look, I'm not making this up," Cooper said. "Now, I know you're looking for Andrew Weaver. I'll help you find him, and then we can sit down and straighten this all out."

"Straighten what out? I'm a Weaver. If you really are my father, I don't care. You abandoned me when I was an infant. Why would I want anything to do with you now?"

"I know I can't make amends, but I hope you'll give me the chance to at least get to know you."

She thought for a moment. "I still don't—Are you saying that orphanage told you who had adopted me?"

"It took some persuasion, but eventually, yeah."

She didn't like the way he said *persuasion*.

"Except the Weavers had gone west. After a while, I learned they took you to Ohio, so I went there. Then I found out you'd come down here." Cooper shook his head. "I've been looking for you for a long time, Janie."

"Don't call me that!"

JOE WATCHED THE TWO FIGURES, wondering if he should interfere. They weren't yelling, but Molly didn't look happy.

Cooper's back was to him, so he couldn't tell much about the conversation.

Emma came to stand beside him. "I don't like this, Joe."

"Me, neither. You never heard of this guy? Not even from the orphanage?"

"No, not a word. I have no idea if he's telling the truth or not. But if not, he at least knew we'd adopted Molly."

"Do you have any papers from back then?"

Emma bit her lip. "When we moved to Ohio, Molly was pretty young. Four or five, I think. And then, in our first house we lived in out there, we had a fire." She let out a sigh. "The adoption papers were burned, along with just about everything else we owned. Except the store. Thank God Simeon was a good businessman. But we lost all our papers—our marriage certificate, the children's birth records."

Joe nodded slowly, still watching Molly and Cooper. He and Emma had given up on the coffee idea when Cooper insisted on going to have a private word with Molly. "What about Andrew? Is he adopted?"

"Yes, but he's not Molly's brother. I mean .." Emma turned pleading eyes on him. "We got him as a baby too. He's older than Molly, and they don't look alike, but I never thought anyone would question ..." She shook her head. "And we took Andrew in more than two years before Molly came to us. I'm sure he's not related to her by blood. We did it all legal, Joe."

"I'm sure you did. I don't know if this Cooper is really her pa, or if he's just a slimy slug trying to get into her life for some reason, but I know I don't like him."

"I don't like him talking to Molly."

"We can fix that."

Emma hesitated. "I confess, I'm afraid she'll be angry with me."

"For interrupting?"

"No, for everything." Emma's shoulders slumped. "Mostly for not telling her. But she and Andrew were so close. They always thought they were true brother and sister. And Simeon and I considered them that."

Joe frowned. "Any idea what Cooper really wants from Molly?"

"None. I mean, if he is what he says, he's waited twenty years to find her. Why now?"

"Not fatherly love, I'd wager. I wonder if he thinks there's some sort of gain in it for him." Joe caught his breath. "Molly's coming back."

"Should we go on now?"

"I think so. Andrew might need us."

"Yes." Emma watched Molly closely. Cooper lingered for a moment then slowly followed her toward them.

As soon as Molly was close enough, Joe said, "Well, what do you think? Emma and I would like to get moving."

"Yes, let's go." Molly flicked a glance behind her. "I wish we could lose him, but now he says he'll help us find Andrew."

"We don't need his help," Emma said.

Joe shook his head, unsure of the best course. Much as he distrusted Cooper, it might be good to have more people along when they arrived at their destination.

"Ma, do I have brothers?" Molly asked. "Besides Andrew, I mean."

"Not that I know of. The orphanage didn't say anything like that."

"And Andrew isn't ..."

"Andrew is no blood relation, dear. But when we find him, if you don't mind, I'd like to be the one to tell him about all this." Tears welled in Emma's eyes. "We never thought ... your pa and I never thought we'd need to prove you were ours, or that anyone would question that."

Cooper was only a few steps away.

"Come on." Joe took Emma's arm and turned her toward the horses. "Let's mount up."

"So," Cooper said cheerfully as he approached, "Heading out?"

Emma stared at him. "We'd rather you didn't come with us."

"Oh. All right." He looked a little flustered, and he took his time collecting his horse and fussing with the cinch strap. Then he pulled a fancy gold watch from his pocket and consulted it.

Molly turned her back on him and pushed herself up and into the saddle. Joe gave Emma a boost into the sidesaddle then mounted Ranger.

"All set?" he asked Molly.

She nodded soberly, and he set the pace by urging Ranger into a lope.

"I'M GOING OUT THERE," Nolan said.

"Are you sure?" Andrew sat huddled at the table, nursing a cup of coffee while Sophie busied herself preparing their midday meal.

"We've sat here all mornin', and nobody's come around. We've waited long enough. I've got to take care of my horse."

Sophie swung around with a spatula in her hand. "What if those men are still out there?"

"Haven't seen anyone since that one fella yesterday afternoon. It was quiet all night." Nolan swore. "We can't keep hidin' in here all our lives. I need to go out and see to the horses."

Andrew pushed his chair back, feeling only a twinge in his side. He'd managed to sleep during the times Nolan kept watch through the night, and he felt decent today. Maybe today he could be free of this place. "What do you want me to do?"

"Bring your rifle and stand lookout for me."

"Out there?"

"Yes, out there. You won't be able to do anything from in here if they come from out back and open fire on me."

"Can't you wait?" Sophie asked.

"How long? Till tomorrow? The next day?"

Sophie turned back to the stove.

Andrew picked up his rifle. "He's right. I'm ready."

Nolan nodded and opened the door. He let it swing inward and waited a few seconds while he stood off to one side.

"Seems quiet," Andrew said.

"So far."

Nolan poked his gun barrel out first, then his head. Andrew waited while the rancher looked around the yard.

"All right, Weaver. You stand at the corner of the house, where you can see 'em if they come down the hill."

Andrew swallowed hard and followed him outside. He wondered what Sophie would do if her husband was cut down in the front yard. With quiet steps, he walked to the corner of the house and peeked around. The range looked peaceful. A few steers had even grazed their way to within fifty yards of the house.

When he turned, Nolan had darted to the corral fence and crouched there. Andrew gave him a nod, and Nolan slipped through the bars and approached his chestnut, speaking softly. The gelding let him examine the wound on his flank.

After a moment, Nolan straightened and approached the third horse, the one belonging to the slain outlaw. They'd caught it in the twilight and turned it out in the corral. It was a sturdy dun, and if they weren't all killed, Nolan would have a good addition to his livestock.

Andrew looked up the hill again, then out toward the road. He mustn't let Nolan's actions distract him from keeping watch. All was quiet as Nolan fed the three horses. He got a bucket of water from the well, with Andrew peering all around while he walked between there and the corral. The rancher watered his own horse and the new one, then fetched a rag and a can of salve from the shed. After wetting the rag, he dabbed at his horse's wound.

When he'd finished, he walked over to Andrew, casting a worried glance up the hill.

"How's your horse?" Andrew asked.

"He'll live. Prob'ly be stiff for a few days. I'll watch now, and you go tend to yours. I gave him some oats."

Andrew swallowed hard and stepped away from the house. Why couldn't Nolan water Blinker when he did the other two? He felt exposed as he carried the bucket to the well. The back of his neck prickled, and he took a slow look all around before entering the corral.

"Hey, fella."

Blinker had his nose in the feed box. Andrew set down the bucket and ran his hand along the horse's withers. Blinker looked all right, but he must have been terrified by all the gunfire.

He looked over at the shed. Their saddles were where they should be, with the bridles hung from their pommels. Maybe they ought to take them inside. He wished they had a more secure place for the horses too. If no one else came to harass them, would he have the courage to leave here alone?

Blinker turned his attention to the water pail. When he'd drunk most of it, he raised his head and swung it toward Andrew, slinging water drops and bits of feed and slime onto his shirt. Andrew sighed and patted him several times.

His body must be healing. The soreness that lingered was mild, compared to what he'd felt two days ago. At least Nolan had done the digging last night. Andrew had helped drag the outlaw's body around the shed. During that little escapade, he'd found his nose was only a few inches from the dead man's belt buckle, which bore the letters CSA. The outlaw had been part of the Confederate Army.

"Lots of former soldiers around these parts." Nolan had said when Andrew mentioned it.

He'd expected the rancher to make him do at least half the digging, but Nolan kept doggedly at it. Was it because he'd brought up the war? Or did he simply realize that the exertion would aggravate Andrew's wounds and maybe make him helpless? The grave was shallower than he liked, but he hadn't complained to Nolan about it. He'd be gone soon. Tomorrow, if the outlaws didn't return. Then any varmints digging up the corpse would be Nolan's problem.

Blinker emptied the bucket, and Andrew fetched another. While the gelding drank, Andrew retrieved his rifle and took a good look at the hillside behind the house. The outlaws had arrived from that direction. He pivoted and studied the landscape in every direction, looking for movement.

Another thing had bothered him about the burial. While keeping watch, he'd seen Nolan remove the man's boots and put his hand in the man's pocket. Had he taken something else off the dead man? He was surprised Nolan hadn't kept more of the man's clothing. Probably he was right to check the poor fellow's pockets before they put him in the ground, but still ... He didn't say he'd found anything. Probably best not to bring it up.

15

Molly's thoughts swirled as they rode onward. Could she possibly be that man's daughter? Even if she wasn't, the fact that she'd been adopted by the Weavers had sent her reeling. Her earliest memories were of Ma holding her in the rocking chair, safe in her warm arms, and of Andrew rolling a rubber ball toward her across the oak floor in the Brooklyn house. The move to Ohio was a blur, but after that there were friends, school, church, Ma and Pa, the store.

That much is true, she told herself. *The Weavers are my family, no matter what came before. They chose me out of an orphanage. They wanted me, even if other people didn't.*

Her birth mother was dead. Emma had said so. Molly couldn't bring herself to even think of another woman as her "real" mother. The implication was that Emma wasn't a real mother. But she was. She loved Molly and Andrew as much as, or more than, any other mother loved her children. Molly didn't doubt that.

"Do you think he's still behind us?" Ma asked, throwing an anxious look Joe's way as he rode up alongside them.

"I haven't seen or heard anything out of him. Would you like to take a rest?"

"How much farther is it?"

"At least another hour."

"It would probably be good to get down and stretch our legs for a few minutes." Ma pulled Harry to a halt.

Molly had hoped she'd say she wanted to keep going. Reluctantly, she slowed Firefly and guided her to the parched grass at the road's verge. They all dismounted, and her mother looked around. She leaned toward Molly and whispered, "I'm going over there where those big rocks are, to freshen up."

Molly nodded. As Ma walked away, she loosened the girth on Firefly's saddle and let the mare put her head down to crop the grass. She took the water bag from the saddle and drank a couple of swallows.

"How are you doing?" Joe asked. He watched her with concern. Molly knew those brown eyes could harden and drill into a person, but right now they were soft and caring. Joe wasn't doing all this for himself. He was doing it for Andrew, and for her and Ma.

"I'm confused." She managed a tight smile. "Thanks for doing this, Joe. All of it. I know it's not what you planned on."

He shrugged. "I'm just hoping for a good ending. For everybody."

"Even Cooper?"

His face sobered, like Pa's used to when he was totting up the mercantile's ledgers. "I figure, once we find out what happened to Andrew, the next thing we do is find out who that fella really is. If he's not your pa, then I reckon the sheriff might have some questions for him."

"And if he is?" Molly asked.

"Well ... think about this, Molly. If he is truly your father, then if nothing else, he can tell you something about your family. Your other family, I mean, before the orphanage. He says you've got brothers out there, though he claims not to know where they are. But you might get information from him that could help you find them if you want to. And there might be grandparents, and aunts and uncles and cousins too."

Molly put the plug back into the opening of the water bag. "I didn't think of that."

"You know, my father died early, and when I went home after my time in the war, my mother was gone too. But I do have a sister. She writes to me now and then. I'm not much for letters, but I do love hearing from her, so now and again I sit myself down and get off a line or two and send it her way."

"That's nice," Molly said. "Ma writes to her sister too."

Joe nodded. "Sure. And there could be other folks out there that remember when you were a baby. They could tell you how it was back then. Tell you what your mother was like, for instance. Maybe even show you a picture of her." He grinned. "Tell you if you look like her. 'Cause I wasn't going to say anything, but you really don't look like Emma."

Molly put a cautious hand up to her hair. "I know. I just thought I was the odd one of the family."

"I wouldn't call it that."

He was still smiling, and a funny little shudder went through her. Not the scared kind like Cooper made her feel. No, she had the distinct impression that Joe was paying her a subtle compliment in his own way. Her face warmed, and she couldn't quite look at him.

She lowered her hand to her throat. Her necklace had slipped out from beneath her collar as they rode. She fingered the coin on the chain, as she often did while deep in thought.

"What is that thing, anyway?" Joe asked.

"What?" She looked up in surprise.

"Around your neck. I saw it once before."

"A coin."

"What, a penny with a hole in it?"

She smiled then. "No, not exactly. I asked Ma about it once, and she thinks it's some kind of foreign money. She said a friend gave it to me when I was a baby."

Joe's eyebrows lowered. "Maybe you should ask her who the friend was."

Molly turned toward the rocks. Her mother was returning, looking a bit self-conscious.

"Ma," Molly said as she came closer, "Joe noticed my necklace and he asked about it. Tell me again where it came from?"

Emma stopped walking, and her mouth gaped open.

ANDREW AND NOLAN took turns watching out the front window. There was no point in watching at the back one that they'd boarded up. They would hear if someone broke through the flimsy barricade. Andrew took his turn peering out into the yard toward the road. Eight of the front window's twelve panes were broken, and several of the mullions were splintered, testimony to yesterday's violence.

If not for the lone rider Nolan had seen the afternoon before, Andrew would think they were safe. He was tempted to just ride away and leave the couple to their own problems. But Sophie didn't deserve that. They still hadn't settled up about the cattle, either, but he was ready to walk away from the deal. He shrank from going out on the range to locate the scattered animals and bring them in. It was too dangerous now.

"What do they want with you?" Andrew ran his fingers through his hair. "If it's the cattle, why didn't they just take them and leave? It doesn't make sense that they attacked the house."

Sophie slowed in stirring her biscuit dough. "Do you think they want the horses, Albert?"

"How should I know?" Nolan slammed his ironstone mug down on the table. "If I knew what they wanted, we'd find a way to stop them."

"If they wanted the horses," Andrew said, "they could have taken them yesterday while they were out there and we were holed up in here. Or during the night. But they didn't even try to take their dead friend's horse. I don't think they're after livestock."

"Then what?" Sophie's face was pale. "Do they want the land? Our ranch?"

"Maybe." Andrew had been thinking about it for hours, but no easy answer came.

"They aren't lawmen, are they?" Sophie asked softly, and Andrew wondered how long she'd wanted to ask that question.

Nolan whirled and glared at her. "Why do you say that, woman?"

Andrew cleared his throat. "We didn't see any badges, and surely lawmen would have identified themselves." At least it seemed logical to him. He'd never had much to do with lawmen.

Sophie said no more. She dumped her dough out on the table's floured surface and kneaded it without a peep. Only after Nolan turned back to his vigil did her lashes flutter. She raised her gaze to meet Andrew's while her hands continued their steady motion. In her eyes was such sadness that Andrew couldn't tear away his scrutiny.

He didn't know what troubled Sophie so deeply—other than her husband's temper, of course—but he wanted to take that despair from her and replace it with joy. Short of that, he would settle for the suggestion of hope in those lovely eyes. How could Nolan treat her so?

Suddenly conscious that he was gawking at her, he turned away. Nolan must never catch him looking at his wife with that much empathy.

"YOU SAID a friend gave me this necklace, Ma. When was that? Because I don't remember."

Emma's eyes darted about, as though she sought the answer somewhere on the simmering grassland.

171

Joe walked over to stand next to Emma. He didn't want to cause a rift between them. They needed to shore each other up today. "It's all right. I was just curious."

"No. No, Molly should know. The time for secrets is past."

Looking into her open, honest face, Joe could tell she was tired, but also that she had strength. As she'd said, she was tired of secrets. Now was the time for openness with her daughter.

She stepped closer to Molly. "Let me see it, child."

Molly held out the thin chain, and Emma took the dangling coin in her fingers. She studied it for a moment and nodded.

"When we brought you home from the orphanage that first day and unwrapped your blanket—" She paused and looked deep into Molly's eyes. "You were crying, and I was ready to change you. And it was there."

"The coin?" Molly's face crinkled as though she was trying to make sense of that.

"Your sock had come off. It was tied on around your ankle with a pink ribbon."

"That's odd," Joe said.

Emma glanced at him. "Yes, it was very odd. I showed Simeon. He looked at it, and he thought it was some Oriental coin. From Japan or China, maybe, or Burma. One of those places in the Far East. He said it was especially odd because our baby wasn't Asian."

"Maybe her birth mother was," Joe hazarded.

Emma shook her head. "I don't think so. I mean, look at her."

Joe smiled. It was true, Molly didn't look Asian—not that he'd had much experience with people from the other side of the world.

"We thought some attendant at the orphanage had put it there. If it was on you when you came there, they made sure you left with it. Simeon had me put it away." Emma gave Molly an apologetic look. "You were so tiny. We didn't want any chance you'd swallow it or choke on it."

"Of course," Molly said. "But you gave it to me later."

Emma nodded. "I wasn't sure if we should, but ... well, it didn't seem right to hide it from you." She looked at the ground. "I'm sorry we hid other things. But this was something real, something we could touch. From your past."

Molly nodded slowly. "You think one of the orphanage helpers gave it to me?"

"I don't know. I thought perhaps one of the women who helped with the infants did it. Maybe there was a Chinese nurse, or ..."

"But you didn't see one," Molly said.

Emma shook her head. "If you came in with it tied to your foot, some worker at the orphanage must have seen it. Maybe not the manager, but somebody. They could have stolen it, but they didn't. They must have thought it was special, and they sent it with you when they dressed you for us, the day we took you home."

Joe's mind was spinning. "Put it away."

Molly frowned at him. "Now?"

"Yes. Tuck it back inside your blouse."

"Joe?" Emma cocked her head to one side. "What are you thinking?"

"It's something special, like you said." He laid a gentle hand on Emma's arm. "If that coin was tied to Molly when she went to the orphanage, it could be that her real father would know about it."

Emma's face cleared. "We could ask Cooper—"

"No!" Joe was still working things out in his mind, but he was sure that wasn't the course to take. "Don't mention it. And, Molly, make sure it stays out of sight. If we meet up with him again, you could ask him something that might lead him to think of it—if he's really your father. If he knows nothing about it, well, it wouldn't prove he's not, but it might tell you that the coin came from the orphanage, not from your first family."

Molly looked at him long and hard. "Yes. That could be helpful, couldn't it? If he does know about this—"

Emma put her arms around Molly and hugged her fiercely. "I'm so sorry. We never meant to hurt you by not telling you everything. We only wanted to give you and Andrew the best life you could have. Well, the best we could give you."

"Oh, Ma!" Molly's eyes filled with tears as she returned the embrace. "You and Pa were wonderful parents. I couldn't ask for a better family. Even if there was another family, ours was the best."

Emma sniffed and drew back. "Thank you, dear. And when we find Andrew, I'll tell him everything. As soon as we know he's all right."

"Of course," Molly said. "Now, let's go find him."

Joe's admiration for the Weaver women climbed even higher. Molly may not have inherited her inner strength from Emma, but she'd certainly learned from her example.

He made sure the ladies mounted safely and climbed into the saddle. He wasn't looking forward to facing another round of gunfire at the place where he'd seen Blinker. He glanced skyward. *Lord, help me keep them safe long enough to learn what happened to Andrew.*

16

He'd lost that no-good Cooper's trail. Ryland took off his hat and wiped his brow. This Texas heat was no joke. A man could bake to death out here. At the next place he stopped to ask about the Weavers, he'd have to make sure to fill the canteen he'd bought in Austin. He didn't come all this way to shrivel up in the sun.

Forget about Cooper, he told himself. Find Molly!

Cooper was a distraction. Up until this morning, at every place he'd learned Mrs. Weaver and Molly had stopped with their friend Joe, Cooper had shown up too.

Well, that suited Ryland just fine. If he crossed trails with the man, he had a few choice words for him. He looked around. The grass looked pretty good here. Well, it was too dry, like everywhere he'd seen in Texas, but still ...

Up ahead was a ranch. He spotted a few head of cattle off to his right, grazing the range, and he could see where horses had turned off into the grass. There had to be a house someplace.

He saw the lane then. It led off across the prairie, and in a few more paces he could see the roofline. He didn't have the heart to make Prince move faster but let the gelding walk. He and Prince had come to an understanding of sorts, but Ryland wasn't sure yet whether the horse would ground tie, so he dismounted and held the end of the reins, pulling the horse along behind him as he approached the front door.

The woman who answered his knock was heavy with child, and Ryland felt his face flush as he struggled not to look at her stomach.

"Uh, my name is Atkins, and I'm looking for Mr. Noyes and the Weaver family. Have any of them come by here in the last few days?"

Her face clouded. "What is your business with them, sir?"

This could be helpful. When someone he questioned didn't immediately say no, but fell into the defensive mode, they generally had some information they didn't want to hand out too freely.

"I'm employed by an attorney, and he's commissioned me to find Miss Molly Weaver." Ryland reached into his pocket for his wallet. "I have a letter of endorsement here."

She studied the paper, frowning. "Perhaps it would be best if you spoke to my husband."

"Oh?" Ryland's empty stomach gave a little hitch. She knew something, all right. If she didn't, she'd have said so. "You've seen Miss Weaver, then?"

"I—We've had some unsettling happenings here, and I—"

She was afraid of him, Ryland knew in a rush. "Oh, ma'am, I assure you my intentions are good. I wouldn't do anything to harm Miss Weaver or—or yourself." He stopped, feeling he was making a hash of it. But there was something. The flicker in her eyes told him that. "Please, ma'am, if you could just indicate to me whether you've seen them, or if they've come this way. I've spent many months searching for Miss Weaver, and it is only for her good."

The woman sighed. "My husband will be in for his dinner within the hour. If you'd like to wait ..."

Ryland hesitated. He'd really rather get on with it, but she was frightened. What had happened here? The last thing he wanted to do was further alarm her.

"All right, Mrs.—"

"Swanson."

He nodded and glanced around the yard. "If you wouldn't mind, I'll water my horse."

"Of course."

After watering Prince, Ryland unsaddled him. If they were going to wait an hour, the horse deserved a break. After all, Prince was his lifeline out here in the wilderness. How did these people stand it, living so far from others? He couldn't imagine his mother living miles from the nearest neighbor and twenty or thirty miles from any town. New England wasn't like that.

A small corral stood nearby, with two mules drowsing in the sun, but there was nothing in there for them to eat. He wanted Prince to have a chance to fill his belly.

He took a rope from the saddlebag. At the livery in Austin, Harry had recommended he carry one so he could stake out the horse at night. Otherwise, this one might take off for home, he'd said with a laugh. He hadn't had Prince long enough to test his training, or so he'd said.

Ryland awkwardly fastened the rope around Prince's neck and tied the other end to the bottom of a fencepost so the horse could graze outside the corral, where a little grass grew.

"There you go, boy."

Prince was already chomping away. Ryland sat down with his back to another post and pulled his hat down over his eyes.

A few minutes later, he was surprised when the door of the house creaked open. Mrs. Swanson stood on the threshold, a mug and a plate in her hands. Ryland scrambled to his feet.

"You must be tired," she said. "You're a long ride from anywhere. Since you seem like a decent sort, I thought maybe you could use a cup of coffee and some cornpone."

Ryland grinned. "Thank you very much. It would certainly hit the spot." He walked over and took the steaming mug and the plate, which held a generous slab of cornbread. "I really appreciate this, ma'am."

"Oh, it's nothing."

He shook his head. "I can't understand how women can cook in heat like this."

She chuckled. "And I wonder how men can stand to drink hot coffee in this weather. Ed shouldn't be much longer." She went inside and closed the door.

Ryland sat down and ate the cornbread, savoring every bite. He'd been on the road so long, he'd had a chance to sample the everyday cuisine at many hotels, restaurants, taverns, and stagecoach stations. But the last few days, food had been minimal as he forged his trail alone on horseback.

Mrs. Swanson's cornbread tasted finer than any he'd ever eaten before. Reluctantly he pressed his finger onto the last crumbs and carried them to his lips, cleaning the plate. He placed it and his empty mug carefully on the side of the doorstep and ambled back to where Prince was still grabbing every mouthful he could reach. Ryland untied his rope and moved him a few yards down the fence to a new patch of grass and sat down again.

Next thing he knew, he jerked awake, knocking his hat off. His head still hurt a little where Cooper—or whoever, but he was pretty sure Cooper was to blame—had hit him. He rubbed it gently as he watched a man riding into the dooryard, looking curiously at Prince.

Ryland stood and walked toward him, hat in hand.

"Mr. Swanson?"

"Yeah?" He squinted at Ryland, as though a little wary.

"My name is Ryland Atkins, and I'm trying to find a young lady named Molly Weaver. Your wife didn't say much, but she implied that you might tell me something if I waited here to talk to you."

Swanson's eyes narrowed. "You're not the fella that spoke to her out by the clothesline the other night, are you?"

"No, I've never seen Miss Weaver before."

"Well, I'm not sayin' I don't know her, but why should I tell you anything, mister?"

Enough of this shilly-shallying. Ryland took out his credential letter and explained his mission. "I promise you, I have only good intentions toward the Weaver family. I'd like to reunite Miss Weaver with her grandmother in Maine."

"Maine?"

"The State of Maine, sir."

Swanson frowned deeper. "That's a long way from here."

"Yes, it is," Ryland said. "I've been traveling a long time, and I'd dearly like to find Miss Weaver and give her the good news that her grandmother is eager to meet her. Truth is, the old lady has been hanging on for several years, hoping to see all her grandchildren again. I've found two of them, and Molly Weaver is the last. I mean, the last of the ones who were missing."

Swanson doffed his hat and wiped a sleeve across his forehead. "Mister, I don't know whether to trust you or not."

Ryland sighed. "Mr. Swanson, here's what I know: Molly Weaver and her mother are in this area. They're searching for Molly's brother Andrew, with the help of his neighbor, Joe Noyes. I've never met Noyes either, but people who do know him tell me he's a decent chap. Anyway, there's another man trying to find them, and I am quite certain his motives are less honorable than mine."

"Cooper," Swanson said.

"Yes. His name is Ben Cooper."

Swanson looked him up and down. "I'm still not sure I should trust you, but you look like a straight shooter."

"I am. I assure you, I am."

Slowly, the rancher nodded. "And this Cooper fella—he's a bad'un?"

"I believe so. He's been trailing the Weavers ever since they left Ohio—to what purpose, I'm not sure, but I think perhaps he intends to defraud them of whatever money or property they have. When I got to Andrew Weaver's ranch, he accosted me and stole my watch and my wallet. I don't believe he will treat them any better."

"Well, now. Cooper spoke to Miss Molly out at the clothesline the other night. Scared her good. When Joe Noyes and I ran out to find him, he'd ridden off. We figured he had something to hide."

"It's clear that you know the Weavers and Noyes."

"Yeah, Molly and Miz Weaver stayed here a few nights while Joe was out lookin' for Andrew. He came back the other night and said he'd seen Andrew's horse. They left early in the mornin'."

At last. Ryland's pulse picked up. "And where was this? Where did they go?"

"Joe told me exactly where it is. It's half a day's ride from here. But you've got to be careful, mister. Somebody at that place shot at Joe when he rode up. He's afraid they've done something to Andrew Weaver and stolen his horse, but he didn't say that in front of the women. They've all gone to try to find out what happened."

"I see. And this has nothing to do with Cooper?"

"I don't know what it's to do with, but I don't think so. Cooper came along after them."

"Did you see this Cooper fellow?"

"No, but I've been cautious since he came around, and I told my Ginny to be careful too. He's sneaky. Wouldn't surprise me if he hid and watched Joe and the women when they left here. You watch yourself, you hear?"

"SOMEONE'S COMING." Nolan flattened himself against the wall next to the front window and moved his head just far enough so he could see to the road.

"They're coming on the road this time? Not down the hill?"

"I see horses."

Andrew stood back. He could see out, but he hoped the newcomers couldn't see him. He stuffed his revolver in his belt and picked up his rifle.

"Mrs. Nolan, you'd best get in the storeroom and keep your head down," he told Sophie.

She looked toward her husband, but he didn't so much as glance her way.

"I got biscuits in the oven," she said to Andrew. "They need a few more minutes."

"If I can, I'll take them out when it's time."

They both knew they might have worse things to worry about than burned biscuits. With a grim set to her mouth, Sophie went into the small storeroom and shut the door.

Andrew wasn't an expert on women, but he sure thought he could tell Albert Nolan a thing or two about them—or at least about Sophie.

"Listen," Nolan hissed. "They're out back too."

Andrew snapped to attention and strained his ears. Hoofbeats seemed to thunder all around the small house. Through the front window, he could see at least three horsemen galloping in from the road. Another charged around the corner, between the house and the corral.

"There's more this time." Andrew ducked down behind the back of a chair.

"They found some reinforcements." Nolan gritted his teeth and stuck his rifle barrel through the window.

"Don't shoot unless they do," Andrew said.

Nolan scowled. He obviously didn't take orders—or even suggestions—well, but Andrew didn't want more trouble than they could avoid.

The first two bullets shattered another windowpane and splintered a hole in the front door. It pinged off the side of the stove, ricocheted to the cupboard and fell spent to the floor. Andrew stared down at the misshapen lead ball. His heart seemed to have stopped working for an instant, then sped on.

Nolan returned fire and ducked back. Andrew crawled across the floor to the wall beneath the window. He wished there were other openings where he could see out and shoot. A bullet slammed through the wall just above his head. If those outlaws shot enough holes in the house, he wouldn't have to worry about seeing out, or anything else.

Carefully, he edged up on the side of the window opposite Nolan, who was reloading. Andrew whipped out for a split second and was rewarded by another bullet breaking a pane and sending shards of glass into the room. At least two perforated the skin on his shoulder. He sprawled on the floor, heart racing, and pulled a sliver from his arm. Blood seeped through his torn sleeve in a growing stain.

Gritting his teeth, Andrew squeezed the wound and flinched. Another piece of glass must be in there. He needed to reload. He'd worry about the small wounds later.

More lead made its way through the window and the wall. One bullet flew over him, and Andrew was sure it came from the end wall nearest the corral. How were the horses? His ears were so numbed by the noise that he couldn't hear their restless movements, but a faint, terrified neigh reached him.

He swallowed hard and made himself rise on his knees and shoot out the window. He didn't have a clear view of his target, but he figured that keeping fire coming out of the house was important.

Ducking down, he fumbled to reload the rifle. He could fire shots from his revolver in between. Would that be wise, or would it just deplete their ammunition? He didn't want to pause long enough to take careful aim with so many out there shooting at him.

Movement to one side caught his eye. The storeroom door

had opened a few inches. He stared at Mrs. Nolan, who peered at him from her position on her knees in the doorway.

"Can I help?" She called.

"Can you reload?"

"Yes." She crawled toward him.

Andrew passed her the rifle and his box of ammunition then scrambled to the window frame. He waited for a shot from outside, then leaned out around the frame. This time he saw one of the brutes slinking toward the shed. He aimed his revolver and fired then ducked back without waiting to see if he'd found his mark.

At once, a volley of bullets whizzed through the opening.

Horrified, Andrew glanced around at Mrs. Nolan.

"You need to go back in the storeroom and lie low."

She slid the rifle across the floor toward him and crawled on hands and knees back into her hiding place.

Had Nolan seen her come out here, or was he so intent on the battle that he hadn't noticed?

An incongruous fragrance hit him, and Andrew looked at the stove. The biscuits. Would he be crazy to rescue them? He crawled over and opened the oven door. Prone, he covered his hand with his blood-stained bandana and reached into the hot interior. He jerked Sophie's pan out and let it sit on the open oven door while he turned back toward the window.

Nolan poised for a second beside the frame, then leaned over to shoot. Amid a burst of gunfire, he grunted and sagged to the floor.

Horrified, Andrew stared at him. Nolan clutched his side. Crouching low, Andrew went to him. Blood soaked his shirt around his hand. Another bullet had grazed Nolan's head, and blood was matting his hair.

"Nolan!" Andrew shook his arm.

The rancher's eyes flickered as sporadic shots continued.

"You're hit," Andrew said.

Nolan's mouth worked, but no words came out.

Andrew looked around for something he could use to stanch Nolan's bleeding. The closest cloth item was one of Sophie's dish towels, on her worktable. He started to crawl toward it but changed his mind and skittered on all fours to the storeroom door. He reached up and opened it a few inches.

"Mrs. Nolan! Sophie! Your husband's hurt."

17

Molly rode along quietly between her mother and Joe, but her jitters increased as they drew closer to the place where Joe had seen Andrew's horse. Was her brother even there? Or had something happened to him, and his horse been claimed by a stranger?

Faint popping sounds jerked her from her reverie, and she pulled back on the reins. "Stop. Joe, do you hear that?"

The other horses stopped, and they all sat listening intently.

"Sounds like gunfire," Joe said after a moment.

"Are you sure?" Emma asked.

"I don't know what else would sound that way, except maybe fireworks, and we're way past Independence Day."

Molly swallowed hard. Joe had enough experience to know gunfire when he heard it. Not only had he been shot at twice recently, but he'd been in the war. She studied his grim profile.

"Is it coming from that ranch?" she asked.

"I can't tell, but it's in the right direction, and we're not that far out."

"What do you think we should do?"

Joe hesitated.

Molly said, "I can sneak a little closer and see if I spot anyone."

"Absolutely not," Emma said.

Joe grimaced. "You two stay put. I'll see what I can find out."

Dread seized Molly. What if they lost Joe? She'd never forgive herself.

"Maybe we should go back to the nearest town and ask for help."

"There's no lawman within thirty miles, maybe more." Joe pointed to their back trail. "Go back to that little stream where we watered the horses. I'll come find you there."

"That was at least a mile back." Molly looked behind them.

"The most important thing is for you and Emma to be safe. Go off the road a little, in case strangers ride by. Get your horses out of sight from the road if you can."

Molly didn't like it, but her mother nodded. "We'll be fine, Joe. We'll take a little rest."

He eyed Molly. "You've got your revolver, right?"

"Yes." While they waited at the Swansons' ranch, Ed had given her a leather holster, and she'd devised a way to carry it on a sash at her waist. She opened her saddlebag and pulled it out, with the sash already threaded through belt slits in the leather. She tied it around her middle then patted it. Joe nodded. His gaze rested on the shotgun's stock, protruding on the off side of her mother's saddle.

"All right. Keep your eyes open, both of you. I'll try to be back within an hour. If I'm not there in two, head on back to the Swansons' place. I'll come to you there."

Reluctantly, Molly turned Firefly to walk beside Harry back to the place Joe had named.

"Ma, he could get killed."

"So could we all, dear. Pray hard."

The road curved slightly along a hillside, and she could no longer see Joe and Ranger. They didn't meet anyone on their way. As soon as they got to the stream, they dismounted and led the horses to its verge. Firefly plunged her nose into the water and took a greedy drink.

"Should we unsaddle?" Ma looked at her over Harry's neck as he stretched down toward the water.

"I don't think so. We need to be ready to move when Joe comes back." Firefly lifted her head, and Molly looked around then led her to a grassy patch that was partially hidden from the road by brush. "Let's loosen their girths, but don't take the bridles off. If we need to go in a hurry, it would take too long to get ready."

Joe had assured her that Firefly would ground tie and wouldn't run off if she let go of the reins. They weren't sure about Harry and hadn't risked letting him loose during their travels. Ma attached the long lead rope and held the end as she and Molly looked for a place to sit. The two women sat down in the grass after carefully inspecting it for noxious plants and anthills.

"I don't hear the gunfire anymore," Ma said after a minute.

"Me either. Maybe they've quit." Or maybe they were just too far away now to hear it.

They sat for fifteen minutes or so, and Firefly stayed within a few yards of Harry. The gelding began tugging on the rope, and Ma moved a few yards so he could reach more grass.

Molly looked up at the sun. She wished she had a watch. She thought she heard faint hoofbeats and listened. They fell silent.

"What is it?" Ma asked.

"I thought I heard something." Molly stood and took a few steps toward the road, staying behind the bushes. She heard nothing, so she went farther and peered along the dusty track. After a pause, she turned back toward her mother. "Nothing, I guess."

"Maybe we should make coffee."

Molly stared at her. "Someone would see the smoke."

"I thought Joe might like some when he gets back."

Molly's heart fluttered. Joe had done so much for them.

What if he didn't return? No, she couldn't keep thinking that way. She sent up another silent prayer. "I guess we could gather some sticks. If he comes back and everything is all right, we might want to have some then and maybe eat our lunch."

Ma stood. "Where can I tie Harry?"

"Here." Molly took the end of the rope and led the horse to a sturdy shrub and tied him. Harry seemed content for the moment. She hoped the arrangement was secure enough to hold him if he pulled on the rope.

"What kind of bush is that?" Her mother had followed.

"I don't know."

"I never saw one like that in Ohio."

"It's a lot drier here than in Ohio," Molly said. "They have lots of plants we didn't have there."

"That's true." Her mother stooped to break off some dry stems from a leafless bush that looked dead. "This will burn, but we'll need something bigger."

"Do you think it's been an hour since we left Joe?" Molly asked.

"No. Well, maybe. Let's see if we can find some sticks."

Molly looked around. "We don't want to go too far." Firefly was still cropping grass but edging in Harry's direction.

As they foraged for firewood, she looked back frequently to check on the horses. She didn't want to get out of sight. Her mother was moving farther away, toward a clump of small trees that might be cedars. Molly decided it was time to carry her meager armful closer to the road and take another look in the direction Joe had gone.

She passed the horses and laid down her pile of twigs. She didn't want to think about what they would do if Andrew was dead—or, perhaps worse, if they couldn't find out what had become of him. And Joe ... Surely his hour to reconnoiter was up now. He had to come back soon. If Ma suggested going back to the Swansons' home, she would put up a fight.

She realized that over the last week or ten days, she'd come to trust Joe completely. Her wariness was gone where he was concerned. He'd willingly gone off and left his own ranch unprotected to help her and Ma. Now he was putting his life in danger in the effort to find Andrew. What was he facing this instant?

Now was a good time to pray. Without thinking about it, she closed her eyes and silently pleaded with God for Joe's safety and Andrew's return. When she opened them, she turned and glanced at the horses and froze.

A pair of feet and trouser legs were visible under Firefly's belly, and a man's hat showed above the saddle seat. Someone was standing on the other side of her horse. Her pulse soared, and she pulled the revolver from its holster on her sash.

Walking as softly as she could, she approached Harry. Yes, she recognized that hat.

When she was about ten feet from the horse, Harry nickered. Cooper looked up and met her gaze over the saddle.

"What do you think you're doing?" Molly pointed the revolver at him.

Silence hung between them for a moment, and then Cooper laughed. "I thought I saw a loose strap. Wouldn't want one of you ladies to have an accident."

"Get away from the horse."

He stood there for a moment, sizing her up. His lips curved upward.

"Oh, come now, Janie." He held her gaze, but his hand snaked toward the shotgun's stock.

Careful of her aim, Molly pulled the trigger. His hat flew off and Firefly squealed, lunging aside and knocking Cooper off his feet.

Harry jerked his head up, and Molly patted his withers, keeping an eye on Cooper. For a moment, she feared she may have grazed his head with her shot, but he rolled away and rose shakily.

"Easy, boy." Molly stepped away from Harry and aimed the

revolver once more in Cooper's direction. "Now you know I'm a passable shot."

Satisfied that he wasn't holding a weapon, she fixed him with her stoniest glare. Her mother had brought along a good chunk of money, and Molly wasn't sure where she carried it. Maybe in her saddlebag. A small sack of coffee lay on the ground by Harry's hind hoof, and a little had spilled out on the grass. "Stealing our coffee? What were you *really* after?"

Before he could say anything, her mother called from behind her, "Molly! Molly, what's going on?"

"We've got company," she replied without taking her eyes off Cooper.

A moment later, her mother came panting to her side. "Mr. Cooper."

He gave her a wobbly smile. "Hello again, Mrs. Weaver."

"He was stealing from us," Molly said.

"Oh, really, I wasn't—" Cooper broke off.

Molly knew her expression and the spilled coffee told the truth.

"Get the shotgun, Ma. He was going to take it." She didn't say she'd feared he would use it on her.

"Where's your friend, Noyes?" Cooper sounded almost affable as he stooped to pick up his hat.

"Why—"

"Don't answer him, Ma," Molly said. "He was looking in your saddlebag."

"What?" Ma stepped around the horse and eyed her gear and the spilled coffee on the ground. "You rascal." She scooped up the sack then moved closer to Harry, reaching for the shotgun.

Molly kept her eyes on Cooper. "He took the coffee out of your saddlebag."

"I see that the buckle's undone."

"Check and make sure he didn't take anything else."

"Please, Janie. I'm not a thief," Cooper said, straightening his spine.

"I told you not to call me that. Right now, it looks like my earlier assessment of you was correct. You're a liar, mister. I don't know who you are, but you're no kin of mine."

ANDREW HELD the towel tightly against Nolan's side, but blood soaked through and stained his fingers.

"Get me something else."

Sophie sprang up and ran into the bedroom. Tearing sounds reached him.

When she returned and handed him a wad of sheeting, he nodded grimly. "I won't lie to you, Sophie. This is bad."

Her face was white as milk as she knelt across from him and stared down at her husband.

"Is he going to die?"

"I don't know." The wound was at the side of Nolan's abdomen, below his ribs. Surely the bullet hadn't hit any major organs. But Andrew wasn't sure where the liver and kidneys were —and Nolan could bleed to death.

"What can I do?" Sophie asked.

"I'm not sure either of us can do anything."

Nolan's breath came in shallow gasps. Besides trying to stop the bleeding, Andrew had no idea how to help him. He'd had cuts and scrapes, and his father had broken his wrist once, but he'd never dealt with a wound like this. Sophie brought him a wad of cloth. He took it and pulled off the towel. Blood soaked Nolan's torn shirt and spread across his stomach.

Andrew stuffed the sheeting against the wound and pushed. Just pressing on it hurt Andrew's ribs, but he ignored his own discomfort. Nolan moaned, and his eyes flickered.

"So ... phie?"

"I'm here, Albert." She leaned over him so he could look into her face. Strands of her wispy brown hair had come loose from her bun and hung down at her cheeks. Her brown eyes were wide with horror. "Albert, I'm right here."

He struggled to lift a hand but let it fall back to the floor.

"What is it?" Sophie bent closer.

"Give them what they want."

She turned her head and stared at Andrew then turned back to her husband. "I don't understand, Albert."

He lay with his eyes closed, hitching in one shallow breath after another.

When she looked his way again, Andrew whispered, "What do they want?"

"I don't know," Sophie said. "I have no idea what he meant."

"He may be delirious."

"Yes, he may." She seemed to take comfort in that.

No sound came except Nolan's labored breathing. Andrew rose and went cautiously to the edge of the window.

"They've stopped shooting."

"Can you see them?" Sophie asked.

"They're taking the horses."

"What? No!"

She started to rise, but Andrew said fiercely, "Stay down!" He'd left his rifle halfway across the room. He grabbed Nolan's and swung it toward the ragged man leading Blinker from the corral. He sure hoped Nolan hadn't fired the gun since the last time he reloaded. Andrew held the stock against his shoulder and fired.

The rifle roared, and the man fell. Blinker jumped over his prone form and out through the open gate. He galloped off around the corner of the house, bucking with every other step. One of the remaining horses—the dead outlaw's—followed his lead. Nolan's chestnut reared, tearing his halter from the hands of another man, and plunged earthward. A shot rang out, and the horse screamed and then fell heavily next to the man Andrew had hit.

"What's happening?" Sophie called from her place at Nolan's side.

"They shot your husband's horse. The other two are loose." Andrew stretched for Nolan's cartridge box and reloaded as fast as he could.

When he took a quick look out the window, the man who'd shot the chestnut was mounting his own horse. Andrew's hands shook, and he hauled in a deep breath. He didn't want to shoot their horses, or they wouldn't be able to ride away. He desperately wanted them to go away and never return.

One ... two ... He fired, and the man slumped in his saddle but urged the horse toward his companions. More glass shattered in Andrew's face. He ducked low, beneath the windowsill.

Sophie lay flat on the floor next to Nolan. Her lips moved, but Andrew couldn't hear her. He swallowed hard, wondering if his ears were permanently damaged. He looked at Sophie again.

"Are you all right?"

Her voice was faint, but he understood and nodded.

"You're bleeding," she said.

Andrew put his fingers to his stinging cheek. They came away bloody. Some glass must have caught him. His sleeve was in tatters, and blood smeared his arm. He pushed the cloth aside and studied his wounds. Glass and a large sliver of wood. Not a bullet, thank heaven.

He quailed from exposing himself again at the window, but he didn't know what else to do. Cautiously, he rose on his knees and took a quick look then ducked back. He cast the rifle aside and pulled his revolver. Peeking from the side of the bullet-riddled window frame, he saw several riders charge away from the house, into the road, and head south. He stayed still, trying to quiet his own breathing, listening.

When they were out of sight, he turned toward Sophie.

She raised her chin, gazing at him. "Are they gone?"

"I think so. I saw them go out the road."

"How many?"

"At least four." He swallowed hard and didn't say anything about the man slumped on the ground in the corral.

She frowned. "Weren't there only four the first time? And Albert killed one of them."

"Yeah, that was all we saw. Maybe there were others we didn't see, or they went and got reinforcements."

"But why? It wasn't a posse, was it?"

"I don't think so. Apparently, Albert has something they want."

She blinked and gazed down at her inert husband. "I can't think what."

Nolan made a strangled sound, and she turned her attention back to him.

"Albert? Can you hear me?"

Andrew holstered the revolver and picked up Nolan's rifle and cartridges. He took another hard look out the now gaping window frame, but all was still. He went to the water bucket, dipped some into a cup, and carried it to Sophie.

"Let me hold him up. See if he can drink some of this."

Sophie took the cup from him. Andrew put an arm under Nolan's shoulders and eased him up a bit, so she could hold it to his mouth. Nolan didn't try to drink, so she tipped the cup a little so that water trickled between his lips. He pulled away and moaned. Another sound that might have been a word came from him. Sophie bent close to his face.

"What is it, Albert? What did you say?"

Andrew listened intently. He thought Nolan whispered something. Sophie drew back, her forehead creased.

"Mick ... milk?" She frowned at Andrew. "I couldn't make it out.

Andrew laid him down gently.

"Nolan, I'm here. Can you hear me?"

The man's eyelids fluttered, and his eyes rolled back and forth. He glanced at Andrew and then away.

"Nolan, it's me, Andrew Weaver. What is it, man? What do you want to tell us?"

Nolan's eyes closed again, and he lay there, taking short, shallow breaths.

After a long moment, Sophie asked, "Is he sleeping?"

"That or unconscious."

"He wanted to tell me something." Her fretful eyes sought Andrew's face.

"I think he's just fainted. He's still breathing. Let him rest a bit. If he stirs, see if he'll tell you anything."

"Do you think they'll come back?" Sophie set aside the cup.

"I don't know." Andrew puzzled over the little he knew about Nolan. He'd served in the Southern army before coming to Texas. That was it. Except that the man he'd killed during the first attack wore a Confederate-issued belt buckle. "Tell me again when you came here. You said about a year ago?"

She nodded.

"So, he was discharged before the war was over?"

"I guess so. He'd been gone over a year, nearer two. When he came home, he wanted to move west right away. He said there wouldn't be as much fighting out here, and we could get some land and start our own ranch."

Several questions presented themselves as Andrew digested that.

"Let me wash your wounds," Sophie said. "Are you shot?"

"No, it's from the window. I can do it." He went to the bucket and dipped some water into the wash basin. They'd have to replenish it from the rain barrel soon. His chest tightened at the thought of going outside. So much to deal with, not the least of which was a dead horse in the corral, and a man possibly dead or badly wounded. He'd like to see that man's clothing up close.

He set the half-full basin on Sophie's worktable. With one of her linen dish towels, he patted his cheek first, and a bloodstain rewarded him, but something stuck in his skin hurt every time he patted with the cloth. His arm hurt worse than his face, and with the help of his pocketknife, he pried out the wood splinter and several shards of glass.

"How are you doing?" Sophie asked.

"There's one I can't get."

She rose and came to his side.

Andrew touched his cheek, just below his temple. "Can you see something there? A piece of glass, maybe?"

She touched the spot and he sucked air in between his teeth.

"Here." He offered his open knife, and she carefully prodded his cheek with the blade.

"I see it."

Her fingers were gentle. Andrew held his breath. Her touch was as soft as Ma's when he was a kid. No one could make a scrape feel better as quickly as Ma. Pain lanced his cheek, then went away.

"Got it." She held out the knife so he could see the tiny bit of broken glass.

"Thank you." He took the knife to the stove and carefully scraped the glass into the firebox. "We'll have to clean up the floor so we don't step on any."

She wrung out his cloth in the basin. "Come back here. You've still got blood on your neck."

He stood still as she dabbed at it.

"You're a sight," she murmured.

When she'd finished, he picked up his own rifle, checked the load, and stepped cautiously to the window. The chestnut's hulk still lay where it had fallen, but he couldn't see the man's body. Had his friends helped him ride away? Or was he still lurking out there somewhere, wounded and full of hate?

Nolan let out a groan.

"Oh!" In a flurry of skirts, Sophie whirled and hurried to crouch beside him.

Andrew watched from the edge of the gaping hole in the wall, but nothing moved. After a couple of minutes, he went to the table, rinsed out the cloth, and scrubbed once more along his cheek, hairline, and neck. He debated taking the basin outside to dump it and decided to toss the water out the window instead. Venturing outside at this point could be fatal.

He'd taken two steps toward the window when a firm knock came at the door. He jumped, slopping a bit of the bloody water. Sophie stared at him, her brown eyes wide with terror.

18

Ryland plodded along on Prince, unsure of what he should do. He'd lost Cooper's trail. At every crossroad he paused, wondering which way he should go. He studied what hoofprints he could make out. The road was dry, which didn't help, and he couldn't distinguish the shoe prints of Cooper's nag from the rest.

Without his pocket watch, he had to judge the time by the sun. He conjectured it was nearly noon when he stopped to speak to a man who was working out in front of a cabin, constructing a rail fence. Since he hadn't seen a lot of trees lately, Ryland wondered how far he'd had to haul the logs. He rode up close and touched his hat brim.

"Excuse me. I'm looking for a woman, Mrs. Weaver, and her daughter, whom I believe are traveling with a gentleman—that is, a rancher. Have you seen them?"

The man paused in his labor and stared at him. Ryland hadn't thought it was that difficult a question. Finally, the man drawled, "You ain't from around here, are you?"

Ah. It was his Maine accent that drew attention, and perhaps his proper grammar.

"You are right, sir," Ryland said heartily, with a smile. "I am from New England. Have you seen the travelers I'm looking for?"

The fellow leaned on the fence post he'd been pounding and considered. "Saw a man, looked like a cowpuncher, with two ladies."

Ryland's heart leaped. "Yes? They passed by here?"

"Yep. 'Bout two hours ago."

"Excellent! And did you speak to them?"

"Nope. Just looked."

"Ah."

"Purty girl, the one."

"Yes, so I'm told," Ryland murmured. In both Ohio and Austin, people he'd questioned had made note of Molly Weaver's golden hair and striking blue eyes.

"They went that way." The man pointed.

"Thank you very much."

Ryland rode on, more hopeful than he'd been since he left Andrew Weaver's ranch. Molly and her mother had passed this way just hours ago.

He tried to keep his mind on the trail, but the hoofprints were indistinct. If only it had rained here recently.

His thoughts flitted back to Maine, to his beloved Abby Benson. Yes, he could think of her that way now. She'd kissed him before he set out on this interminable journey. Well, he'd initiated it, but she kissed him back. Who could say what would happen when he returned? He knew what he wanted—a wedding, that's what. And he had half a hope that Abby would accept his proposal.

He kept Prince jogging along, hoping to spot another person he could ask. He came to a place where a narrower dirt road—almost a trail—veered off at an angle.

"Whoa." He stared down at the ground, frowning. It had been used quite a bit, but not as much as the road he was on. With a sigh, he nudged Prince forward, in the direction he'd been traveling. This was getting tiresome, and the cruel sun beat down relentlessly. He removed his jacket and tied it behind the saddle with his satchel and blanket roll. He supposed he was going to have to sleep on the ground again tonight.

The unmistakable report of a gun made him jerk in the saddle. It wasn't all that close, but it wasn't that far away, either.

"Easy, Prince." His heart racing, he patted the horse's neck, where the pale mane spilled down in front of Prince's withers. If the truth were told, the horse was calmer than Ryland felt. He'd been close to a couple of gunfights before, and he didn't want to be in that position again. He sat rigid, listening, but he didn't hear any more shots.

"Come on, boy." He lifted the reins. "Let's put some distance between us and whoever's trigger happy."

As Prince resumed his lazy jog, remorse stabbed Ryland. It could be that Molly and Mrs. Weaver were in trouble. Was he riding away from them?

He decided to go on until he either found the Weavers or another friendly person who might help him. When he came to a fork in the road, he sat staring at the ground, feeling stupid.

"Maybe we need a little break, Prince." He dismounted and took a rope from the near saddlebag. He wouldn't risk tying his horse by the reins again. As he concentrated on tying the knot, his head ached. If he ever caught up with Cooper, they had a score to settle.

Ryland took inventory of his weapons. His sword cane was lost back at Andrew Weaver's, or perhaps Cooper had taken it. The morning after he left the place, he'd realized it was missing. But his knife was in the pocket of his jacket. He got it out and, after some puzzlement, slid the sheath into his pants pocket. He wouldn't be caught weaponless again.

He rummaged in the saddlebags and came up with a few crackers. Better than nothing. As he turned away from Prince, he spotted a ring of stones where someone had built a campfire a few yards off the road.

Eyeing the trampled grass, he walked toward the fire circle.

Not a lot of people had camped here last, he decided. Maybe only one. A little more investigating showed him where a horse had been staked. Someone had no doubt camped here overnight, and not that long ago. The horse droppings were fairly fresh.

Ryland crunched the crackers slowly, ambling around the campsite while Prince grabbed at the grass. He really ought to have stocked up with more edibles before leaving Austin. He'd only come through one town with a general store since, but he'd gone through the small stash of canned goods he'd bought there and was down to this last handful of saltines.

Another collection of rocks lay several yards off, near what looked like a small cedar tree. It only grew as high as his waist, but it wasn't the shrub that caught his attention. He walked over and knelt beside the rocks. On top of a flat stone lay a smaller stone, about three inches in diameter. His pulse quickened, and he picked up the small rock.

An *X* was scratched on the bottom of the stone.

Ryland replaced the rock, stood, and looked around quickly. Could this be something Andrew Weaver had left? Or even Molly? They both knew the configuration of rocks Andrew used for a cache.

While he thought about it, Ryland walked away from the stones. If someone came along the road, he didn't want them to see what held his interest.

Molly had left a note for her brother under a similar arrangement at his ranch. Was another message buried here?

Any information hidden here could help him find the Weaver siblings. He'd have to dig it up. But he didn't have a shovel. No houses stood nearby. With a sigh, Ryland popped the last cracker into his mouth and began kicking through the weeds. Maybe he could find a pointed rock or some sort of stick that he could dig with.

A half hour later, with filthy hands and stained trouser knees, Ryland examined the contents of the tin can he'd found buried.

The battered label was for peaches, but the hoarder had washed out the can and stuffed it with something more precious. Money.

Ryland sat back and pondered. Certain that either Molly or Andrew had left the cache—or possibly Emma Weaver, if the entire family was familiar with the method of hiding valuables— he thought about why they would leave so much cash here.

Andrew had set out to buy cattle. Perhaps he'd hidden his money until he made sure the person he wanted to deal with was honest. Molly and her mother had sold a valuable business in Ohio, but surely they'd put the proceeds in a bank. Still, they were traveling to new surroundings, and rough country at that. It was possible the women had left this trove and planned to retrieve it after they found Andrew.

Suddenly frightened that someone might see him kneeling on the ground beside a hole, Ryland looked all around. He put the money in the can and placed it back where he'd found it. He started to shove dirt in but then stopped, thinking.

With another quick glance about, he hurried to Prince's side and pulled a small notebook and a pencil from the inner pocket of his jacket. What to write? He puzzled for a moment, then carefully wrote,

Dear Weaver family,

Do not be alarmed. I found this but have left it as it was. I wanted to alert you, in case we do not meet before you read this, that I am trying to help your family. Also, a man named Ben Cooper is following you.

Ryland frowned. How much did the Weavers know about Cooper? Did Molly know he was her father? Did they even know of his existence? Or had he approached them and wormed his way into their confidence? He put the pencil to the paper once more.

Do not trust that man.

He thought about the best way to make sure Molly Weaver could contact her grandmother, even if Ryland never caught up to her. With Cooper skulking about, Ryland could be waylaid out here in the middle of nowhere and never accomplish his mission. But he didn't want to spill too much, in case someone other than Molly got their hands on his note.

In case we do not meet, please be assured I mean you well. If you have not met me when you read this, make all haste to contact Mr. Jeremiah Turner, Esq., 177 Market St., Portland, Maine. I assure you it is for your good.

Sincerely,
Ryland Atkins

He reread the entire message and gulped. Not finding Molly was something he didn't want to contemplate. He was so close! But never returning to Maine would be even worse. He wished he'd mailed one last missive to Abby when he was in that last little town. *I love you!* That's what he'd say, and he wouldn't care if her grandmother saw it.

After another careful surveillance of the clearing and the nearby road, he went back to the hole and pushed his note into the can with the money. He placed it back in the hole and covered it carefully with dirt.

When he'd finished, he wasn't satisfied. There was too much dirt sprinkled about and too big a disturbance. If he left a sloppy cache, someone else would no doubt find it. On the other hand, if he didn't finish soon, someone could come along the road and see what he was doing. He pulled in a deep breath and made himself work slowly and precisely, until even he couldn't tell he'd dug there. Then he put the rocks back exactly as he'd found them.

He stepped back to give it the once-over. Perfect.

Thundering hoofbeats yanked him out of his thoughts. A wiry dun horse tore out of the rough prairie beyond the bushes, toward the road. Prince jerked his head up with a startled squeal. Ryland was too shocked to do anything but stare for a moment. His heart hammered, and adrenaline gushed through his veins. He was thankful he'd tied Prince.

The dun veered away from Prince and galloped into the road. Before Ryland could recover, a second horse loped into the clearing and slowed as it neared him.

"Hey there." Ryland held out a hand and tried to keep his voice steady. "No need to cause a commotion."

The gray stopped and stood shivering a couple of yards from Ryland.

"That's a good fella. Easy, now."

Neither horse was saddled, so he probably didn't need to worry about them having lost their riders. The pair must have broken out of their enclosure. But why were they running so hard? The gray's sides were drenched in sweat, and he hauled in short breaths.

Ryland took a small step forward, and the horse didn't move away. Maybe he could help its owner. The gray had a halter, and within moments Ryland was able to grasp it. "There now. Aren't you a nice horse?" He stroked its long nose.

Cautiously, he led it toward Prince. His palomino was wary, but Ryland was able to take the rope off Prince without losing his hold on the gray gelding. Prince whickered and took a couple of steps but didn't run off. Ryland fastened the rope to the gray's halter and tied the end through the right stirrup on Prince's saddle. He hoped he wasn't asking for trouble. He was still somewhat inexperienced with horses.

The two stayed put, and after a moment the gray stretched his neck down. He was just able to reach the grass and clip off a mouthful.

Now, if only he knew where the horse came from. He

supposed he could ride Prince in the direction the two horses had come from and hope he found the farm or ranch where they belonged.

He took one last look at the cache and checked Prince's gear, untied the rope from the stirrup, and climbed into the saddle. The lead rope was just long enough for him to hold it comfortably, but he feared that if the new horse shied or decided to run away, he wouldn't be able to hold it. But when he nudged Prince forward, the gray followed. Heading past where the scrubby cedars grew, he eyed the ground carefully.

He certainly wasn't a tracker, but Mory had taught him a few things, and he sat for a moment scrutinizing the grass. He thought he could see where the two horses had passed through the open ground. The gray seemed willing to plod along with Prince. Ryland wondered where the dun had got to, but quickly dismissed the idea of looking for it. That horse would be somebody else's problem.

"Up, Prince. Come on, boy."

ANDREW SET down the basin and pulled his revolver. Stepping to one side of the door, he called, "What do you want?"

"I'm looking for a friend," came a man's voice.

Andrew caught his breath. It couldn't be.

"Joe?"

"Yes! Joe Noyes. Is that you, Andrew?"

Shoving his gun back in its holster, Andrew leaped to the door. He put his hand on the latch and hesitated. One of the bullet holes in the door's planks gave him an opening, and he put his eye to it. Relief washed over him as he took in his friend's face.

"Joe!" Andrew looked over his shoulder at Sophie, who started to rise. "It's all right. I know this *hombre*." He threw off the bar and the deadbolt then flung open the door.

"Andrew! Am I glad to see you." Joe stuck out his hand.

Grasping his friend's hand, Andrew pulled on it. "Get in here, fast."

"What's going on?" Joe stepped inside.

Andrew pushed him out of the way, shot the bolt, and replaced the wooden bar. "We've been under attack, that's what."

"I came yesterday, and someone shot at me," Joe said. "I was sure I saw old Blinker in the corral, but he's not there now. I saw the dead horse, though."

Andrew couldn't keep the regret from his voice. "The outlaws that have been plaguing us started shooting the horses. That one out there's Nolan's. They ran off the other two."

"Who else is here?"

"Oh, sorry. Come on in." He led Joe to where Albert Nolan still lay on the kitchen floor with Sophie kneeling beside him. She rose awkwardly. "This is Mrs. Nolan. As you can see, her husband has been grievously wounded. It's just the three of us."

"I'm sorry, Mrs. Nolan." Joe held out a hand, and she shook it.

Andrew said, "Sophie, Joe Noyes is my closest neighbor, and a good friend."

"I'm pleased to meet you." Sophie flicked a glance toward the woodstove. "There's coffee. It's been simmering quite a while, but it's probably still drinkable."

Joe hesitated.

"Come on," Andrew said. "You might as well have some. We've done all we can for Nolan."

"Where's the nearest doctor?" Joe asked.

"Too far. New Braunfels, I think. It would take hours to get there, and I doubt if one would come all the way up here."

Sophie nodded. "There's at least one doctor in San Antonio, but I honestly think we're closer to Austin."

"Austin? That's even farther." Joe took the empty mug Andrew thrust into his hand.

"Besides, we have no horses," Andrew added.

"Well, I have Ranger, and your mother and Molly have horses—"

"Ma and Molly?" Andrew stared at him.

"We came looking for you."

"But ... They're in Ohio."

"I'm sorry, pal. Your father ... he passed away. I didn't mean to have you hear it this way. Em—er your Ma wrote to you, but ..."

"It's been weeks since I picked up my mail."

Joe nodded. "The ladies came down here hoping to stay with you, at least for a while. I don't know all the details. I do know they've sold your family's mercantile."

Andrew blew out a breath. "Whoa. That's a lot. Where are they?" He picked up the coffeepot and poured Joe's cup full.

"Back down the road a couple of miles. There's a stream. I told them to wait there while I sorted things out."

Andrew set the coffeepot back on the stove. "You're telling me my mother and my sister are a mile away? I can't believe it."

"Well, two or three miles." Joe took an experimental sip of the coffee and made a face.

"You don't have to drink it," Andrew whispered.

"No, it's fine." Joe took another sip.

"Are they coming here?"

"If I tell them to."

"No." Andrew glanced at Sophie. "A gang of outlaws is attacking this ranch, and we don't know why. I'm surprised you didn't run into them. Which way did you come?"

Joe pointed. "We heard some shooting, and I made them wait for me."

"The outlaws rode off in the opposite direction not half an hour ago." Andrew frowned. "But they could come back anytime. I don't want Ma and Molly walking into it."

"Well, I don't want to leave them out there alone for long, either. I should probably ride back there and get them."

"Look, this outlaw band seems to have targeted this ranch, or maybe Albert Nolan himself. I'm not sure which. Or why. Mrs. Nolan doesn't seem to know either. But they've come here twice, shooting the place up. It's not safe here."

"Then why are you still here?"

Andrew's jaw tightened. "I couldn't leave them alone like this. The first time was bad enough. We didn't dare go outside for hours. They came back this morning. That's when Nolan was shot. I couldn't leave his wife here alone with him. Surely you understand that. And there was the question of whether they were watching the place, and whether we could even get out of here alive. And now I don't have Blinker."

Joe sighed. "So these men who've attacked you—what, twice?"

Andrew nodded. "You have no idea who they are or what they want?"

"At first Nolan and I thought they wanted his cattle, but in that case they'd have just taken them after they chased us inside, right? But they came back."

"Mr. Weaver!"

Andrew whirled. Sophie beckoned him to her husband's side.

"He's trying to talk," Sophie said.

Andrew crouched beside the wounded man. "Nolan, what is it?" He touched the wounded man's shoulder and leaned close. "What are you trying to tell us?"

"Mick ... army ..."

Andrew looked at Joe and Sophie in confusion. "Mick army?"

"Albert was in the army," Sophie said with a tentative shrug.

"The Confederate Army," Andrew said, for Joe's benefit. "They're from Arkansas."

"Do you think this could have something to do with his service in war, ma'am?" Joe asked, eyeing Sophie intently.

"I—I don't know."

Andrew caught his eye. "I noticed the outlaw Nolan killed in the first attack was wearing a gray tunic and a belt with CSA on the buckle."

"What rank was your husband?" Joe asked Sophie.

"Just a private. Arkansas Sixth Infantry."

"How long was he with them?"

"Uh, maybe two years. His enlistment was two years. But I didn't really expect him to come home as soon as he did."

"How's that?" Joe kept his voice calm and sympathetic, and Andrew sat back on his heels and kept quiet.

"I thought he wasn't due home yet, but he showed up one morning, and he said his unit disbanded."

Joe frowned. "Why?"

"Something about the commanding officer being killed. I'm not really sure. Albert doesn't talk about the war."

Andrew jerked his head, signaling Joe to step aside with him. "Does that sound right? I mean, would a unit be disbanded because the commanding officer died?"

"Not that I ever heard of. But then, I was with the Union. Maybe things were organized differently in the South. It doesn't sound right, though."

Nolan let out a little groan, and Sophie hovered over him. "Albert, what is it?"

Joe leaned closer to Andrew and lowered his voice. "When we went to buy your ma a horse in Austin, Harry at the stable told me there's bands of marauders in this area. Near where we live too. In fact, when Emma and Molly got to your place, a couple of fellas were squatting in your cabin."

"What?" Andrew eyed him in alarm.

"Don't worry, I made them leave. And before we left to come find you, I asked the sheriff to ride out there now and again to check your place and mine. He said he'd try to keep an eye on things while we were gone."

Andrew didn't like the sound of that one bit. The sheriff wouldn't have time to go out there very often. "So, when we get home, there could be a bunch of outlaws holed up in my house. Or yours. Or both."

Joe sighed. "It was a tough decision to leave, but it seemed like finding you was the most important thing at the moment. If I didn't volunteer, I was afraid your ma and Molly would go off alone, looking for you."

Realizing how much he owed his friend, Andrew swallowed hard. "Thanks. For everything. I'm not happy that Ma and Molly are here, but it sounds like they could have been in the situation I'm in right now if you hadn't helped them."

"We were shot at, back at your place."

Heat swept over Andrew, and he could feel his face flush. "My mother was shot at?"

Gritting his teeth, Joe nodded. "'Fraid so. But she and Molly are fine." A sudden grin burst over his face. "Say, your sister's quite the crack shot."

"Well, yeah, she's better'n I am." Andrew rubbed his forehead. "We'd better go get them right now."

"Like you said, we oughtn't to leave Mrs. Nolan alone here with her man in the condition he's in."

Andrew leaned close and said quietly, "Yeah, Nolan's got quite a temper. If he starts feeling better, he'll be like a bull on a rampage."

"That right?"

"He hits her," Andrew whispered.

Joe shook his head. "Look, pal, I think you'd better stay here. I'll go get the ladies. They're not safe where they are."

"And then what? Get all your horses stolen tonight? Have this house shot to pieces with all of us inside?"

Joe put a hand on his shoulder. "One thing at a time, Andrew. We need to be all together. Safety in numbers, you know? And Molly can help with the shooting if we need her, or at least the loading."

"We need to get away from here, Joe."

"I agree, but you said so yourself—we can't leave Mrs. Nolan alone with a dying man—"

Andrew let out a grunt of frustration. He wasn't sure Nolan was dying, but he supposed it could happen. His bleeding had slowed, but that didn't mean he'd heal, and there was always a risk of infection.

"You were in the war. You'd have a better idea about his chances of recovering than I would."

"I could look at him, but I'm not sure he'd want me to. Are your weapons loaded?"

"Yeah, mine and Nolan's both," Andrew said. "You're lucky I didn't shoot you right through the door."

"You can give me some cover from the window. I'd best go now. I've already left your ma and Molly alone too long."

"All right." Andrew gulped and went to the window, peering out from the side and then looking from the center of the window. Nothing moved except Joe's horse, Ranger, who stood patiently outside the corral.

Joe went to where Nolan lay and murmured in low tones with Sophie. A few minutes later, he came to Andrew.

"Nolan got out the name MacKenzie. His wife says that was his captain's name when he was in the Reb army. Some Arkansas outfit. I don't know what to make of it."

"That's what he was trying to tell us before." Andrew puzzled over it. "That's the officer who was killed."

"And now a bunch of ex-Rebel soldiers are attacking this house." Joe let out a low whistle. "I'll go get the women. We'll only have three horses, but maybe they've got a wagon."

"I think they do."

"All right then. Ranger can work in harness. I'm not sure about your mother's horse, but we'll figure it out." Joe clapped Andrew on the shoulder and drew his revolver. "Take another good look. When you count to three, I'm going out the door."

19

Molly stared at Cooper over the gun barrel. If he didn't do as she demanded, did she really have the courage to pull the trigger?

"Ma? What do we do now?"

Her mother stepped up beside her. "Mr. Cooper, I assume you've left your horse nearby. I believe it's time you left here. And do not return."

Cooper stood still for a moment and gave a slight nod. "As you wish, ma'am." He turned toward the road and melted into the brush along the verge. In less than a minute, Molly couldn't make out his form. He was gone.

She lowered the gun. "Ma, check your bags." Her voice shook, and she hauled in a steadying breath.

"Check yours as well." Ma went to Harry's side and opened the unbuckled flap of the saddlebag. "Everything seems to be here." She moved to the other side.

Molly walked slowly to Firefly. She moved jerkily as she opened each saddlebag and her satchel. Nothing was wrapped in her blanket roll, so she didn't bother with that. Her mother was beside her when she finished.

"Well?" Ma asked.

"Everything's here. What about the money you brought?"

Ma smiled. "Oh, that's not on my horse."

"You've hidden it on your person?" Molly asked then looked around in case Cooper was lurking within earshot.

"Absolutely. And it will stay there, unless you think we should hide it somewhere else."

"No. It would be too dangerous to make a cache now. He might be ..." Again she swung around and peered at every rock and bush that could possibly conceal a person. "Ma, do you think that awful man is really ..." She gulped.

Her mother put her arm around her. "I don't know, dear. He's certainly not like you, either physically or temperamentally."

"Thank you for saying that."

"But he makes me uneasy."

"Yes. Me too." Molly lifted her chin. "Listen."

Ma stood still beside her. After a moment, she nodded. "I hear it. But it's not coming from the way he went."

They both turned toward the road and the sound of regular hoofbeats. Molly held the revolver, willing her hands not to shake. A moment later, Joe came into sight, riding Ranger. He waved when he saw them and trotted down to meet them by the stream.

"Thank heaven." Ma let out a deep sigh and closed her eyes for an instant.

"What's going on?" Molly asked before he was out of the saddle.

"I have good news. I've found Andrew."

Molly let out a little squeal. She wanted to throw herself into Joe's arms but managed to hold herself in check.

"Praise God!" Ma beamed at Joe. "And he's all right?"

"Yes and no. There's a ranch about three miles away. There was a lot of shooting. I got as close as I dared, and then the gunfire stopped. I got a glimpse of several men riding off in the opposite direction. Everything was quiet, but I waited fifteen minutes or so, then I rode up to the house."

Molly wished he'd just get on with it. She hadn't thought of Joe as a talker, but he spun this tale with obvious relish.

"There weren't any horses in the yard this time, and I was afraid I was too late. But when I knocked on the door, who do you think opened it?"

"Andrew," Molly cried.

"Yes. He has some minor injuries, but in general he's all right physically. But his host, a fellow named Nolan, was shot in the skirmish they'd come through. Andrew wants to leave the ranch, but he's too much of a gentleman to leave Mrs. Nolan there alone with her badly injured husband."

"I would expect as much of Andrew," Ma said. "Can we help them?"

"I'm not sure. Andrew seems to think the outlaws are after something in particular, and he thinks Nolan might know what it is."

"Well, let's get going!" Molly ran to Firefly and tightened the cinch strap on the saddle.

Portland, Maine

ABBY BENSON CARRIED the tea tray into the parlor and placed it on the low table before her grandmother. Mrs. Rose poured cups for Abby, herself, and their guest, Jeremiah Turner. Abby carried a cup to the silver-haired lawyer and handed it to him with a smile.

"Have you news from Mr. Atkins?" Grandmother asked, pouring a dollop of cream into her own cup.

"The latest word I had was the telegram from Austin. I told you about that on my last visit."

"Yes." Grandmother waited expectantly.

"A letter came today that he wrote a week prior to that

telegram, when he embarked on a stagecoach line. In it, he told me something that concerns me."

"Oh?" Grandmother took a sip of her tea.

"Mr. Atkins learned that another person has been inquiring about the Weaver family." Mr. Turner took a sip and set his cup and saucer on the end table beside him.

"To what end?" Grandmother asked.

"That is precisely what I would like to know." Turner eyed the plate of hermits Abby had baked that morning. "Benjamin Cooper."

"Do tell."

Abby watched the old woman. How could she be so calm? Abby's own heart had lurched at the name Cooper. That could only be her uncle—her cousins' father. But what was he doing out west?

"We had learned more than a year ago that Cooper made inquiries about the children in their old neighborhood, but we'd heard no more of him since then."

"He's a no-good scoundrel." Mrs. Rose nodded firmly.

Mr. Turner ignored her comment. "I don't know how he learned of young Jane's whereabouts, but apparently he followed the Weaver family to Ohio. You know from Mr. Atkins's earlier communications that Simeon Weaver had passed on by the time he got there, and Mrs. Weaver and her daughter—whom we are quite certain is your granddaughter, Jane—had left the area."

"Yes." Grandmother frowned over the rim of her bone china cup. "They were going to Texas to join the Weavers' son, he said."

"That is correct." Mr. Turner eyed the cookies again.

Abby wished he would get on with his tale. Perhaps it would speed things up if she urged him to eat. She leaned forward and took a hermit.

"Please, Mr. Turner, help yourself." She smiled at him.

"Thank you, Miss Benson. Those look delicious." He

selected one at last and took a small bite. Chewing, he smiled at her. "Very tasty. I have a suspicion you are the cook responsible."

"Why yes, I am. And thank you. I'm glad you like them. So, Mr. Atkins ...?"

"Yes, Atkins. He's a good young man, very diligent. I was hoping to hear from him with more current news, but I fear he's gone beyond the reach of the telegraph lines. I hear Texas is in chaos at the moment. Washington is sending in a military governor, I believe."

Grandmother frowned and set her teacup aside. "It is such a pity they went into that place. Not even a state now! How do they expect to do business?"

"I'm sure all the Confederate states will be readmitted eventually," Mr. Turner said. "These things take time."

"Indeed. Meanwhile, my granddaughter is in the middle of all that turmoil. Why, just last month their treasury in Austin was robbed. Did you read about it in the papers? I understand they haven't caught the miscreants."

"Yes, I read about it," Mr. Turner said. "It's difficult with the government and everything disrupted by the war. Of course, there are a lot of returning soldiers demanding recompense, and Atkins said he's been warned of outlaws swarming about in gangs." He looked up and said quickly, "Not that I mean to alarm you, Mrs. Rose. No doubt they'll get things under control quickly."

"It's a very large territory," Abby ventured. She'd read all she could find in recent weeks about Texas. She always read up on the places to which Ryland traveled. Of course she was worried about Cousin Jane, but she didn't really know her. She'd disappeared when she was an infant. But Ryland Atkins was another story. Her own future was bound up with his—or at least, she hoped it was.

"It is indeed." Mr. Turner looked very unhappy as he chewed the rest of his cookie.

"Don't they have rangers of some sort who keep the peace?" Grandmother asked.

"I'm told the Texas Rangers disbanded for the war," Mr. Turner replied. "I'm not sure if they've reorganized or not. I assume there are appointed marshals there, or perhaps locally elected sheriffs. The larger towns might even have their own police forces. But still ..." He shook his head. "I cannot say what they're allowed to do under the federal mandates."

"There must be some sort of law-keeping contingent," Grandmother protested.

"Do you think Mr. Atkins could be in danger?" Abby asked with a swift glance at the old woman. Her grandmother knew of her attachment to Ryland, and Abby didn't think she'd mind her inquiry. Grandmother herself was becoming quite fond of the young man who'd done so much for them.

"I certainly hope not." Mr. Turner picked up his teacup and drained it. "I assure you ladies, I will keep you informed of anything I hear from that quarter. And now I should go back to the office. Mr. Wicker is due in court this afternoon, and I must accompany him."

"How is he getting on?" Abby asked.

"Oh, fine, fine. He's still in the early stages of tutelage. This will be only the third time he's represented a client in court, and I am keeping a close eye on him. So far, he's doing fine."

Did she sense a shadow of doubt there? Ryland had confided in Abby that Mr. Turner had hoped he would read law with him, but Ryland had declined the offer. He was happier out in the field investigating than sitting in an office reading dull books or trying to convince a judge to change his mind. So, the attorney had taken on Joshua Wicker, a friend's nephew, to read law with him.

Abby rose when Mr. Turner did. After a pleasant goodbye to her grandmother, he went into the entry. Abby went with him and handed him his hat.

"Thank you, Miss Benson. Your grandmother looks a little pale."

"Well, she doesn't get out much, you know. She has been a bit subdued since the boys visited. Since they left, I mean. She was very happy while Matthew and Jack were here." She was still learning to call her cousins by their new names, but their reunion two months previously had been a time of joy. Since they returned to their far-flung homes, her grandmother had seemed listless. She hoped Janie would be found soon.

"Yes, I must write to both of them with what news we have so far about Jane."

After bidding Mr. Turner goodbye, Abby returned to the parlor. Grandmother was sitting where she'd left her. On the table sat her teacup, still nearly full.

"May I heat up your tea?" Abby resumed her seat.

"No, thank you, dear. I was thinking about poor Jane. She's lost her father now—her adoptive father. And that Cooper rascal is out there. What could he want from her?"

"I'm sure I don't know. I hope Mr. Atkins is speedy in finding her."

Grandmother smiled gently. "Yes. We want him to return as well." She reached over and patted Abby's hand. "Your heart is set on him, is it not?"

A wave of heat crawled up Abby's neck to her face. "I am fond of him, yes. But he's always the perfect gentleman, Grandmother."

"I know. I wondered at first, but I don't think he's tried to take any liberties ..."

"Never!" Abby's face felt on fire. "He did say in his last letter to me that he hoped we could talk when he'd found Jane and brought her home."

"How noble of him. He wants to complete his mission before thinking of himself. And you." The corners of Grandmother's eyes crinkled. "But he shouldn't wait too long."

"Wh-what do you mean?"

"Oh, nothing. Only that he shouldn't make you wait for an intolerable period of time."

"I see." But she didn't. It wasn't as if she would transfer her affections to another young man. No, Ryland Atkins was the one for her. She'd known that before he even brought Jack Miller home to Grandmother. And now he was in a land overrun by robbers and marauders. As she cleared the tea table, she prayed silently for all her cousins, and especially for Ryland.

"I believe I'll go lie down for a while," Grandmother said. She rose a bit unsteadily, and Abby hurried to her side.

"Let me help you to your room."

Her grandmother didn't protest, which was not a good sign. If she felt well, she'd have snapped that she was perfectly capable of making her way down the hallway on her own. As she helped the dear lady remove her shoes and tucked a quilt over her, Abby renewed her prayers for her cousin Jane. If Ryland failed to find her, to what new depths would Grandmother sink?

WHEN HE SAW three horses approaching at a comfortable lope, Andrew drew a deep breath. Molly's form and fair hair were unmistakable, and that must be Ma riding the paint horse, though he'd never seen her on horseback before. "Thank you, Lord." He strode to the door and flung it open. He couldn't help grinning as they turned in at the lane and trotted closer.

"Andrew!" Molly gave a whoop. She rode up close and dropped her horse's reins, sprang down, and ran to him.

He accepted her embrace but caught his breath and flinched away from her.

"Easy. My ribs are a little tender."

"Your ribs? What happened?"

"I took a fall a few weeks ago. Blinker wasn't paying attention, and neither was I. But I'm on the mend now." Joe was helping his mother down. Andrew couldn't believe she'd ridden all this way sidesaddle, and in a black dress to show her mourning state. He moved off the doorstone to accept her hug.

"Ma, he's got some injuries, so be gentle," Molly said.

Andrew kissed his mother's cheek and stepped back. "Let's get everyone inside. It might not be safe to stand around and talk out here."

"I'll put the horses in the corral," Joe said. "Do we want the saddles inside?"

"Might be a good idea, until we decide what to do." Andrew led the women in.

He and Sophie had managed to get Nolan into the bedroom while Joe was gone, though it hadn't been easy. Andrew was afraid they'd aggravated the rancher's wound. But it had roused him to the point of talking too.

First he'd lashed out at Sophie with bitter words, but that was the pain talking, Andrew thought—or just Nolan's innate meanness coming out.

After he was settled, Sophie had plied him with some willow bark tea. He managed to get half a cup down, and then he'd finally given some useful information. As soon as Joe came in, they'd discuss what to do about it. Meanwhile, Andrew wanted to know everything that had happened in Ohio, how his father had died, and all about Ma and Molly's journey.

Sophie stood near the stove, wringing her apron in her hands.

"Ma, come and meet Mrs. Nolan," Andrew said. "Sophie, this is my mother, Emma Weaver, and my sister Molly."

Ma held out her hands to Sophie. "Mrs. Nolan, I can't thank you enough for giving my son hospitality."

"Oh, well, the truth is, he's done a lot more for us than we have for him." Sophie grimaced. "I fear we've brought him, and now you folks, into a very bad situation."

"Sit down, Ma," Andrew said. "Tell me everything."

They'd just started to catch up when Joe came through the doorway lugging two saddles. Andrew jumped up to help him.

"One more," Joe said, "unless you want me to bring in the ones in the shed."

"Leave them for now."

"Right. I'll get my gear." He went out again.

Andrew felt remiss in keeping watch. He seized Nolan's rifle and stood guard at the window while Joe retrieved the last saddle and bridle. The three horses nudged each other and paced around the fenced area, dodging the dead animal that still lay there.

When he opened the door, Joe came in with his burden. "You got anything we can feed those nags? I don't think we want to turn them out."

Andrew turned to look at Sophie, who was preparing a fresh pot of coffee for the travelers. "Oh, yes, of course," she said. "Our horse is gone. Use from the oat bin, by all means."

Joe went out, and Andrew stood by the window to watch him, but he saw nothing to alarm him outside.

When his friend returned, he came to the window with his own rifle. "I see this house took plenty of bullets."

"That's an understatement," Andrew said.

"It's a wonder any of you lived through it."

"Well, we're afraid it will happen again."

"Go sit down with your mother and Molly," Joe said. "I'll keep watch."

"I think we'd be wiser to get out of here while we can."

"We all need to know the situation better before we decide what to do."

Andrew bowed his head for a moment. He didn't want to argue with his best friend, but Joe didn't know the panic of being trapped in a flimsy house with a band of cutthroats outside.

"All right, but we have to be quick." He dragged the table closer to the window so Joe could hear the conversation while he watched. "Ladies, please sit down and let us talk over what to do next."

His mother and Molly took seats. Sophie brought over a

plate of her fresh biscuits, and Andrew was glad he'd saved them. He ended up on the bench beside Molly.

"Here's the situation." Quickly he ran through the events of the past three days. When he'd finished, he looked around at them.

"So, you and Mr. Nolan had to bury a dead man?" Molly asked, wrinkling her nose.

"I'm afraid so."

"We saw the dead horse in the corral," Ma said.

"Yes. Unfortunately, I think burying it is too big a job for us right now." Andrew touched his ribcage. "It's been about three weeks since I was injured, but I don't think I'm up to that much shoveling yet."

"You can't just leave it there," Ma said. "It will rot quickly in this heat and draw scavengers, not to mention the possibility of disease." She shook her head. "Well, there's a lot to consider, including our own situation."

"Did Joe tell you about the man who's been following us?" Molly asked.

Andrew eyed her sharply. "What man?"

"Some oaf by the name of Cooper."

His mother stirred. "He came to where Molly and I were waiting for Joe today."

"He was gone by the time I got there," Joe put in without turning from the window. "Molly ran him off with her gun."

"My sister's totin' a gun now?" Andrew smiled incredulously.

"You have to in these parts." Molly wasn't laughing.

"What did this fellow want?" Andrew looked to his mother for the answer.

She hesitated, and Molly said, "I caught him going through Ma's things."

"He followed them down here from Ohio," Joe said grimly.

Andrew's eyebrows shot up. "Whatever for?"

"We think he wants to rob us." Molly threw her mother an

apologetic glance. "Maybe someone in Ohio told him Ma had just sold the mercantile."

Andrew eyed his mother gravely. "Are you carrying a lot of cash?"

"We left a large part of it in a bank," Ma said. "We did bring some along in case a need arose."

"I see."

"There's something else." Molly seemed reluctant to say more, but she hauled in a deep breath. She looked at Ma and then met his gaze. "Cooper says he's my father. Andrew, I'm adopted."

"Wha—" He stared at her and then at his mother. "Ma?"

"I'm afraid it's true, son. You and Molly were both adopted when you were very small. First you, and a couple of years later, Molly. You aren't blood kin, and your pa and I should have told you that. When we first took you in, you were too young to understand, and it seemed best just to go on letting you think you were natural brother and sister. I see now that was a mistake."

Everyone was silent for a moment. Sophie rose from her stool. "Perhaps I should prepare something more to eat. I've got the makings of a stew simmering."

"No, we have to get out of here. Ma, you can tell me more later. We really need to leave this place." Andrew looked at his friend, who slouched against the wall by the window. "Joe, after you left, we got a little more out of Nolan and pieced things together. He thinks the leader of the gang that's been attacking us is the brother of his former commanding officer. Captain MacKenzie was killed, and apparently the brother blames Nolan."

"Does he have reason?" Ma asked.

"We're not sure, but I have my suspicions." Andrew threw a sidelong glance at Sophie.

"It's all right," she said. "My husband isn't even-tempered ... we both know that. I've seen him pick fights, and ..."

"And we think Nolan may be behind the captain's death," Andrew said softly.

Molly gaped at him. He returned her gaze evenly and gave a little nod. Yes, he was suggesting that Sophie's husband had murdered an officer.

Tears leaked from Sophie's eyes and streamed down her cheeks. "Albert told us about ... a letter ..." She paused with a sob.

"He took a letter off the man he'd shot during the first attack," Andrew said. "We found it in the wardrobe."

Sophie rose abruptly and went to the stove. Andrew wished he could go to her and offer her some comfort, but his duty lay in explaining the mess to his family.

"MacKenzie's younger brother was enlisted in their unit," he said. "Apparently Nolan recognized him when those men were out near the corral. He was leading the gang that attacked. The letter was one written by one of his followers to his wife, but he hadn't posted it yet. They came here to kill Nolan."

Sophie broke down in ragged weeping. Andrew stood, his heart in turmoil. His mother rose and went to Sophie's side.

"There, there, my dear." Ma put her arms around the crying woman.

"I'm sorry, Sophie," Andrew said, wishing he could do more. Her face showed her misery. Nolan had done that to her, but Andrew felt he was also at fault for exposing her shame to others.

"No, it's better if your family knows it all." Sophie turned toward the stove.

"Nolan arrived home from the army earlier than expected," Andrew said, resuming his seat. "Sooner than he should have, in fact. Sophie wondered if he'd deserted, but she never asked, and he never said. Nolan wanted to leave their home in Arkansas immediately. We've hashed it over, and the approximate dates seem to fit with Nolan leaving his outfit about the time the captain was killed."

"You think he murdered his captain?" Molly breathed out softly, with a surreptitious glance toward Sophie.

Andrew shrugged. "From what Nolan was able to tell us this morning, we fear MacKenzie's young brother has rounded up some of his comrades in arms, now that the war's over, and come after Nolan."

"My dear, I'm so sorry," Ma said. Sophie sagged against her, and Ma patted her shoulder.

"We have no proof that he killed the captain," Andrew said. "He didn't exactly confess."

"How bad off is he?" Molly asked.

"Pretty bad."

Ma's face skewed. "Perhaps I could take a look. Mrs. Nolan, do you have some warm water and a clean cloth?"

"There's cloths in the bedroom," Sophie said. "I'll bring hot water."

"We need to get out of here," Andrew said, "but we weren't sure we should move him."

"Is there a wagon?" Joe asked, still vigilant at the window.

"Yes. Out back. Sophie says it's in decent condition."

"I can rig up Ranger to pull it if you'll keep watch," Joe said.

"Let me meet Mr. Nolan and examine his wound." Ma carefully poured hot water from a kettle into the wash basin.

Molly rose and went to Mrs. Nolan's side. "Ma has a lot of nursing experience. She'll tell us if your husband can be moved without further injury."

Sophie nodded.

"Now, how can I help?"

Sophie swallowed hard. "If we decide to go, perhaps you'd gather the blankets from the storeroom, over there, so we can make him a soft place to lie in the wagon."

When the three women had left the room, Andrew went to Joe's side. "If you're ready, let's go get the wagon."

They stepped outside, both with guns at the ready. The humid air seemed too placid.

"We may have stayed here too long," Andrew said.

Joe frowned. "All's quiet now."

"And it was quiet last night. But this morning it was like another war erupted." He led Joe around the house, cautiously leading with his revolver as they turned the corner. Nolan's plain wagon stood peacefully in the grass.

"It's rigged for two horses." Andrew threw an anxious glance at Joe.

"We'll have to work with what we have. Let's haul it around front." Joe grasped the tongue. "That's better than bringing Ranger and Harry out here, where nobody inside can see."

"We could put Molly at the window with another gun." Joe bent and took hold, and together they hauled the wagon around into the dooryard.

"I'll get the harness. Bring Ranger, if you think he's the most reliable."

Joe winced. "I wish we knew if Harry will pull. Firefly isn't trained for it. She's only four years old, and I've never had her in harness. And we don't have time to give her lessons."

Andrew walked to the shed, staying alert as he went. He took Nolan's harness from its peg. He and Joe worked swiftly on each side, fitting the harness in place on Harry and Ranger then hitching it to the evener.

Joe's brow furrowed as he connected one of the tugs. "Where do we go? We'll be wide open out on the road."

"I know. How far is that ranch where you all stayed?"

"The Swansons'? No, we can't put them in danger. Mrs. Swanson's expecting pretty soon."

"Look, I buried some money not far from here. I'd like to get it before we leave these parts."

"How far away?"

"A mile or so. It's off the main road. I camped there overnight. I can run for it now, or we can go that way when we leave."

"And then head home?"

Andrew considered that. He wanted nothing more than to get back to his ranch with Molly and his mother, taking them out of danger. "Unless you think it would be safer to head for a town with some lawmen."

"What, New Braunfels? San Antonio?" Joe shook his head. "Let's at least be pointed up Austin way. Maybe they'll leave us alone once we vacate this place."

"They don't want the land, I'm afraid."

Joe glanced around then said quietly, "Have you considered leaving Nolan to them? Take his wife with us and hit the trail?"

"She'd never go. Not while he's alive." Even as he spoke, Andrew wasn't sure it was true. She'd admitted to him that she wanted to leave Nolan.

Once the horses were hitched, Joe put his saddle in the wagon bed, and Andrew loaded his. If he had to buy another horse, at least he'd already have a saddle and bridle.

They went into the house, and Molly came to meet them. She whispered, "Ma thinks Mr. Nolan's not long for this world."

20

Ryland paused to get his bearings. He studied the angle of the sun, but it was still high overhead, and he still wasn't sure exactly which direction he was headed.

Before him and just a little to one side lay a wooded area. "Let's try that," he said to Prince. "Maybe we'll find a stream. At least there'll be some shade."

He hadn't ridden much farther when he heard a distant whinny. Pulling back on the reins, he listened. The gray horse gave a nervous nicker.

"What is it, fella?" Ryland eyed the gelding sharply. "Are we near your home?"

Cautiously, he rode a little closer. He thought he made out more than one horse near the trees. He sat for a full minute, staring and thinking.

"All right," he said at last. "I'm not riding in there with two horses. Whatever happens, Prince, I don't want to lose you."

He found a place to hitch both animals in a dip in the ground and made sure they were secure. He didn't think anyone at the distant grove could see them.

"All right." He hauled in a deep breath. "You two stay here and behave yourselves. Here I go."

Staying low, he made his way toward the horses. He took advantage of every bush and rock, every low place in the ground, to conceal him. When he was close to the tied mounts, he realized there were at least six of them, and listening carefully, he made out male voices in the near distance.

Ryland studied the horses, and his pulse quickened. One of them was a thin bay with a white sock on its left hind foot. He slipped quietly around to where he could see the bay's face, and sure enough, a white strip graced its nose.

Cooper.

Ryland caught his breath. Were the other men friends of Cooper's? And did they have anything to do with the gunfire he'd heard earlier? He looked closely at the others. One carried saddlebags with CSA stamped into the leather. He frowned at it. A run-in with a band of former soldiers was the last thing he wanted, especially since they'd peg him as a Yankee the moment he opened his mouth.

A good-sized tree stood close by, and he flitted closer, putting its bole between him and the men. He hoped none of them would come check on the horses. After a few minutes, he dared move even closer, behind a pine with low branches.

Perhaps he was mistaken about Cooper. A lot of horses must have the same markings as the one Cooper bought in Austin.

But a few minutes' surveillance convinced him the man who'd ambushed him was nearby. The roughly dressed men he was watching were peppering another man with questions, and that man had a different style of clothing, more fitting for business in town, though it wasn't particularly fashionable. The big tipoff was his speech. Ryland had heard that accent many times while searching for the Cooper children in eastern New York.

He couldn't make out most of their words, but at one point he heard Cooper say distinctly, "All I want is to find my daughter. If she's at this killer's house, let me get her out safely before you do your duty."

Ryland thought about that. Killer? Duty? Sounded like

Cooper was hitching up with the wrong people. These must be ones involved in the shooting he'd heard. And Molly Weaver was somewhere in the middle of that?

Time to sneak away, before someone spotted him. Soldiers usually posted a guard. He was surprised he'd approached this close without being seen.

A thought struck him as he wove his way quietly between their mounts. He could sabotage Cooper's horse somehow.

No, that wasn't right. Cooper wanted to keep Molly safe as much as Ryland did.

But if he did something to slow the others down ...

Ryland took his throwing knife from his pocket and approached the nearest horse, a compact chestnut. His nature wouldn't allow him to hurt the horse, but he could damage the equipment.

The horse grunted and sidestepped as he slid the blade under its belly, but the animal couldn't go very far. Ryland clenched his teeth and painstakingly sliced through the strap that attached the woven girth to the saddle. He moved to a second horse and gave it the same treatment. Better not stay any longer. He pocketed his knife and slunk away, looking frequently over his shoulder.

When he reached Prince and the gray, he held his breath and looked back. He'd actually done it. He'd escaped after pulling his trick without getting caught.

He stroked the gray's neck. Unless this horse had fled from that group of men, it had to belong to a nearby ranch. "All right, fella. What do you say we make a big circle around those men and maybe you can show me and Prince where your home is?"

He swung into Prince's saddle and held the gray's lead line loosely. "Come on, boy. Show us."

The gray merely pulled toward the grass at his feet.

Ryland sighed. "All right, Prince, I guess it's up to us. Where's the nearest ranch?"

He rode slowly away from their hiding place, toward the

road. When they reached the crest of a hill, he looked all around. He could barely make out the line of trees now, where he'd cut the cinch straps. His conscience was already plaguing him. What if he'd delayed the wrong side? And what if they thought Cooper had cut the straps and retaliated against him?

"Too late now." His gaze swept the simmering landscape. This spot wasn't far from the hidden cache he'd found. He thought he saw a wisp of smoke about a mile away from where he now sat. "All right, boys, let's head thataway. Maybe someone over there can help us make sense of this."

MOLLY PLACED HER BEDROLL, satchel, and saddlebags in the bed of the Nolans' wagon. Then she picked up Harry's saddle and set it in by Andrew's and Joe's gear. Her mother's things came next. Joe held the horses' heads while she performed the tasks, stroking them and murmuring endearments. She walked over to him, laying a light hand on Ranger's side and speaking to him as she passed the horse.

"I'm not happy that we'll only have one rider in the saddle."

"Not much we can do about it. Losing Blinker was a hard blow for Andrew." Joe looked over at the dead horse in the corral. "I wish we had time to bury that one, but we'd be foolish to do it, especially when Andrew's not in the best shape."

Molly peered into his eyes. "Do you think he'll be all right?"

"With rest. It sounds like he's already improving over what he was a couple of days ago. But he won't get any rest here. Can you stay with the horses while I help him bring Nolan out?"

"Let me help too."

"I don't like to tie the horses."

"But Andrew might injure himself worse if he lifts a heavy load like that."

Joe eyed the paint horse critically. "Harry's stayed calm so far."

"I could drive them around the yard once, and you watch. If Harry doesn't spook, we should be all right on the road."

"I guess that's sensible." Joe glanced at the house. "Yeah, let's do it."

Molly climbed to the wagon seat, and Joe helped her gather the four reins. She had driven a single horse now and then in Ohio but had only driven a team a couple of times. She wove the reins between her fingers carefully while Joe held Harry's bridle. She hauled in a big breath. "Let them go."

Joe released the team, and she made a clicking sound. "Up, boys!"

Ranger set out, and Harry matched his step. Both pulled against the evener between the team and the wagon. Molly couldn't help grinning. She drove them off onto the grass and took the wagon in a circle around the well and back to Joe, where he stood in front of the house.

"Whoa." She pulled back gently, and both horses stopped.

"Good job." Joe stepped up to pat the animals' noses, and Molly wasn't sure whether he was praising her or them.

"We'll be fine," she said. "I can drive, and Andrew can sit beside me as guard. Ma and Sophie can sit in the back with Mr. Nolan." It would be close quarters, with three saddles and everyone's packs, but they could do it.

Joe helped her down. "I'll tell them we're ready. You're a peach, Molly."

She blinked up at him, too startled to speak.

Joe was still holding her hand. He squeezed it gently. "Stay alert."

"I've got my gun." She wore the revolver in plain sight on her sash, in case the marauders returned.

Joe hurried inside, and she moved to the front of the team and talked quiet nonsense to the horses as she scratched Ranger's brow and beneath Harry's chin.

A couple of minutes later, her mother came out carrying several blankets and a pillow.

"I'm to make a pallet for Mr. Nolan, and the men will bring him out."

"Need help?" Molly asked.

She shook her head and clambered over the back end of the wagon.

A sudden flurry of hoofbeats yanked Molly's attention toward the road. Several horses appeared and slowed, clustering at the end of the lane. Molly's heart lurched.

"Ma, get down!"

Her mother opened her mouth then looked past Molly toward the road. Without a word, she flattened herself in the wagon bed.

Options flashed through Molly's mind. She couldn't run inside, leaving the horses loose and unattended. She could try to tie them to the corral fence, but would the outlaws shoot them as they had Nolan's horse?

A third course seemed better. She jumped onto the wagon and stretched for the reins. One fell down at Harry's side, but she had a firm hold on the other three.

"Stay down, Ma!" she snapped the reins against the horses' rumps and clucked. They moved forward, jerking the wagon. She concentrated on the lines that controlled Ranger and turned him as tightly as she could across the grass, to the far end of the house and around it.

Behind the building, she hauled back on the lines. "Ho, now!"

Ranger stopped immediately, and Harry jostled him but halted as well.

"What are you doing?"

She glanced over her shoulder. Ma was kneeling on the pile of blankets.

"I wanted to get the horses out of sight, in case they started shooting."

"Are those the men who attacked before?"

"I don't know, but it seems likely." Molly wrapped the ends of the reins around the brake lever.

"Maybe you should just drive away. It might save the horses."

Molly was tempted, but she shook her head. "Andrew and Joe might need us. I don't want to abandon them here. You don't have a gun, do you?"

"I left our shotgun inside."

"Pray, Ma."

After a moment, her mother said, "See that boarded-up window? That's in the Nolans' bedroom. Maybe we could tear away the boards and get in that way."

"Our friends might think we were outlaws and shoot us. Come on." Molly jumped down and ran to the back of the wagon. Ranger had ground tied faithfully for Joe throughout their journey, and she hoped he'd stay true now. Her mother scrambled to meet her, and Molly took her arm and helped her to the ground. "Stay behind me."

Ma nodded.

Molly drew her revolver and crept to the end of the house. As they tiptoed along it toward the front, hoofbeats thudded on the dirt lane. Reaching the front corner, Molly peered around it. The lead riders were about halfway between the road and the house.

"Run!" Molly scurried toward the front door, keeping her gun pointed toward the intruders. Behind her, Ma panted.

"Hold it right there, missy!" The leader stopped his horse and raised a rifle, aiming it toward Molly.

She stopped, her heart hammering, but kept the handgun pointed in his direction.

"What do you want?" she managed to call out in a squeaky voice.

The bearded man surveyed her for a long moment. "We want Albert Nolan. Have you got him in there?"

She sensed movement to her left and glanced toward the door. A rifle barrel poked through a three-inch opening along the doorjamb.

"Get out of here," Joe growled.

The rider let off a shot, and Ma screamed.

Molly caught a quick breath, steadied her aim, and fired. The canteen hanging from the man's saddle sprouted a leak, and his horse snorted and shied to the side.

"We've got women and injured folks in there!" Molly was angry now, and her strong voice had returned.

"We don't want to kill any women," the man said. His followers edged their horses closer to his. All of them wielded weapons.

Molly hauled in a deep breath and squared her shoulders. "Are you Mr. MacKenzie?"

He frowned and held up a hand to stop his men from crowding closer.

"I'm only one person, but I'm a good shot, mister," Molly said. "Your men might shoot me down, but I'll kill you first if they try. Now, tell me what you want with Nolan."

"How do you know my name?"

She gave a tight smile. She'd thought that might rattle him, the way Ben Cooper had rattled her by using her name when she had no idea who he was.

"I heard your brother was killed in the war, and you were out to avenge him."

"He wasn't killed in the war. He was murdered. And Nolan's the one who did it."

"You got proof?"

"Yeah, I've got witnesses. Two of these men were there. Nolan was under arrest for desertion. He escaped, but he killed my brother on his way out and stole a horse."

Two witnesses. Molly looked beyond him, at the other men's faces. They all looked scruffy and dirty, as if they'd been on the trail for months. All but one. She stared at the fellow in the background.

"Ma."

"What?" Ma whispered, inching closer to her.

Without looking away from the men, Molly said, "Can you

see that man in the back? The one on the bay with the white strip on its nose?"

Her mother stirred. After several seconds she said incredulously, "Is that Cooper?"

RYLAND TROTTED ALONG, trying to let the gray horse choose their path, but the gelding seemed more interested in grazing. He wanted to be angry with the horse, but that wouldn't do him any good. Maybe the poor, dumb animal wasn't from around here after all, so he wasn't eager to return home.

He kept on, roughly toward where he'd seen the wisp of smoke. It was gone now, as though someone had let the fire in their stove go out. He couldn't blame them. It was too hot to cook. As he guided the two horses along, he drooped in the saddle. When this business was over, he wanted a warm bath and a soft bed.

A shot rang out, not too far ahead, and then another. He sucked in a shaky breath.

"Seems they're at it again, Prince." Instantly, he was more cautious, more aware of his surroundings. He rode forward slowly, pausing frequently to listen. Soon he heard faint voices.

"I think I'll leave you boys here." He dismounted and tied the gray to a stunted tree, hoping Prince would stay near his companion. They weren't far from that ranch house, he was certain now.

He crept toward the muted voices, ducking low and seeking cover wherever he could. At last, he was looking at the back of an outbuilding, and beyond it he could see the edge of a small house. He slipped closer and hugged the wall of the board shed.

Slipping along the wall, he came to a corner and squinted as he peered around it. Half a dozen mounted men filled the house's dooryard. They all look unkempt and road weary. Except one. Ryland eyed the better dressed man cowering behind the others. That horse. Yes, that was the one. How did they get ahead of him? "I shouldn't be surprised with all the dawdling that gray horse did," he muttered.

Their leader was talking to someone outside Ryland's sight. He leaned a little farther past the corner and caught his breath. Two women stood in front of the house, and one was aiming a revolver at the big, bearded man at the front of the pack.

"We're not going to give you Nolan so you can kill him," she yelled.

"Even if he's a murderer?"

"No. If you want him, you need to go get some lawmen. A sheriff or some of those state police they've got now. Bring them here to get him, and we'll hand him over."

The horses shuffled.

Ryland was sure his gasp was loud enough to be heard by the men, but perhaps their horses' shifting covered it. Could that young woman possibly be Molly Weaver? And the woman beside her, dressed in black ...probably Emma Weaver. He couldn't let any two women, but especially these two, get caught up in violence. "What can I do?" he said softly. Prince wasn't there to ask, and he wouldn't answer, anyway. "Lord God, give me some wisdom here."

From this angle, he noted that a couple of the horses' saddles seemed to have lengths of twine hanging from the girths. So much for his prank, cutting the cinches. It had hardly slowed them down at all. If they were going to get rough, he'd have to do something more drastic.

Ryland fingered the hilt of the knife in his pocket.

21

"Molly, you need to get inside," Joe said through the crack at the doorway.

She startled, as though she'd forgotten he was there. "I don't think he'll let me. Ma, you go in."

"I won't leave you alone out here."

"He's talking to me," Molly said. "As long as he's talking, they're not shooting. Go behind me."

She was only about four steps from the door, but Emma was beyond her. Molly took a step forward, and Joe caught his breath. Of course, she was trying to protect her mother and give her room to pass between her and the wall. What about protecting herself? They'd seen enough violence. If Molly was hurt today, he'd never recover.

Emma bent down and scuttled toward him.

Joe opened the door a few more inches. "Come on, Emma!"

She looked plaintively toward her daughter. "But Molly—"

Joe grabbed her forearm and yanked her inside. At least one of them was comparatively safe now.

"Go into the storeroom with Sophie."

Emma pulled her arm away. "All right, I will, but Cooper is out there with them."

"Cooper?" He studied her face. Emma was certain. "I'll tell Andrew. You get in with Sophie."

"What about Mr. Nolan?"

"Ask Sophie."

Emma frowned at him, but Joe didn't have the heart to tell her the rancher had slipped out of the world moments after she'd carried the blankets outside. Sophie had come from the bedroom with tears streaking her pale cheeks and announced to him and Andrew that her husband was dead.

Joe hurried to Andrew's side, where he crouched beside the gaping front window.

"We've got to get Molly in too," Andrew said.

"Why don't we just tell them about Nolan?"

Andrew took a slow breath. "Probably the best way out of this."

"They may demand proof. And Andrew, that Cooper fellow's with them."

For the first time, Andrew looked away from the window. "The one who says he's Molly's pa?"

Joe nodded. "He's hanging back behind them, but it's him."

Andrew edged toward the doorway, and Joe stood. A bullet whizzed past his ear, and the report of a gun thundered. Joe dove to the floor, panic surging through him.

Andrew looked toward him, and Joe gave a little wave to signal that he was unhurt. Crouching by the doorjamb, Andrew pulled the door inward a few inches.

"Molly," he whispered, and then louder, "Molly, get in here quick."

"They'll kill us all if I do," came Molly's muffled voice.

"Nolan's dead," Andrew said. "Tell them."

Joe rose cautiously and peered from the bottom corner of the window hole. His pulse rocketed as one of the riders lit a match and set fire to a stick with a rag bundled around the end. The rag must have been soaked in kerosene or some other fuel, because instantly the stick became a flaring torch.

"Andrew! They're going to burn us out!" Joe ducked down and stared at his friend.

This time, Andrew yelled. "Tell them, Molly! They're going to burn the house."

After a moment, Molly's voice rang out, strong but with a slight tremor. "Let us be! Albert Nolan is dead."

Another shot boomed. She gave a squeal and dove over the threshold, landing prone at Andrew's feet and rolling away from the door still holding her revolver. Several bullets crashed into the wall. Joe flattened himself on the floor and covered his head.

"Get in the storeroom," Andrew yelled.

Joe reached toward Molly. "No! There's no window in there. If they set the house on fire, you won't be able to get out."

"They said they didn't want to hurt women." Molly's voice quavered.

Joe shook his head. "I guess they're all liars."

All was quiet for a moment, then he heard hoofbeats. They came closer. Joe wanted to look, but he didn't want to get his head blown off. Instead, he crawled to Molly and covered her head and shoulders with his upper body.

"Lie flat."

"They'll burn us."

"We'll see."

"Pray, Joe," she choked out.

Shouting broke out in the dooryard, and then another flurry of hoofbeats. It sounded as if they were retreating. Had they thrown torches at the house and fled?

Andrew crawled to the door and rose to his knees, peering outside through an inch-wide opening.

"Joe, come look!"

Joe scrambled over to him on all fours. "What is it? What did they do?" He looked over Andrew's shoulder.

The yard in front of the doorstone was empty. Five horsemen tore toward the road, with a riderless horse following several yards behind.

On the ground lay a solitary man. From his back protruded a knife, buried to the hilt.

"What—"

Slowly, Andrew stood and opened the door. "Looks like someone was fighting on our side." He stepped out, and Joe followed.

Beside the fallen man, the torch laying smoldering in the dirt, putting off foul-smelling smoke. Andrew kicked at it, then stomped on it with his boot until it lay quite harmless beside the man.

Joe knelt and felt for a pulse. "I think he's dead."

Andrew grabbed the man's shoulder, and together they rolled him onto his side.

"He's the one I saw light the torch," Joe said.

"Yeah, but who killed him?"

"Someone must have thrown the knife from behind."

Andrew stared bleakly at him. "Maybe it was Cooper."

"I guess he might have done it, to protect Molly."

Joe shook his head, trying to reconcile that with what he'd seen.

They both looked around the yard. Nothing stirred except Firefly, in the corral. She gave a shrill whinny. The riders were gone, with only a cloud of dust hovering over the road to testify they'd been there. That and the body at their feet.

The door's hinges creaked. Molly came out first, then her mother and Sophie. They all stood gazing at the man on the ground.

Emma turned to her son. "Who did this?"

"We don't know."

Joe frowned toward the road. "Maybe Cooper. But he rode off with them."

"It doesn't make sense," Andrew said.

"Whoever it was, he saved our lives." Molly looked down at her right hand and raised her revolver, staring at it as if she'd never seen it before. She pulled in a breath and holstered it.

Sophie let out a sob, and Emma sidled up to her and put an arm around her. "There, dear. You go ahead and cry."

"Is it true about Mr. Nolan?" Molly asked.

"He's gone," Emma confirmed.

Molly let out a long sigh. "I'm sorry, Mrs. Nolan. For all of this."

Sophie's weeping became a torrent, and Emma turned her toward the house.

"Let's go inside, dear. You need to sit down."

Joe looked all around the yard once more, unable to believe it was over. A flicker of movement drew his attention to the well, and a man rose slowly, behind the stone wall that protected the water supply.

"Are they gone?" he asked.

Joe stared at him. On either side, he could feel Molly and Andrew's shock peeling off them.

"Who are you?" he called.

The man stepped around the well and walked slowly toward them. He wore a black suit of good quality fabric, smeared with dirt. His outfit included a necktie and a hat that might grace the head of a banker.

He stopped two yards in front of Joe. "My name is Atkins."

"You weren't one of them," Molly said.

"No. I stumbled into your predicament, I'm afraid. I wouldn't have taken such actions if I hadn't seen they intended to kill all of you. I don't know who this MacKenzie was, or the man Nolan you say is dead, but—well, it appeared you were good folk and could use a helping hand."

Andrew's brow wrinkled. "That's your knife, then? You threw it?"

Atkins peered down at the fallen man and the knife protruding from his back. "I didn't ... is he dead?"

"He is," Joe said.

Atkins swallowed hard. "That wasn't my intent. I thought perhaps I could hit his arm and make him drop the torch.

Throwing a blade is a skill I acquired earlier in my travels. I don't carry a gun, you see, and a stagecoach tender told me I needed a weapon on the trail." His voice trailed off, and his face looked a little green. "I really killed him, then."

Joe let out a puff of breath and glanced at the Weaver siblings. "I'm afraid so, but you saved all our lives in doing it. Mr. Atkins, we're getting ready to leave this place, but I think we could all do with a cup of coffee and a little something to eat first. Come on inside."

"I wouldn't like to disturb the ladies." Atkins's anxious gaze flitted to the splintered door. "And of course, those miscreants might come back."

"They might. We'd best rearm you." Joe bent and pulled the knife from the dead man's back. He looked it over, eyeing the molded hilt and the razor-sharp blade. "Nice weapon."

"Thank you." His voice quavered when he looked at it.

Joe stooped and wiped the blade on the grass near the doorstone.

Atkins accepted his mostly clean blade. "I also noticed that Benjamin Cooper was with those outlaws."

"You know him?" Joe's hand moved toward his holstered sidearm.

"No. Never met him." Atkins added with a rueful smile, "At least, not face to face. Did he speak to you?"

"Earlier today, but not while they were here."

Molly stepped forward. "Please come in, Mr. Atkins. We have a lot to discuss before we leave here."

"Er, if I may ask, what are your plans when you decamp?"

Joe eyed him closely. "Maybe we should be asking about *your* plans."

Atkins nodded. "Fair enough. I assure you, I have no bad intentions. I will explain everything to you, but it may take a few minutes."

Andrew raised his chin. "Joe and I have ranches near Austin. We plan to go back there. My mother and my sister will accompany us." He flicked a glance toward the house. "Of course, we've got Nolan to attend to now."

Joe nudged the fallen outlaw with his boot. "And this fellow."

"Perhaps I can help with the—er—digging," Atkins said.

MOLLY WATCHED the newcomer as she and her mother fixed coffee for the group and took the cornbread, apples, and biscuits they'd packed out of the food box. Sophie had left her soup stock on the stove, and it was beginning to smell like a palatable meal.

Atkins puzzled her. Like Cooper, he'd shown up out of nowhere. But he was different from Cooper. Very different. Not just younger. He was more polite, and he seemed credible.

When the coffee was ready, her mother leaned close to her and whispered, "Go tell Mrs. Nolan we have refreshment. She may want to stay by her husband's side, but I don't want to neglect her."

Molly hurried to the bedroom door and tapped lightly.

"Come in."

She opened the door. Molly had expected to find Sophie weeping beside the bed where her dead husband lay. Instead, she was sorting through some clothing and laying some items on a chair. She met Molly's gaze.

"What are we going to do now?"

"The men are planning to—to bury Mr. Nolan, if that's what you wish." Molly was sure Sophie would want that. Any alternatives were repellant to even think about. Still, they had to hear her say it.

"Of course."

"And the dead man outside. They'll take care of him too. Joe says he'll check the man's pockets to see if he has anything on him that will identify him."

Sophie's features sharpened. "He's not that MacKenzie's brother, is he?"

"No, he's one of his companions."

"Do you think they'll come back? Because if they do, and they demand proof of Albert's death after we've buried him, what will we tell them?"

Molly clenched her teeth and thought about that. "We can talk that over with the others, but I think they'll have to take our word for it. That and the fresh graves of Mr. Nolan and their friend."

Sophie held her gaze. "Let's pray they don't return."

"Yes. We're all doing that."

With a quick nod, Sophie turned to the clothing she'd sorted. "I unpacked Albert's things. I thought perhaps your brother and Mr. Noyes could use some of them. His shirts and his boots, perhaps. Anything that would be useful for them. Of course, Mr. Noyes is taller than my husband."

"That's kind of you, Sophie. Why don't you come sit down for a few minutes and have a bite to eat? We can talk about all this later."

When they entered the outer room, Andrew jumped up and offered his chair to Sophie.

"Thank you." She walked slowly to it and sat down.

Mr. Atkins rose and relinquished his chair to Molly. He and Andrew leaned against the bullet-riddled wall, holding their mismatched mugs.

"That's good coffee, Mrs. Weaver," Atkins said, lifting his cup a little in Ma's direction.

"Thank you," Ma said. "I don't wish to be nosy, Mr. Atkins, but we all have reason to be wary of strangers. Would you be so good as to tell us why you're here? You tell us you've spoken with Mr. Harry Weston in Austin, where we bought my horse, and yet, now you're down here. That seems more than coincidental."

Atkins drew in a deep breath and looked around at them all. "It is, Mrs. Weaver. It's deliberate. I admit, I was hoping to find you and your daughter. But I assure you, it is for good purposes. I mean you no harm."

"Does it have anything to do with Mr. Cooper?" Molly asked.

"Not directly, no." Atkins cleared his throat. "There is much to be done here, and rather than take up time and waste daylight, perhaps Mr. Noyes, Mr. Weaver, and I should get about the business of digging graves. You ladies, if you're willing, can prepare the bodies. And I will tell you all about my mission—my most benign mission, I assure you—once this is all settled."

Joe pushed back his chair. "That sounds reasonable. We can't leave them here unburied."

Sophie sobbed.

Ma reached for Sophie's hand. "Is there anything you'd like to do for your Albert, other than bury him here?"

Shaking her head, Sophie choked out, "No. Let us lay him to rest here on his ranch."

"We buried one of the outlaws behind the shed," Andrew ventured.

Sophie looked up. "There's another grave, nearer to the stream."

"The hired hand who ... who died?" Andrew asked.

She nodded.

"If you tell us where it is, we'll go out there now and get started."

Tears flooded Sophie's eyes and spilled down her flushed cheeks. "Thank you all. Andrew, you've been so kind to us."

Molly set down her cup. "You'll need someone to stand guard while you dig. I'll come along."

Mr. Atkins glanced at Andrew. "I can help, and your brother can stand guard, Miss Weaver. I understand he was recently injured. Perhaps you can stay here with your mother and Mrs. Nolan, and we three men can—"

"That sounds good," Joe put in quickly. "Molly, if they come back while we're busy, you shoot three times. We'll come back at once."

"I hate to waste ammunition." She quirked an eyebrow at Joe.

"My husband has plenty in the storeroom," Sophie said. "I was going to make sure we packed it all up to take away with us. You should all take some, if it will fit your guns. And use Albert's guns too. They'll give you extra protection without reloading."

"That's settled then." Joe turned to Andrew. "You know where there's a spade?"

"I sure do."

"Oh, there's one other thing," Atkins said, and they all turned to gaze at him. "I found a horse running loose. He's tethered with my own mount a short distance away."

"What kind of horse?" Andrew had an edge to his voice.

"A nice, healthy gray gelding that—"

"Blinker!"

"Praise God," Ma cried, grinning broadly.

The three men went out together and Molly exhaled. Her mother was already clearing the table.

"Sophie, what do you wish to do next?" Molly asked. "Will you go with us?"

Ma turned with mugs in her hands. "Surely you won't stay here alone, child?"

"I ... I think I'd like to come with you." Sophie's bloodshot eyes sought Emma. "If it's not too much trouble. At least to Austin. I may be able to find a place to stay there. At least I can send a telegram to my family back in Arkansas."

"That sounds like a good plan." Emma smiled at her and carried the dishes to the worktable. "Oh, dear, did we already pack the dishpan?"

"I'll get it from the wagon." Molly hurried to the door.

"Oh, and the horses. We mustn't leave them standing for hours while we take care of—you know." Her mother's face once more sported lines of worry.

"I'll unhitch them and water them. Should I take the harness off?"

"No, I think the men still plan to leave here today."

Molly hurried out to where the horses stood patiently. She was glad the dead outlaw's body had been removed. She found the dishpan and took it inside.

"I've put water on to heat for the dishes," her mother said. "Meanwhile, Mrs. Nolan and I will prepare her husband's body and finish packing up their things. You can mind the horses and keep watch."

Outside once more, Molly found Ryland Atkins riding toward her on a nondescript horse that was two shades too dull to call a palomino. Behind him, he was leading Andrew's gray.

"You can leave them here, and I'll give them some water," she said. "I can't tell you what it will mean to my brother to have Blinker back."

Atkins smiled and dismounted. "I'm so glad I was able to catch him. There was another horse, but it galloped off."

"I think that one belonged to the outlaw they shot."

"Ah." He put the reins and the lead rope in her hands. "This is Prince, and I guess you know Blinker."

"Not really, but I'm pleased to make his acquaintance."

Atkins went off around the house to find the other two men. Molly watered Prince and Blinker and tied them to the fence. Then she untied Firefly and led her to the well. Ranger and Harry shuffled their feet and pawed the ground. Blinker responded with a whinny. Firefly lifted her head, flinging water drops at Molly, and neighed.

"Easy, girl." Molly patted her silky neck. "I guess you're glad to see Blinker. I'll see if I can get you something to eat, and in a little while, we'll all head home." Firefly stretched her neck downward and greedily gulped more water from the trough. Andrew's ranch. Home. That sounded good.

22

Andrew watched as Joe uncovered his tin can cache with Albert Nolan's spade. The women and Mr. Atkins waited at the roadside, forty yards away.

"Thanks for doing that, Joe."

"I could tell you were hurtin'. I shouldn't have let you help with the graves." Joe turned another spadeful of earth.

"I wanted to get out of there fast, so's we can make it at least as far as the Swansons' before full dark."

Joe glanced up at the sky. "We'll be cutting it close. But Ed Swanson's a good man. He'll let us camp near his house and probably take in all the ladies."

"Molly's tough." Andrew gave him a crooked smile. "If there's not enough beds, she'll sleep in the wagon."

"She's a good sport." Joe paused and wiped a sleeve across his brow. "Do you think she'll make a good rancher?"

"Or a good rancher's wife." Andrew chuckled at Joe's startled expression. "Come on, Joe. I've seen the way you look at her."

If his friend's face wasn't already red from exertion, Andrew would have thought he blushed.

"She's a fine woman. Rides, shoots, cooks." Joe bent to the

task again, and his next shovelful of dirt turned up the peach can. "There you go."

Crouching by the shallow hole, Andrew lifted it from the dirt and bent the lid up, careful not to cut himself on the edge, where he'd opened it with his knife a few days ago. Atkins had told him about the note he'd written, so Andrew wasn't surprised when a folded paper came out with his pouch of money.

"Looks like it's all here."

"I'll take it."

Andrew and Joe jerked around to find Ben Cooper standing a few feet away in the shade of a stunted tree, aiming a pistol squarely at Andrew's chest.

"Thought you rode off with MacKenzie and his men," Joe said.

Amazed at his friend's calm, Andrew pulled in a breath. "What do you want, Mr. Cooper? Because I don't think my sorry little bit of money is the reason you came all the way to Texas."

Cooper smiled and took a step forward. "Nope, you're not one of mine. Both my boys had blue eyes. Cornflower blue like Janie's. Like their mother's. I had to know if you were Zeph or Elijah, but you're not."

Andrew clenched his teeth to keep back a vicious reply.

"Is that gang hiding someplace, ready to ambush us again?" Joe asked.

"No, we parted ways. They figured the little lady was telling the truth and that Nolan character they wanted is dead. They'd already lost two of their band and didn't want to lose any more. I left their company and came back to make sure Janie was all right."

"Janie?" Andrew frowned.

"Your sister. Molly. Now, hand over the money, kid. You're right, it's not what I came for, but I could use a little cash to ease my travels."

Joe couldn't let it go at that. "What *did* you come for? And don't tell me you love your daughter. Your twenty years of neglect say different—and that's assuming you really *are* her father. I'm not sure I believe it."

"Oh, you can believe it all right." Cooper smiled almost apologetically. "I ran into some bad luck in New Jersey and figured it was time to turn elsewhere. Thought I'd go home— back to Brooklyn. With a little digging, I managed to learn who took in my baby girl. Ohio seemed as good a place as any, so I went there."

"And learned Mr. Weaver had died, and that the family had recently sold a valuable business. Is that about it? You started trailing the widow, hoping to profit from your travels?"

"You think me crass, Mr. Noyes?" Cooper's features hardened. "Hand over the money. Now."

"Drop the gun, Cooper."

Andrew whirled toward the road. Molly stood ten feet behind Cooper with her revolver aimed squarely at his back.

Cooper didn't bother to look. He smiled.

"Oh, come now, Janie dear. You wouldn't shoot your dear old father."

"Wouldn't I just? You're a liar and a thief, and who knows what more? Drop the gun now or your spine will have a hole in it."

Joe moved aside a couple of steps, but Andrew's feet seemed glued to the ground.

"Drop it *now*," Molly said.

With a sigh, Cooper stooped and laid his pistol on the ground at his feet.

"Now step to your left. Four steps. Get moving."

Cooper edged sideways with a reluctant glance at his weapon.

"Andrew, pick up his gun."

He swallowed hard and followed his sister's instructions.

"Now, hand it to Joe," Molly said. "We don't know but what he's got another hidden in his clothes."

"Oh, come on!" Cooper threw his hands in the air.

"Uh-uh. You hold still." Molly's voice was so stern, Andrew

certainly would have obeyed her. Cooper seemed to consider it and took the prudent course.

Andrew walked over to Joe and gave him Cooper's gun.

"Unload that, Joe," Molly said. "It's a dangerous land we're in, and I won't take his weapon away from him."

Joe opened the action and removed all the cartridges.

"You can't leave me with just an empty gun," Cooper protested.

"Sure we can. We'll leave you one bullet a mile down the road under a rock." Molly jerked her head, signaling Joe to give Cooper back the handgun.

Joe hesitated. "Don't you think we'd do better to turn him over to the law?"

Molly huffed out a breath. "What do you think, Andrew?"

"It would mean hauling him all the way to Austin with us." That would be tiresome, if nothing worse. He arched his eyebrows. "We could ask the others what they think."

"Go tell them," Molly said. "Joe and I will watch him."

Andrew needed only a few minutes to explain the situation. Emma and Atkins had seen Cooper's arrival but had stayed back with Sophie under Molly's instructions.

"He tried to rob you," Emma said.

His mother had aged, Andrew thought. She needed some sleep, not restless nights worrying about Cooper.

"What's the alternative?" Atkins asked. "Just let him go?"

"I suppose so."

Atkins shook his head. "He may have *tried* to rob you, but he succeeded in robbing me, and he whacked me over the head. If Prince hadn't got away from him, I'd be without horse, money, or weapons, back at your ranch. He stole my watch and what funds I had in my wallet. I'm glad I had a bit of common sense and left some of my cash in the saddlebags."

"We should take him in." Sophie's voice startled them, and they all turned to look at her. "He was with the men who killed my husband. He may not have pulled the trigger, but he associated with them."

Andrew looked at Atkins and his mother.

"We'll take him," Atkins said. "I'll help watch him."

Ma nodded. "Go tell Molly. And somebody keep an eye on him while he fetches his horse. Then we can tie him up in the wagon."

FIVE DAYS LATER, Andrew drove the wagon down the streets of Austin and stopped in front of the sheriff's office. He climbed down wearily and offered a hand to Sophie Nolan to help her down.

After the first night in the Swansons' yard with Cooper tied up in their barn, they'd made their way as quickly as they could directly to Austin. Several miles back, Andrew and Atkins had unhitched Ranger from the wagon and sent Joe, Molly, and Emma to the ranches.

Since Andrew had put his mother on Blinker, he was left with only Cooper's bay, Prince, and Harry, so Andrew warily put the harness on the bay. Hitched beside Harry, the bay didn't fidget, and both horses seemed to accept their lot. They'd probably been friends when they were both at Weston's livery, Molly had said. Andrew didn't know, but he was glad they didn't make a fuss. Atkins rode beside the wagon on Prince, with Cooper trussed up in the wagon bed.

"Well, we made it." Atkins climbed slowly from the saddle.

"Yeah," Andrew said, arching his back to stretch. "Don't care if I never have to go anywhere again. At least, not for a long time."

"How are you doing, Mrs. Nolan?" Atkins asked.

"Much better now that we're safely here. I suppose I'll need to tell the sheriff everything before I look for a place to stay."

"We'll help you find a place," Atkins said.

Andrew smiled at her. "Don't worry, Sophie. We won't leave you until we know you're settled in a good place."

During the long trip, he'd had several chances to sit on the wagon seat with Sophie or lounge with her beside the campfire and talk. Her bruises had faded, and he'd found himself extremely interested in her. The whole group liked her and wanted to see her settled where she could start a new life, but Andrew's interest went deeper. He imagined that Sophie's future might be entwined with his own.

But it was too soon. Molly had agreed when he'd confided in her. "Give her some time to get used to things," she'd counseled. "She was under that man's thumb for quite some time. She may just want to be independent for a change."

Andrew couldn't argue with that. Hadn't he wanted to go off on his own and see what he could make of himself?

But Sophie was ...

All right, she was a couple of years older than he was. But she was a sweet-natured woman, and she knew how to make do with short resources. She feared God. That was important. Molly was right about her subservience to Nolan, though. Andrew would wait a while. Give her a chance to get used to being free of him.

"The sheriff might be able to tell us about a respectable boardinghouse," Ryland said.

Andrew smiled. "Right, or the lady at the post office. She'd know a place."

In the wagon bed, Cooper wriggled against his restraints. "Would you get me out of this infernal wagon?"

"Gladly." Andrew put down the tailboard and climbed into the wagon bed. The sooner they were rid of this bird, the better.

The door to the office opened, and a man emerged.

"Deputy," Ryland said, stepping toward him. "I'm Ryland Atkins. We spoke when I was here a couple of weeks ago."

"I remember." The deputy eyed the bound man in the back of the wagon. "What have you got here?"

"We brought you a man we apprehended at a ranch some

distance from here." Ryland looked toward Andrew. "I'm not sure if it happened in Travis County, but this man assaulted me at Mr. Weaver's ranch not far from here and then followed Weaver's family until they found Andrew."

"Cooper's a thief, and he was with a gang of outlaws that attacked a ranch and killed the owner. This woman's husband." Andrew reached for Sophie and nudged her forward.

The deputy's eyes widened. "Seems like we ought to get a statement. Let's take the prisoner inside and get him locked up. I'm sure the sheriff will want to speak to all of you."

They sat in the sheriff's office for over an hour, going over and over the events of the past ten days. Sophie confirmed much of Andrew's story, and he gave the sheriff detailed directions to the Nolan ranch and described the location of the graves they'd left there. Nothing was said about Albert Nolan's violence toward his wife. They hadn't discussed it, but Andrew knew without asking that Sophie wouldn't want it mentioned.

He wrote out an account of the siege for the sheriff. The lawman hadn't asked Sophie to write one, which was a relief in a way, but Andrew felt he was underestimating Sophie. Because she was a woman, was her word worth less than his? On the other hand, maybe this way, she'd never be called to testify against Cooper in court, or MacKenzie and his bunch, if they were ever caught. Meanwhile, Atkins wrote out an account of his part in the adventure.

The sheriff sighed and looked down at the papers they'd written. "Atkins, you say Cooper bushwhacked you and stole your watch and some money?"

"Yes, sir," Ryland replied. "We found my watch in his pocket when we captured him."

"That was while he was trying to rob me at gunpoint," Andrew put in.

"And that happened out to Weaver's place, in this county?"

Ryland nodded gravely. "Yes, sir, he assaulted and robbed me there."

"All right, that there's enough for me to hold him on, since it happened in my jurisdiction. I'll see what I can find out about the rest of it. It's hard these days. Some counties have got no law. Some have got police, and some have appointed constables. But we'll do what we can. Now, Mrs. Nolan ..." He turned to face Sophie.

"Yes, sir?"

"What are your plans? Are you going back to that there ranch?"

"I don't want to. We buried my husband, and I'd like to find work and a place to stay here. Eventually, I might want to go back to Arkansas. I have two brothers there, and some cousins. But mostly I'd like to start over. Texas was not ... kind to me."

The sheriff nodded. "You got a place to stay?"

Sophie shook her head.

"We'd appreciate it if you could recommend a decent place for Mrs. Nolan," Andrew said. "A boardinghouse, maybe, or a widow who wants a female companion?"

The sheriff nodded. "The Landons on Bowie Street let rooms. That would be a good place to start. Ma'am, I'd appreciate it if you stuck around for a few days while we try to sort this out, or at least let me know if you're going someplace else."

"I'll do that," Sophie said.

"Oh, and you say your husband owned the ranch?"

"That's right." She lifted her pocketbook. "I have the deed here."

"Well, hang on to it. Once this is settled, you can get an agent to sell it for you."

They walked outside, and Andrew helped her up to the wagon seat.

"To the boardinghouse?" Ryland asked.

"Yes, I'd like to get Sophie settled there."

Ryland nodded. "I want to send a telegram to my employer, if you don't mind, and perhaps drop a quick note to our client."

"Fine. You can go on out to the ranch when you finish, if you want. I think I'd better stop at the post office and the general store. Ma probably won't find much to cook with at my place right now." Since he hadn't bought any cattle, Andrew had a fair amount of money on him. He wouldn't stint on buying supplies.

"That reminds me," Ryland said with a rueful smile. "I'm nearly out of funds. I'll ask my employer to wire me something at the bank here, and when I get it, I'd like to contribute to the expenses. You and your mother have fed us all the way here from Nolan's."

"I would as well," Sophie said.

"First of all, thank you, Ryland." Andrew eyed Sophie sternly. "As to you, no. You'll need whatever your husband left you. And besides, you contributed this wagon. What do you want me to do with it?"

Sophie's forehead wrinkled. "I have no use for it now. I don't have a horse. If you or Mr. Noyes can use it, please take it."

"We could do that," Andrew said, "but Joe and I each have a wagon. Maybe I can sell it for you at the livery."

"Oh, that's kind of you. Thank you."

Andrew nodded. "I'll take it out to my place and unload all our stuff and bring it back to the livery as soon as I can. Let's get you to the Landons' now. Ryland, I'll run my errands and meet you back at my place. You know the way."

On the way to the boardinghouse, Andrew started to speak several times and stopped. He hated to leave Sophie alone, but he couldn't invite her to his ranch. He'd have a houseful as it was, and she ought to be where she could look for a job, as she'd said.

But he didn't want to lose track of her. His instincts told him she was a person he wanted to spend more time with. Perhaps a lot of time.

He swallowed hard and guided the horses around a corner onto Bowie Street. What did he really know about her? Not much. She was from Arkansas, and she'd married a violent man. He'd met her at perhaps the worst time of her life. How did he know she'd turn out to be the person he hoped she'd be? A person he could love?

There. He'd admitted it, at least to himself. His empathy toward her had remained platonic at first. After all, she was Nolan's wife. But he hadn't been able to help wishing things were different for Sophie. Now that her husband was dead, could she start a new life with a man who would care for her tenderly and value her as a fine woman and a worthy partner? A man like him?

He gulped. Was he letting his imagination run away with him? If he had any sense, he'd stop that train immediately. But what would stop him from keeping in touch with her? Getting to know her better? If he took it slow and easy ...

"There it is," she said, and he realized she hadn't spoken since they'd left Ryland in front of the sheriff's office.

He pulled the wagon over to the side of the street in front of the boardinghouse.

"Sophie ..."

"Yes?" She lifted her chin and gazed at him.

"Is it all right if I come around in a couple of days and see how you're doing?"

She smiled. "I'd like that."

Andrew nodded. "I ... I'd like to stay in touch. As a friend. And I think you'd like Molly and my ma if you had a chance to know them better."

"I already like them."

He was able to return her smile then. "Who wouldn't?"

"From what bits I've heard, I think your family has some business to settle. Whatever Mr. Atkins came here for."

"Yes." Andrew was sure that matter concerned Cooper somehow, but he wasn't sure how it all fit together. Ryland had asked them if they minded waiting to discuss the matter when only the Weaver family was present—particularly after they had delivered Cooper to the law. "Maybe I can come into town soon and tell you all about it." He frowned. "What day is it, anyhow?"

Sophie gave a musical little laugh. "I'm not sure. I think maybe it's Wednesday."

"Friday, then. Or Sunday. Ma and Molly might want to come into town for church. We could come by here after."

"That would be lovely."

He reached for her hand. "I ... I really like you, Sophie. I don't want any more bad things to happen to you."

She drew in a slow breath. "We can't keep bad things from happening, Andrew. I'm just glad you were there when the worst happened." Tears glistened in her eyes. "I'm not sure how I could have handled it if those evil men had come while Albert and I were alone. I'd likely be dead now."

It was true, but he didn't want to think about that. Instead, he redirected the conversation.

"Do you know what you can do for a job?"

"I thought maybe sewing. Or perhaps I can apply at a mill."

He nodded, wishing he could relieve her of the anxiety puckering her brow. They hadn't discussed her background much —schooling and talents. He hadn't seen a single book in the Nolan house, but that might not mean anything. Honestly, he didn't know much about her. Yes, he needed to do something about that before getting any wild ideas.

"I'll come on Friday, or if anything prevents that, on Sunday for sure."

"Or if we find out today's really Thursday."

She was smiling again. Andrew laughed. He was still holding her hand. How did that happen? He squeezed it gently. "Come on. Let's see if these people have a room for you."

23

Molly held out her arms for the heavy saddlebags Joe handed her. They'd already carried a load inside Andrew's house, and Ma was in the kitchen now, trying to scare up a meal.

"That's it, except for the saddles," Joe said. "Where should I put them?"

"In the shed, I guess."

"Andrew planned to close it in this fall. I hope he can do that."

Molly nodded soberly. "Joe, what will happen if he can't get himself some cattle?"

Joe worked at Firefly's cinch strap, his mouth quirked to one side. "I expect you folks could make it through the winter all right. It mostly stays warm here, but Andrew and I will go into the hills for some firewood."

"I'm sure we could get by over the winter, too, but we'd be using up the money we saved."

Joe pulled her saddle off the mare. "I expect things will settle down soon, and he'll find some stock. People are just upset after the war, and a lot of folks aren't thinking right. They do need to build up their herds, but they'll need to sell some, too, to keep

263

going. Andrew should be able to buy some young stock in the spring, if nothing else."

Hoofbeats coming from the direction of town caught their attention. Molly fumbled for her revolver, since Joe had his hands full with the saddle. Ryland Atkins trotted into view, looking rather jaunty in his suit, riding his dull palomino. He grinned and doffed his hat then rode up close to them.

"Greetings, travelers."

"Is Cooper in jail?" Joe wasn't one to beat around the bush.

"He certainly is, and Andrew's taken Mrs. Nolan to a boardinghouse. Should I put Prince in the corral?"

"Andrew fenced a field behind the house. You can put him there or stake him out." Joe turned toward the shed and took the saddle inside.

Molly looked at the overgrown yard. "There's some grazing out here, but it would be easier to put him out back. I'll show you."

"I remember it. Prince ran out there last week, when Cooper brained me."

Ryland swung down from the saddle. His movements around horses weren't nearly as awkward as they'd seemed when she first met him. She'd been amazed that he'd actually caught Blinker and led him for several miles. Now he looked—almost—like a horseman. He would need more time in the saddle to look like a ranchman, though.

"I expect old Prince would appreciate some time to graze." He began removing his saddle.

While he took care of his mount, Molly carried the saddlebags inside.

"Oh, there you are," Ma said. "I hope there's some food left in what you're carrying, because I have no idea what we'll eat for supper."

"I don't think there's much." Molly slung her burden on the bench by the table and unbuckled one of the pouches. "We could dig up Andrew's cache. There were some beans and coffee in there."

"Let's not do that unless he says to." Ma frowned at the nearly empty coffee sack Molly held out. "We can hope he thinks to buy some supplies before he heads out here."

"He might, but he may not have the wagon. It's Sophie's, remember."

"But most of our things are in it."

"True. I expect he'll bring it here and take it back to her tomorrow."

"Well then, I guess it's a bit of cornmeal mush and coffee all around tonight, and tomorrow we'll have to shop."

Molly held back a groan. Another day on the road, away from the ranch. She'd hoped they could rest tomorrow.

"Mr. Atkins is here."

Ma blinked. "That's good, I suppose, but it's one more mouth to feed."

The door opened as she spoke, and Atkins came in carrying his bedroll and satchel, with Joe close behind.

"What's this about feeding me?"

"Oh, Mr. Atkins, forgive me." Ma's cheeks flushed. "I was just bemoaning our lack of foresight. We should have stopped for some groceries."

"Andrew said he'd stop at the store after he sees Mrs. Nolan settled."

"Wonderful," Emma said.

"That's a relief." Molly smiled at the men. "Sit down, you two. We have enough coffee to fix you about one cup each."

Joe cast a worried glance toward the door. "I think I'd better go check on my stock."

"Do that, and come back for supper," Ma said.

He smiled. "If nothing's amiss, I will, Emma. If I feel like I need to stay home, I'll flag Andrew down when he passes my place and let him know." Joe looked at Atkins. "Oh, and Ryland, you'd probably better bunk at my house tonight. This place is pretty small."

"Thank you. I'd love to be your guest."

Joe nodded and went out.

"Ma, I'll make up the bed." Molly headed for the bedroom. Andrew would have to sleep on the floor, but they'd work things out over the next few days.

A few minutes later, she returned to the main room and found her mother puttering about the stove while Ryland sat at the table, sipping from a steaming mug. She approached him uncertainly.

"Is now a good time to talk, Mr. Atkins? About why you're here, I mean, and that Cooper fellow."

He raised his eyebrows. "First of all, please call me Ryland. Anyone who's camped on the road for near a week together should be on a first-name basis."

"All right, then, Ryland."

"Emma, what do you say?" he asked.

Ma turned around. "Wouldn't it be best to wait for Andrew to get here?"

"Maybe. On the other hand, what I have to say concerns Molly, not Andrew. I think we've established that, while they're both adopted, they're not blood brother and sister."

Emma walked stiffly to the table and pulled out a chair. "All right, let's hear it. I guess my girl's waited long enough."

Molly rounded the table and sat on a stool. What her mother said was an understatement. On their journey, she'd started a hundred times to question the man but held back. He'd said to wait, and the last thing she'd wanted was for Cooper to overhear them.

She met Ryland's gaze. "So, Cooper. Is he?"

"Is he your father, you mean?"

"Yes."

"I believe so. If he's not, then he's assumed the identity of your birth father. But he fits the description I have, and I took the liberty of having a private word with him last night."

Molly nodded. "I noticed you were huddled with him when I came back to the camp with some firewood. What did you talk about?"

"I asked him for some details about the Cooper and Rose families. His answers convinced me he's the genuine article, but I told him nothing substantial about the family situation. If he's released from jail, I don't want him bothering your extended family."

Molly's pulse quickened. "You said 'Rose family.' Tell me—"

"It was your mother's maiden name," Ryland said. "Catherine Rose. Without revealing anything, I prompted Cooper to give me his late wife's name, and he not only said Catherine Rose, but he gave me the name of her father, Zephaniah Rose."

Molly frowned. Her grandfather. The name Rose didn't seem to fit a weather-beaten old farmer, but she rather liked it as a name for her shadowy birth mother.

"He was a ship's captain," Ryland went on.

Molly jerked her chin up. "A captain? Are you sure?"

"I'm certain. Captain Rose, unfortunately, died several years ago, but he did try to find you and your brothers."

Patiently, Ryland laid out the family's story. Captain Rose was at sea when word came to his wife, Edith Rose, in Maine, that their daughter Catherine had died. At once, Edith wrote to her son-in-law, Benjamin Cooper, but received no reply. By the time the captain returned home, she was frantic. Zephaniah sailed to New York in search of the children. He learned to his dismay that Cooper had abandoned them, and they'd been taken to an orphanage.

After a heartbreaking search, the captain returned home without his grandchildren. Edith was devastated. Captain Rose eventually went back to sea, and life went on. Their second daughter, Isabelle, also died in her twenties, and her only child, Abigail Benson, went to live with her grandmother.

"Your cousin still lives with Mrs. Rose," Ryland said. "She's a great comfort to her grandmother."

In 1861, he went on, just before the war broke out, the ladies received crushing news. Captain Rose's clipper had gone down in the Bay of Bengal the previous fall, and all hands were lost. Mrs. Rose grieved anew. So much of her family was taken from her! Abigail was all she had left. She decided to reopen the search for her other grandchildren. She hired an attorney, Jeremiah Turner, in Portland, to spearhead the search.

"Mr. Turner is my employer." Ryland took a folded, much creased paper from his inner pocket. "Here is my letter of credential from him." He handed it to Emma, who unfolded it and read it then passed it to Molly.

"He hired you to find my Molly."

"And her brothers."

Molly scanned the letter. It said nothing about the Weavers directly.

"I'm not sure I understand."

"Sorry. There's so much to tell you." Ryland pulled in a deep breath. "The orphanage in White Plains, where the Cooper children were left, is now under new management. It took some time and a lot of investigation, but two years ago, I was able to find your oldest brother, Zephaniah Cooper. His new family named him Matthew Anderson, and he has a prosperous ranch in Colorado. He's married and has an infant daughter, named Catherine Rose Anderson, in honor of your mother."

Molly was stunned. Two years. This man had known her brother that long. "I ... I want to know more, but ... it's a bit overwhelming."

Ma reached over and patted her shoulder. "There, dear. A happy ending, I hope."

"If you'd care to take a pause?" Ryland watched her carefully.

"No, no. What happened after that?"

"Well, the war was at its height. Matthew and his wife did go back with me to visit Mrs. Rose in Portland, and then they returned to their ranch. But travel was becoming difficult. I tried to locate you and your second brother, Elijah Cooper, without much success. Finally, last year, I learned that Elijah's new name was Jack Miller, and he had joined the army."

"Union?" Ma asked sharply.

"Yes. His adoptive parents were from Pennsylvania. But I had a terrible time trying to track him down. His outfit was sent all over the place. Florida, Louisiana ... I assumed he stayed with them."

"If he wasn't killed." Molly was struck with a wave of grief, which was nonsense. He hadn't said she'd lost a brother. But if she had ...

"Months later, I learned I'd been following the wrong path. Elijah was now honorably discharged from the army and had been taken into the War Department in Washington as a telegrapher."

Molly stared at him. "He's a telegraph operator?"

"Yes. His father taught him. Mr. Miller, that is. But he can tell you all about that when you meet him."

"He's still alive, then?" Emma's eyes almost sparkled.

"Indeed," Ryland said. "Jack Miller is now married to Miss Marilla Buckley, and his adoptive family has moved to Connecticut. Jack's father is also a telegrapher, and he found his son a job in the business in a town not far from them. However, I'm told Jack has been offered a position in Portland, Maine, and is considering moving close to Mrs. Rose."

Molly let out a long, slow breath. "When did you find him?"

"Not until last January. It was quite an adventure, but we'll save that for another day."

"But ... how do you know for certain that I'm ..."

"Jane Cooper?"

She nodded.

"I learned that Jane was adopted by a family in Brooklyn by the name of Weaver. I know there are quite a lot of Weavers—trust me, I've met dozens who were no relation. But I had an address, and after a great deal of spadework, you might say, I found Emma's cousin, who still lives in Brooklyn."

Emma grinned. "Cousin Pearl. Of course!"

"Of course," Ryland agreed. "It seems obvious now, but it took me nearly two years to connect with Mrs. Pearl Hillier. Communication and travel have been terribly disrupted. Be that as it may, I learned at last that you'd moved to Ohio. Unfortunately, I arrived there a few weeks after Mr. Weaver's death. The two of you had set out for Texas. So now you know why I'm here. I followed your trail from Ohio to this place, and here I ran afoul of Cooper."

"You knew about Cooper," Emma said.

"Yes, and I knew he'd made inquiries about the children recently, but I didn't expect him to show up out of nowhere." Ryland picked up his mug and peered into it and set it down regretfully.

"I'm sorry there's no more coffee," Emma said.

"Don't worry about it. I've survived much worse than a shortage of coffee."

"I'm surprised Pearl didn't write me about your visit to her."

Ryland shrugged. "Perhaps she has, and I've outdistanced her letter."

At the sound of a wagon approaching, Molly jumped up and ran to the window.

"Andrew's back, and he brought the wagon."

"Is Sophie with him?" Emma pushed back her chair.

"No, but Joe's returned." Molly looked over her shoulder at her mother. "More unloading to do, I expect."

They all went out into the yard, and Andrew waved with a tired grin. "I hope you wanted vittles, Ma, because I stocked up."

"Bless you!" Emma ran to peek over the sideboard of the wagon.

"I went to the post office too. You've got more mail than I have." He held up a sheaf of envelopes.

"Goodness, I didn't share your address with many people. I

guess we'll have some reading to do tonight." Ma seemed happy about that, and Molly was glad. She'd probably heard from Pearl and her sister, at least.

Andrew made a face at Molly. "Nothing for you, sis."

"I don't mind."

In half an hour, they'd unloaded everything and put away the supplies and Harry and the bay's saddles.

"That horse," Molly said. "We can't keep Cooper's horse."

"No, I told the sheriff we'd bring him back tomorrow. I'm going to take Sophie's wagon to the stable and see if Harry Weston can sell it for her." Andrew began unbuckling the harness.

"We thought we might have to shop tomorrow," Ma said, "but you've brought enough for a month!"

"If I missed anything, make me a list and I'll get it tomorrow." Andrew led Harry toward the pasture, and Joe took the bay's halter and followed.

"Well now, I'm going to start a real meal." Emma strode to the door and went inside.

"Your mother likes to take care of people," Ryland said.

"I don't think anything makes her happier than cooking for the people she loves—except maybe news from loved ones." Molly's smile faded as she turned to Ryland. "What happens now, Mr. Atkins?"

"That's up to you. Edith Rose and Abigail Benson would very much like to meet you, not to mention your two brothers, Matt Anderson and Jack Miller."

She pulled in a deep breath. "I think I'd like to meet them."

"They're lovely people. In fact ..." Ryland's face turned a brighter pink than the lowering sun allowed for.

"What is it?" Molly couldn't keep from smiling at his expression.

"Well, Miss Benson ... Abigail ... holds my regard. And, all right, I'll admit it—my heart."

"How wonderful!" Molly laughed. "We'll have to see if our

finances will allow us to both stock this ranch with cattle and take a trip to Maine."

Ryland nodded with satisfaction. "I'll write to Mr. Turner and Mrs. Rose telling them that. I've already sent a telegram saying you're found, but I know they'll want to hear more. Mrs. Rose is especially eager for news. I can give you her address, if you'd like to write to her."

"I'm not sure I'm ready for that."

"It's all right." He hesitated. "There is one more thing I wanted to ask you about, Molly."

"Go ahead."

"I didn't mention this to Cooper, because I didn't want to give him any private information about the family that might enable him to worm his way back in with his children—"

"That will never happen with me."

"I didn't think so. The boys, however, aren't aware of his recent behavior. Anyway, it's a family tradition or heirloom ..."

"With the Rose family?"

"Yes. You see, when Captain Rose was at sea, he picked up various curios. His wife has a great many boxes and cabinets he brought her from the Orient. And on one of his voyages, he picked up something for his grandchildren. It's nothing of great value, but more of a keepsake. I've learned that you and your brothers, as well as your cousin Abigail, all had them when you were younger."

She stared at him. What on earth?

"Matt and Jack still have theirs, as does Abby. She wears hers as a necklace."

Molly felt lightheaded. "You can't mean ..." She fumbled at her collar and drew out the chain from around her neck. "My mother said this was tied to my ankle with a pink ribbon when they got me from the orphanage."

Ryland smiled. "That's it. The cousin coin. You don't know how much joy that odd little trinket is going to spread when I tell them you're wearing it."

THAT EVENING MOLLY leaned on the pasture fence, watching the horses grazing in the moonlight. They all seemed content, which was exactly how she felt.

Brothers. A grandmother. A cousin who wore the same coin she did.

Abby. Ryland Atkins was in love with her. Molly dreaded the thought of another, even longer, arduous trip, but it would be worth it to meet her grandmother and Abby. But not yet. Not until they'd settled in, and Ma felt at home here.

Quiet footsteps approached, and she turned toward the house. Joe walked softly to stand beside her and rested his forearms on the top rail. There was no one else she'd rather have join her in her reverie.

Joe gazed out at the quietly munching horses. "Peaceful."

"Yes." Molly drew in a breath of the evening air, still pleasantly warm but not stifling as it had been earlier.

"Do you think you'll go to Maine?" Joe and Andrew had heard the tale over supper.

"Someday. Not immediately. I can't ask Ma to make another journey right now. Not one like that."

"Maybe in a few years, a railroad will come to Austin."

She sighed. "I don't think I can wait that long. Ryland says Mrs. Rose is somewhat feeble. If I wait too long, I might never meet her."

Joe was silent for a long moment then stirred. "You're right. He said she wants to meet you, and to see all of her grandchildren together if possible. Molly—"

"Yes?" She turned to study his face. Something was troubling Joe.

"I know we haven't known each other long, but ..."

"What is it, Joe?" His manner was beginning to make her nervous. Was it something about her family?

He heaved out a sigh. "I think you're the finest young woman

I've ever met, Molly Weaver. I don't like to think you might up and leave Texas, because ... well, because I've got a mind to come calling on you, if that's all right."

She stared at him, unable to form words.

Joe swallowed hard. "If you like, I can ask Andrew or your ma, but ... seems to me you're a woman who makes up her own mind. What do you say?"

Her heart pounded like a steam engine, and she was sure her face was about to erupt in flames.

"If you'd rather not, I'll shut up now." He eyed her cautiously. "But I sure do admire you, Molly. I'd hate to see you go. I mean —well, it would be nice for you to see your grandmother before she dies, but if you had any notions of not coming back—" He broke off and lowered his head, staring down at the grass.

"Joe."

He raised his chin and met her gaze.

"I ... I like you too, Joe. More than like you. You took care of me and Ma. You saved our lives, or at least helped do that. You took an awful chance for my brother. And you've been a loyal friend. I don't know how you are as a rancher yet, but—"

He gave a nervous laugh. "I guess that remains to be seen. But there weren't any squatters in my house when we got back, and most of my cattle seem to be accounted for."

"Beyond that," Molly said, "you seem like a square shooter. I know Andrew trusts you implicitly, and I have to say, Ma and I do too. You've proven you're a solid, reliable fellow." She stopped talking. This wasn't a job interview.

"So ... may I court you, Molly?"

"Yes. I'm pretty sure I'd like that."

She reached toward him, not quite certain what was supposed to happen now, but in the next moment his arms were about her.

He leaned toward her then pulled back. "Would it be all right if I kissed you?"

She smiled. "I believe so, but I'll warn you, my lack of experience is appalling."

Joe laughed. "It's been a long while since I kissed a girl, only Sarah Davison, in fourth grade, behind the grammar school."

Molly arched her eyebrows. "And what became of Miss Davison?"

"She broke my heart. Moved away the next summer, and I heard ten years later she'd married a sawmill owner."

"Then she's not an impediment to your suggestion."

Joe's eyes widened. "What? Oh, no. Not at all."

Molly stood on tiptoe, and Joe met her halfway. She'd always thought kissing was overrated, but not anymore. With Joe's strong arms encircling her and his warm lips on hers, an entire future raced through her mind, one she hadn't an inkling of before that moment.

When he released her, she smiled up at him in the moonlight. "Miss Davison doesn't know what she's missing."

"Ha!" He pulled her to him again.

One more kiss, Molly decided. Then they'd have to go in, or Ma would have a fit. She hoped no one had looked out the back window to see what they were up to. Or did she care?

EPILOGUE

Four months later

Molly shivered and rearranged her scarf about her neck. She hadn't considered how uncomfortable traveling would be in early December. Her feet were freezing.

"We're almost there." Joe reached for her hand. His warmth radiated through her gloves, and she gave his fingers a light squeeze.

"I'm so glad we decided to do it this way."

"Well, your mother was torn, and I know she didn't want to leave Andrew."

"She didn't want to intrude," Molly corrected him. "I assured her Mrs. Rose would be happy to meet her, but I honestly think Ma didn't want to get in the way when I meet my other family."

"Maybe. But it would have been fine."

"I know." Molly leaned back against the leather seat cushion and gazed at him. Joe Noyes, soon to be her husband. She smiled, certain she'd made the right choice on that matter. "Thanks for agreeing to get married in Maine."

He shrugged. "Your cousin sounded so mournful in her letter, about how your granny wouldn't get to see the wedding. Seems she's missed them all so far."

Molly laughed. "My granny. Don't call her that to her face. I get the feeling she's a proper lady."

"I won't. I'll be on my best behavior."

He was a little on edge, Molly decided. A fish out of water. Instead of the dude visiting the frontier, he was the cow puncher visiting a New England city. She wasn't completely at ease herself. Were her clothes fashionable enough? Style hadn't mattered on the ranch.

"Next stop, Portland," the conductor called, walking up the aisle with a practiced cadence.

Molly inhaled deeply. "This is it."

"Yeah, it is. You ready?"

"About as much as you are."

Joe laughed and snagged his wide-brimmed hat from the overhead rack. At least he'd bought a new hat.

"Will someone meet us?" He plopped down on the seat.

"I'm sure they will. Abby said she and Ryland plan to be at the station, and she expected Matthew and Rachel to arrive yesterday. I'm not sure about Jack and Marilla."

The train's brakes screeched, and she braced herself as it slowed.

A couple of minutes later, they made their way to the door. Joe jumped down first and turned to give her his hand as she moved carefully down the steps onto the platform.

"Molly! Molly Weaver!"

She looked around, astonished to see a crowd moving toward her, or what seemed like a crowd by ranching standards.

"Are you Molly?" a young woman in a long woolen coat and a fur hood asked breathlessly.

"Yes. And this is Joe."

"I'm Abby." She threw herself at Molly, engulfing her in a hug.

"Shall we move aside?" Ryland asked, smiling at her with twinkling eyes.

"Mr. Atkins, so good to see you." Molly held out her hand as she stepped away from the train's door.

"And you. Joe, welcome." Ryland extended a hand to Joe.

After that came a confusing round of introductions and embraces, with their breath forming little clouds in the air as they spoke rapidly, overlapping one another's greetings.

"We left little Catherine at the house with Grandmother," Rachel said—at least, Molly thought it was Rachel. "It was too cold to bring them out."

"But we've got two cabs waiting to take us all home, after we get your luggage," her husband said.

That was Matthew. Matt belonged with Rachel, Molly told herself.

Joe went off with Ryland to secure their baggage, and she sneaked shy glances at her brothers.

"You look like them," Abby said in a confidential tone.

Molly grinned. "How did you know what I was thinking?"

"They've been asking each other, 'Do you think Janie looks like us now?' for the past two days. Oh, sorry—Molly."

"It's all right. I'm still absorbing it myself."

She found herself in a carriage with Joe, Marilla, and Jack.

"Grandmother's beside herself to meet you," Jack said. "She was hoping the rest of your family could come."

"Andrew's leery of leaving his ranch right now," Molly said. "He's got several cows due to calve before we get back."

"He's watching my herd too," Joe said.

"What about your mother?" Marilla asked softly.

"She was torn, but she decided it was best to save the money and stay there to help Andrew and his wife, Sophie. They've only been married a month."

"So she did get to see one child's wedding," Jack said.

"Oh, yes. And Sophie is a dear. She helped stitch my wedding dress. She's quite a seamstress." Molly gulped. She hoped her wedding dress would pass muster in Maine.

"I can't wait to see it," Marilla said.

Joe grinned mischievously. "Me either."

Molly poked him with her elbow. "You have to wait for the wedding." She looked out the window. One more week, and all would be ready. Then she would be Mrs. Joe Noyes.

The horse clopped along paved streets, and some of the buildings they passed were several stories high. In the distance, she glimpsed an odd-looking tower. "What's that?"

Jack ducked low to see what she pointed toward. "Oh, the observatory. They run up signal flags whenever a ship is sighted, so the merchants know whose vessel is coming in."

"Ships. Have you ever seen the ocean, Joe?" Molly turned to look at him.

Joe shook his head. There were lots of things neither of them had seen, Molly decided, even though Joe had been through the war and she'd traipsed hundreds of miles with her mother, and now thousands, to this remote corner of the country.

"Well, you'll have to see it. After all, our grandfather was a sea captain," Jack said.

She nodded. "I'm eager to learn more about him."

"We can take you all around the harbor. I'm sure Abby and Ryland can show us lots of things. Maybe we can even go up in the observatory, or the lighthouse down on Portland Head."

"Or visit one of the merchant ships in port," Marilla added.

Molly grinned at them. "It sounds like great fun."

The carriage came to a stop.

"We're here." Jack opened the door and hopped out, then helped her and Marilla down. Joe followed, his eyes wide as he surveyed the large house before them. On top stood a cupola with a platform like a roofless porch.

"That's the widow's walk." Marilla was at her elbow, gazing upward too. "Mrs. Rose used to go up there and watch for the captain's clipper ship to return."

"How exciting. And how sad. I was told he didn't return after the last voyage."

"It's true," Jack said as the second cab pulled up. "Come on, Grandmother's been waiting a long time to see you."

EDITH ROSE'S HEART FLUTTERED. Looking around her spacious parlor at her grandchildren, she couldn't blink back the tears that filled her eyes.

Abby pressed a lace-edged handkerchief into her grandmother's hand. "Here you go."

"Thank you, dear." Edith dabbed at her eyes.

"Not crying, are you, Grandma?" Matthew turned his daughter on his lap so little Catherine could see her great-grandmother.

"Just happy." She must look rather silly, beaming at them all, but she didn't care. Abby had talked her into putting on a green dress, without so much as black piping or a jet button. She had mourned long enough. Today, celebration took precedence over all the sadness of the past.

She smiled at Molly. Somehow it had been easier to adjust to Jane's new name than it had with the boys—perhaps because she hadn't seen her when she was a child.

"My dear, thank you so much for agreeing to be married here. You, too, Mr. Noyes."

"Please call me Joe." The affable Texan grinned.

"We're happy to do it, Grandmother," Molly said. "Four months ago, I had no idea I had such a large family. Having you all at my wedding brings me more joy than I can express."

Edith could gaze at her all day long. Molly was the exact image of Catherine, who'd married and left them more than thirty years ago, and then permanently departed this earth ten years later. Her eyes brimmed once more, and she applied Abby's handkerchief.

"You said you brought your wedding dress," Abby said

cheerfully, perhaps to move the attention away from Edith, for which she was grateful.

"Yes. My new sister-in-law, Sophie Weaver, helped make it, and my mother—that is, Emma Weaver."

Jack grinned at her. "We know who you mean, sis. We've all got our second families, and we're thankful for them."

"And they all hope to meet you someday," added Matthew, who bore an uncanny resemblance to the captain.

"I hope I have the chance." Molly gazed around at them all, her face a portrait of bliss.

"Do you have a veil, child?" Edith asked softly.

"Why, no. I couldn't find one in Austin, and Ma said perhaps my hat would do."

Edith's pulse accelerated. "If it's to your liking, we have the one your mother, Catherine, wore at her wedding." She wouldn't mention what a disappointment Catherine's marriage had turned out to be. All of them now knew the story of their father, Ben Cooper, who at this moment was languishing in a jail in Austin, Texas. But the day held happier memories.

"Our grandfather brought it from France," Abby said. "It's lovely Calais lace."

Molly's eyes shone. "It would be an honor."

"Good!" Abby grinned. "I'll show it to you later. I unpacked it from the attic, and it's good as new."

Edith cleared her throat, which ached a little with all the memories squeezing it. "I have a portrait of your mother in her wedding attire. You—you look a great deal like her, my dear."

Molly's cheeks stained a becoming pink. "Thank you. That makes me happy."

Joe reached for her hand. "I guess I'd better ask my future brothers-in-law to take me to a tailor tomorrow. I didn't have time to buy a suit in Texas, and Mr. Atkins assured me I could buy one here."

Ryland, who'd been studying Abby's profile with a wistful

look, jerked to attention. "Hmm? Oh, yes. There's time, if you're holding the ceremony next week."

"That's the plan," Abby told him.

"I know just the place. Maybe we men should make an afternoon of it tomorrow and leave you ladies to ... whatever it is you need to do to prepare for the wedding." Ryland shrugged, and Edith found his manners endearing. There had been no formal announcement yet, but she was certain he would offer for her Abigail soon.

Ryland might not be rich or brilliant, but he was kind, persistent, hardworking, and quite smart when it came right down to it. She couldn't think of a better man to take his place by Abby's side.

"There's something I'd like to ask you about, Grandmother," Molly said, fidgeting a little in her chair.

"What is it, dear?"

"I ..." She stuck a finger inside the collar of her dress and drew out a chain. "I've had this coin since I was a baby, and I only learned recently that it came from you and my Grandfather Rose."

Edith smiled as Abby drew out her own necklace and Matt pulled a leather thong from around his neck. Jack opened his wallet and took out a coin.

"We all have them," Jack said.

Edith nodded in satisfaction. "My Zephaniah brought them home from China, along with a great many other curiosities. He gave one to Abigail, one to Zeph, and one to Elijah. And he had several extras, for any future grandchildren we might have."

"That's you," Jack said.

"Yes, as soon as I received news of your birth, I sent one to Catherine to lay aside for you. I'm amazed you still have it."

"Thanks to some kind person at the orphanage, it found its way with me to the Weavers, tied to my ankle with a ribbon."

"Actually, I put it there," Matt said.

"You?" Molly turned and stared at him. "How ..."

"After Ma died, I made sure it was on your foot. I never knew if they let you keep it at the orphanage, but I always imagined finding you someday, and we'd know we were brother and sister for sure because we both had them."

Tears filled Molly's eyes. "I can't tell you how happy I am to know that." She leaned toward Edith and patted her hand. "Thank you so much for sending it."

Edith sat back, smiling broadly. "I loved you all then, and I love you now. Today, it's my pleasure to present one to my great-granddaughter, Catherine Anderson. Abby?"

Abigail stood and went to the mantelpiece, where a small, lacquered box stood between two candlesticks. She opened it, took something out, and turned to Matt and Rachel.

"Here you go—a cousin coin for Catherine. There are actually a dozen more in the box, so if any of you are blessed in the future ..."

Edith looked around at them. "I hope I have so many great-grandchildren that there aren't enough to go around."

The end

DISCUSSION QUESTIONS

1. Was Emma Weaver foolish to set out for Texas when she did? Is she really the strongest member of the family?
2. What advice could you give Molly and Emma for traveling without a male escort?
3. If you were with Molly and Emma, would you have trusted Joe Noyes the first day you met him? Do you think Joe was justified in misrepresenting himself to the squatters?
4. What could Andrew have done to avoid much of the trouble he found on this trip?
5. Ryland learns to throw a knife in this story. What other skills would he do well to learn?
6. If you were Molly, what would you have done when Cooper turned up at the clothesline?
7. What else might Andrew have done to help the Nolans?
8. Do you think Ryland is the best match for Abby? Should he consider reading law instead of continuing as an investigator?

9. How is Joe helping Molly make peace with her past? Do you think she will make a good ranch woman?
10. The Rose family has started a tradition with the Cousin Coins. Does your family have a tradition that draws them together?

ABOUT THE AUTHOR

Susan Page Davis is the author of more than one hundred books. Her books include Christian novels and novellas in the historical romance, mystery, and romantic suspense genres. Her work has won several awards, including the Carol Award, two Will Rogers Medallions, and two Faith, Hope, & Love Reader's Choice Awards. She has also been a finalist in the WILLA Literary Awards and a multi-time finalist in the Carol Awards. A Maine native, Susan has lived in Oregon and now resides in western Kentucky with her husband Jim, a retired news editor. They are the parents of six and grandparents of eleven.

Visit her website at: https://susanpagedavis.com.

OTHER BOOKS IN THE HOMEWARD TRAILS SERIES

The Rancher's Legacy

Homeward Trails - Book One

Matthew Anderson and his father try to help neighbor Bill Maxwell when his ranch is attacked. On the day his daughter Rachel is to return from school back East, outlaws target the Maxwell ranch. After Rachel's world is shattered, she won't even consider the plan her father and Matt's cooked up—to see their two children marry and combine the ranches.

Meanwhile in Maine, sea captain's widow Edith Rose hires a private investigator to locate her three missing grandchildren. The children were abandoned by their father nearly twenty years ago. They've been adopted into very different families, and they're scattered across the country. Can investigator Ryland Atkins find them all while the elderly woman still lives? His first attempt is to find the boy now called Matthew Anderson. Can Ryland survive his trip into the wild Colorado Territory and find Matt before the outlaws finish destroying a legacy?

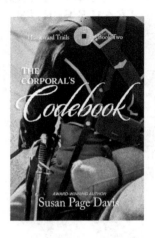

The Corporal's Codebook
Homeward Trails - Book Two

Jack Miller stumbles through the Civil War, winding up a telegrapher and cryptographer for the army. In the field with General Sherman in Georgia, he is captured along with his precious cipher key.

His captor, Hamilton Buckley, thinks he should have been president of the Confederacy, not Jefferson Davis. Jack doubts Buckley's sanity and longs to escape. Buckley's kindhearted niece, Marilla, might help him— but only if Jack helps her achieve her own goal.

Meanwhile, a private investigator, stymied by the difficulty of travel and communication in wartime, is trying his best to locate Jack for the grandmother he longs to see again but can barely remember.

ALSO BY SUSAN PAGE DAVIS

Novella Collection

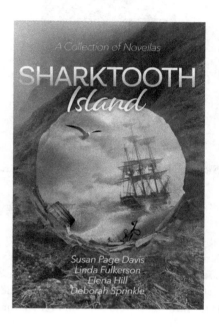

Sharktooth Island

by Susan Page Davis, Linda Fulkerson, Elena Hill, and Deborah Sprinkle

Romantic Suspense

A fabled island that no one dares to tame. In four tales of adventure, over the centuries this troublesome island becomes a place of healing and love.

Skirmish Cove Mysteries

Cliffhanger

by Susan Page Davis

Skirmish Cove Mysteries - Book One

A charming themed inn, breaking waves, and a missing guest. What more could one ask?

The Novel Inn's reopening goes smoothly until a guest vanishes. The new owners prepare for their first large group—a former squad of cheerleaders meeting for a reunion. Things go awry when the head cheerleader fails to show up. Sisters Kate and Jillian, the innkeepers, enlist the help of their brother Rick, a local police officer. They're confident the missing woman will be found, but they soon learn to expect the unexpected, even during a walk on the beach.

True Blue Mysteries

Blue Plate Special

by Susan Page Davis

Book One of the True Blue Mysteries Series

Campbell McBride drives to her father's house in Murray, Kentucky, dreading telling him she's lost her job as an English professor. Her father, private investigator Bill McBride, isn't there or at his office in town. His brash young employee, Nick Emerson, says Bill hasn't come in this morning, but he did call the night before with news that he had a new case.

When her dad doesn't show up by late afternoon, Campbell and Nick decide to follow up on a phone number he'd jotted on a memo sheet. They learn who last spoke to her father, but they also find a dead body. The next day, Campbell files a missing persons report. When Bill's car is found, locked and empty in a secluded spot, she and Nick must get past their differences and work together to find him.

Ice Cold Blue

by Susan Page Davis

Book Two of the True Blue Mysteries Series

Campbell McBride is now working for her father Bill as a private
investigator in Murray, Kentucky. Xina Harrison wants them to find out
what is going on with her aunt, Katherine Tyler.

Katherine is a rich, reclusive author, and she has resisted letting Xina
visit her for several years. Xina arrived unannounced, and Katherine
was upset and didn't want to let her in. When Xina did gain entry, she
learned Katherine fired her longtime housekeeper. She noticed that a
few family heirlooms previously on display have disappeared. Xina is
afraid someone is stealing from her aunt or influencing her to give them
her money and valuables. True Blue accepts the case, and the
investigators follow a twisting path to the truth.

Persian Blue Puzzle

by Susan Page Davis

Book Three of the True Blue Mysteries Series

An antisocial cat, an elusive investment broker, and a hope-selling psychic raise suspicions in a western Kentucky community.

Someone's broken into Miss Louanne's house. Campbell McBride and her father Bill have moved their home and detective business into an old Victorian house. Their new neighbors bring in unexpected cases for True Blue Investigations to unravel.

While helping Miss Louanne look for her missing cat, Campbell learns of other suspicious activities in Murray. Another neighbor tells the detectives about a stranger in town who's peddling an investment plan. They aren't sure any crimes have been committed, but they're intrigued enough for Campbell to visit a psychic along with police detective Keith Fuller's mom and to start checking up on the financier.

Things heat up when a customer threatens the psychic and then she vanishes.

COMING SOON FROM SUSAN PAGE DAVIS

Skirmish Cove Mysteries Book Two

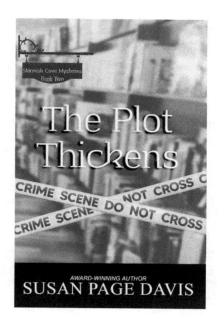

The Plot Thickens
by Susan Page Davis
Skirmish Cove Mysteries - Book Two

Jillian only wants to redecorate one room at the Novel Inn—but first she has to deal with murder.

Murder strikes Skirmish Cove during the coastal town's winter carnival. Jillian Tunney, part owner of the nearby Novel Inn, discovers the body of a clerk at her favorite bookstore. With her sister Kate and brother, Officer Rick Gage, she tries to find out who killed him.

Meanwhile, Jillian is immersed in redecorating one of the themed rooms, but Kate is annoyed when a mysterious guest at the inn doesn't want to leave his room. The innkeepers find they have way too many secrets to solve.

Coming November 2022!

Scrivenings
PRESS
Quench your thirst for story.
www.ScriveningsPress.com

Stay up-to-date on your favorite books and authors with our free e-newsletters.

ScriveningsPress.com

CPSIA information can be obtained
at www.ICGtesting.com
Printed in the USA
LVHW021817060922
727712LV00003B/511

9 781649 172228